DEATH NOTES

A Phineas Fox Mystery

Sarah Rayne

This first world edition published 2016
in Great Britain and the USA by
SEVERN HOUSE PUBLISHERS LTD of
19 Cedar Road, Sutton, Surrey, England, SM2 5DA.
Trade paperback edition first published
in Great Britain and the USA 2017 by
SEVERN HOUSE PUBLISHERS LTD

British Library Cataloguing in Publication Data
A CIP catalogue record for this title is available from the British Library.

ISBN-13: 978-0-7278-8660-6 (cased)
ISBN-13: 978-1-84751-762-3 (trade paper)
ISBN-13: 978-1-78010-828-5 (e-book)

All Severn House titles are printed on acid-free paper.

Severn House Publishers support the Forest Stewardship Council™ [FSC™],
the leading international forest certification organisation.
All our titles that are printed on FSC certified paper carry the FSC logo.

MIX
Paper from
responsible sources
FSC   FSC® C013056
www.fsc.org

Typeset by Palimpsest Book
Falkirk, Stirlingshire, Scotlan
Printed and bound in Great B
TJ International, Padstow, Co

DEATH NOTES

Recent Titles by Sarah Rayne from Severn House

The Phineas Fox Mysteries

DEATH NOTES

The Nell West and Michael Flint Series

PROPERTY OF A LADY
THE SIN EATER
THE SILENCE
THE WHISPERING
DEADLIGHT HALL
THE BELL TOWER

ONE

'I do not want,' said Phineas Fox, 'to take a commission involving researching the life of a nineteenth-century murderer. I don't care how gifted a musician Roman Volf was, he was hanged for murder and I don't want him. Give him to somebody else.'

'But it's for a TV documentary, Phin,' said his agent in a wail down the phone. 'Hugely prestigious. All factual, but probably with some of those reconstruction scenes woven in. They want dark romance and mysterious tragedy, and . . . No, I didn't make that up, hold on and I'll forward the email to you.'

'You can't romanticize Roman Volf,' said Phin. 'Not even darkly. He was a villain and a womanizer and he was hanged for helping to assassinate a Russian tsar.'

'Nicholas?'

'No, an earlier one. Alexander II. 1880 or thereabouts. Roman was hanged in St Petersburg, and it was all very squalid.'

The forwarded email pinged in at that point. It did indeed refer to dark romance and wistful tragedy, and it said that the programme's editor very much hoped Phineas Fox would be available, because he had been highly recommended and he was their first choice. Phin tried not to feel too flattered by this.

'And have I mentioned,' said his agent persuasively, 'the very generous fee they're offering?'

'You haven't mentioned a fee at all, but I still don't want . . . *How* much did you say?'

'Very nice, isn't it?' said his agent, gleefully. 'It'd be useful with you having moved to that new flat, I should think.'

Phin had recently moved to a large, and worryingly expensive, flat, which took up about one fifth of a huge old Victorian house. He had done so on a wave of fiscal euphoria following a lucrative research project into the energetic amours of an eighteenth-century composer, but a disconcertingly protracted period of silence from commissioning editors and music biographers had followed, and he was starting to wish himself back in his studio apartment in Bayswater.

As well as that, the wall of the study, which he had enjoyed furnishing and lining with all his books, had turned out to back on to the bathroom of a lively neighbour, who had the amiable habit of singing rugby songs to start the day. Phin had realized after the first week that he would have to build in some kind of sound-proofing across that wall in order to blot out the strains of 'If I Were the Marrying Kind' and 'Oh, Sir Jasper' when the neighbour was in the shower. He thought the first song dated to the fifteenth century, but while it was interesting to find such an old song surviving, he did not want to hear it at half-past seven every morning, except for Sundays when the rugby player was usually sleeping off the excesses of Saturday night.

He brought his attention back to his agent, who was explaining who had recommended Phin for the Roman Volf project.

'It's that Canadian editor you worked with on the Oscar Peterson tribute a couple of years back. She seemed to think rather highly of you.'

'She was just a work colleague.'

'Red hair and long legs, I heard. She's supposed to have said something about you having silver eyes. Still, you know editors, they like to wax lyrical from time to time. What about this Roman Volf thing? Will you accept it?'

Phin thought for a moment, then said, 'I'll have a look at him and phone you tomorrow.'

A good researcher should be able to plumb the depths of all kinds of darknesses and remain objective. Especially when his bank balance is dwindling with alarming rapidity, and even more especially with the looming prospect of either sound-proofing half of his flat at his own expense, or moving to another one and hoping for quieter neighbours.

Accordingly, after his agent's phone call, Phin plundered his extensive bookshelves for references to Roman Volf and the infamous assassination of the tsar.

The first mention he found was couched in colourful terms, and said, 'Roman Volf was a virtuoso violinist – charismatic and brilliant. But a dark and suffocating web of tragedy wove itself around the last months of his life, and it was believed by some that his descendants would be trapped in the spider-strands of that dark web for many years into the future . . .'

This had been written by a Russian journalist called Feofil Markov, and a footnote explained it had been translated from the original Russian, and that most of Mr Markov's articles had been for the Russian political and literary newspaper, *Golos*. The book's author could attest that the words were Feofil Markov's, but regretted that it had not been possible to verify the truth of any of the content, and added that Markov's imagination had been known to be lively.

Phin accorded this warning a mental nod, and read the rest of the article.

'Two days after the official announcement of the tsar's death,' wrote Feofil, 'Roman Volf led an exultant midnight march of the rebels across the Pevchesky Bridge and along the banks of the Catherine Canal. He played his violin as he went, the anarchists and rebels prancing along behind him, as if he were some fantastical Scaramouche incarnation or a latter-day Pied Piper.'

No other reports referred to this incident. Most focused on Roman's part in the assassination, with some saying he had been a minor player in the plot, but others stating he had master-minded it. The date of the assassination had been March 1881, and Phin was pleased to find his memory had only been one year out.

He wondered if that extraordinary Pied Piper march could be verified. Because if so – and always supposing he accepted the TV commission – it would make a terrific dramatic recon-struction. Could he draft a possible screenplay? He would need more verification, of course, and he would also need to know the music Roman had actually played. He burrowed into several more books, and finally found a further snippet – again from the ubiquitous Mr Markov – who said that the maestro's choice of music on that march had been outrageous.

'He played Berlioz's "The Brigands' Song" – that celebration of the freedom of life enjoyed by outlaws,' wrote Feofil, 'and followed it with the "March to the Scaffold" from Berlioz's *Symphonie Fantastique*. It was not until one o'clock in the morning that the Russian police, along with a number of imperial Cossacks, finally surrounded him on the Pevchesky Bridge. They arrested him, and took him to the dread Peter and Paul Fortress – the "Russian Bastille".'

And, thought Phin, as far as Roman Volf was concerned, that was the day the music died.

At the end of the article Feofil had written, 'Roman Volf faced Death disdainfully, as if he was auditioning it to provide accompaniment for one of his performances. Throughout the trial he protested his innocence, although no one believed him. His judges certainly did not.'

Phin closed the books, having marked the places, and set out to trawl his favourite antiquarian bookshops. There would be plenty of material about Roman on the internet, but he enjoyed secondhand bookshops and there was nothing quite like holding a leather or vellum-bound book in your hands, and knowing that the last person to do so might have lived half a century earlier. It was a pity that the old bookshops were gradually vanishing from the landscape and that the Charing Cross Road was not what it had once been in this respect.

He began with a tucked-away shop in a small courtyard two – or was it three? – turnings off St Martin's Lane. Phin always suspected the shop might stand on time-slip land – that this was a sliver of London that straddled the centuries. The shop had an unobtrusive façade, as if it did not especially want to be noticed, and it was narrow and cluttered in a Dickensian kind of way. It specialized in Russian literature and it was said to have originally been bought and run by an aristocratic Russian émigré immediately after the 1917 Revolution. Its more romantically inclined clientele liked to spin improbable tales about refugee Romanovs having started the business with the proceeds of imperial jewels smuggled out of the Winter Palace. On occasions the Anastasia legend was inevitably dragged out for an airing, although Phin suspected this story might have been fostered by the original owners as a marketing ploy.

He nodded to the proprietor, who was involved in a discussion with two academic-looking gentlemen, and moved slowly along the shelves. Most of the books were in Russian, but Phin thought he would at least recognize Roman's name. After a fruitless hour, he found his way down to a semi-basement, which housed a section of books on architecture.

There was only one English title – *Lost Buildings of Old Russia* – and the book resided so unassumingly at the end of the shelf that Phin nearly missed it. Remembering this afterwards he almost felt sick. The book was cloth-bound and worn, and its spine was so cracked that it was in danger of disintegrating altogether. When Phin opened it, it emitted the dry, brown scent peculiar to all old books, but the pages fell apart at a section where several black and white photographs were reproduced. There were blurred shots of places with onion spires, but on one of the pages was a large, surprisingly clear image. It showed a burned-out building, clearly once massive and elaborate, and the caption identified it as the Skomorokh Theatre near Tchaikovsky Street in Odessa. The theatre, it seemed, had been almost completely destroyed by a fire in 1878, and this was a photograph of the ruined façade and shell, taken in 1881. Preliminary talks were apparently about to commence for the possible rebuilding of the theatre – a grant had been promised from an anonymous donor.

The anonymous donor could have been anyone, but the year was 1881. The year of the tsar's assassination. Phin's mind sprang to sharper attention, and he studied the photograph more closely, seeing for the first time that a figure stood in the foreground. It was a man with strong, slanting cheekbones and narrow, slightly tip-tilted eyes, as if the cheekbones had pushed the eyes up slightly at the outer edges. A man with dark hair, a little too long and somewhat untidy, as if he often pushed it back impatiently. Such as when he was playing a violin in a crowded concert hall or opera house . . .?

It was Roman Volf. There could be no mistake. Phin would check up on the Skomorokh Theatre and its exact location, but there was no reason to doubt what the caption said. Which meant that in 1881 Roman had been in Odessa.

It proved nothing – the assassination had been on 13 March, and Roman could have been at the burned-out Skomorokh Theatre in Odessa on any day before then, and still been in St Petersburg to help kill the tsar. But it was worth looking into, and Phin carried the book to the cash desk, and handed over the modest £15 requested. He made his way back to his flat, barely aware of crowded tubes and jostling, impatient people, at intervals patting his jacket pocket to make sure the book was still safely there, and had not been filched by an enterprising street thief in quest of a wallet.

Back in his flat, he examined the photograph more closely. Was there anything in the shot that might pinpoint the exact date it had been taken? He searched the flat for a magnifying glass, finally finding one at the back of his sock drawer. Focused on the photograph, the glass brought Roman Volf's features into sharp clarity. Even like this, even from an era when photography was basic and chancy, the magnetism of the man was evident. No wonder he was said to have had numerous mistresses, and thousands of adoring followers. He was wearing a dark jacket with the collar turned up, and under his left arm – the arm nearest the camera – he was carrying something white. Phin tilted and rotated the magnifying glass every possible way, until he could make out what it was. A newspaper, folded over. And newspapers had dates on them. It might not be possible to make that out, of course, even if the paper was folded to show the date. And the paper would be a Russian one anyway . . .

The print was tiny, but after a bit more manipulating of the magnifier, it was possible to see that the newspaper was called *Golos*, and the date was 13 МАРТА 1881. *Golos* was the magazine Feofil Markov had written for – it translated as *The Voice*. The date hardly needed a translator, but Phin made quick use of an online translation website. Sure enough, it was 13 March 1881. The day of Alexander's murder.

He stared at the grainy images, then a spike of doubt suddenly raised itself, a spike adorned with the words 'Gregorian Calendar'. There had been two weeks or so around the end of the 1800s and the start of the 1900s when dates and calendars had been adjusted because people – countries – were switching from the old, imprecise Julian calendar to the more exact Gregorian one. What if 13 March was one of them? What if this was the thirteen-day gap, and it was 1 March when Roman had been in Odessa?

Phin carried the book over to his desk, booted up the computer, and typed in a series of search requests for Julian and Gregorian dates. It took a few moments, but eventually he found what he wanted and sat back with a huge breath of relief. Russia had not adjusted its calendars to catch up on those lost thirteen days until 1918. So the date on Roman's newspaper really had been 13 March – the day Alexander II had been murdered.

Could the photo have been taken a day or two after the 13th, with Roman holding an old newspaper? No, it could not, because he had been in St Petersburg by the night of the 15th – he had led that bizarre midnight procession over the Pevchesky Bridge, pouring defiant, near-treasonous music into the night. In the early hours of the 16th, he had been arrested and taken straight to the Peter and Paul Fortress. Could he have travelled from Odessa on the 13th and been in St Petersburg on the 15th? Phin called up a map website, typing in a request for details of the journey between the two places. The distance was just over 1,000 miles and, on today's roads, it would take approximately twenty-two hours of driving. How long would that journey have taken in 1881? Two days at least – probably nearer three. On that basis Roman would have had to leave Odessa on the 11th. And if this photo had been taken on the 13th, Roman could not have been in St Petersburg on the day the tsar was murdered.

It did not prove his innocence. He could have been involved up to his sardonic eyebrows in the plot, and deliberately been 1,000 miles away when the deed was done. And yet . . .

Was it possible that the photo had been faked? But that would only have been done with the aim of proving his innocence, and it would have been put forward at the trial as an alibi. At the very least it would have raised a massive doubt as to Roman's guilt. It might have transmuted the death sentence to life imprisonment.

Or had the imperial, imperious Romanovs wanted scape-goats at any cost and seized on Roman as one of those scapegoats? Phin wondered how difficult it would be to get hold of a transcript of Roman's trial, and if such a transcript still existed.

The *Lost Buildings* book had been published in 1920 – forty years after the assassination. By then nobody would have been particularly interested in a forty-year-old murder, even though it was the murder of an imperial ruler. Another assassination had happened in 1914, a Great War had been fought as a result, and in 1917 a Revolution had toppled the Russian Imperial House, ending the line of the Romanovs. The story of Alexander II and Roman Volf had faded. The Skomorokh photo had probably turned up in some obscure library or collection, and been included without the publishers even realizing what it was or what it suggested.

But Phin realized. It was potential proof that Roman Volf had been wrongly executed. And if it were true, how would that square with the programme makers of the TV documentary? A small voice in his head said, What a terrific scoop it would be if you produced definite evidence that Roman was innocent!

Before he could change his mind, he typed an email to his agent, accepting the commission. He was about to send it, when he remembered something else, and he reopened the email to send carefully non-committal regards to the red-haired Canadian editor who had described his eyes as silver.

If Roman had been guilty, he must have known that leading that defiant march along the banks of the Catherine Canal was courting disaster. It was two days after the assassination – why would he draw attention to himself in that way?

As for Feofil's suggestion that Roman's descendants might become tangled in the black spider-strands of his actions – how much of that could be ascribed to the Russian trait for wringing as much angst and melodrama from a situation as possible? But what spider-strands? Had there been any consequences of Roman's execution? To his family? Had there been family? If so, how easy would it be to track down the descendants?

Mortimer Quince's diary

This morning I went to an audition at Collins' Theatre. It went splendidly, even though it's always difficult to give a performance of any real quality in an empty theatre – empty theatres always echo so dismally.

I gave them 'O, Moon of My Delight,' from the 'Persian Garden' song cycle. It's remarkable to think that was written twenty-four years ago – 1896, I believe – but it's still stirring stuff, and I reached the top notes with such piercing energy that I swear the very rafters shook. I followed it with 'Love's Old Sweet Song,' which is even older, of course – a Victorian parlour ballad, in fact, and I remember it being popular when I was a boy. I put such a sob into my voice that two cleaners who had been sweeping the back of the auditorium were so deeply affected they had to leave by the nearest exit. I count this a true accolade.

This afternoon will be devoted to following a new line of enquiry which may help me uncover the last weeks of my father's life. I have always hidden the fact that I was Roman Volf's son. Quite apart from all other considerations (such as the fact that he was hanged in a St Petersburg gaol for murder), the connection is not what could be termed legitimate, and I should not care to have slurs cast on my mother, even though I do not remember her.

But my carefully casual enquiries among the Russian émigrés in this part of London recently brought me the name of Feofil Markov. It seems Markov was a well-known journalist and music critic in St Petersburg around the time of Alexander's assassination – and therefore during the time of Roman's execution.

My Russian acquaintance is a bookseller; a charming, somewhat elderly, gentleman who came to this country a year or two ago – almost immediately after the 1917 Revolution in fact – and somehow scraped together enough money to open a bookshop near St Martin's Lane. The shelves are crammed full of books and periodicals and newspapers, most of them in Russian. Everywhere is pleasantly untidy and slightly dusty, and my friend sits at a high desk, wearing fingerless gloves and a brocade dressing gown, chuckling gleefully over some new and arcane acquisition which he will never sell, and looking like a Russian version of a Dickens character.

He met Feofil in 1914 when the two of them downed a couple of bottles of vodka in a bar overlooking the Moskva River, after which my friend fell off the chair while drinking death and destruction to the Romanovs.

Feofil published several critiques of some of Roman's performances, as well as an obituary and articles about him after the execution. He also somehow managed to inveigle his way into the condemned cells, and interview some of the assassins after the murder of Alexander II.

Most of the articles appeared in a reactionary Russian newspaper called *Golos* – my bookseller friend tells me that *Golos* translates as 'The Voice'. He adds that the paper was closed down in 1885 and Feofil was lucky not to be arrested for sedition, but that he might be able to track down a few copies for me. Would it help my studies? There would be a small cost, naturally.

'Purely to cover my time – perhaps travelling – perhaps the buying of drinks or meals for people who could provide the copies . . . Would that be acceptable?'

'Naturally,' I said.

I have started this search largely because the nightmares that plagued me as a child – later as a young man – have returned. They had been quiescent for so long I had begun to believe they had left me for good. But they are back, and they are as vicious and as fearsome as ever. I am increasingly convinced that they have their root in my father's shameful death and that I will only get rid of them by finding out exactly what happened to him.

Tonight the nightmare was waiting for me as soon as I fell asleep. It did not, God be praised, take on complete substance, but the outlines of it were there – the stone courtyard, the shouting crowds, and, most dreadful of all, the stench of burning . . . Hands were pulling at me, and I was enveloped in terror, because I was afraid they were pulling me towards something dark and dreadful . . .

I have tried to tell myself that the nightmare cannot be a

real memory. But always, for some half an hour after waking, it is difficult to believe that.

A clock somewhere in the city was chiming three o'clock, when, as Keats has it, I 'awoke to find me here on the cold hill's side,' except that the reality was that I awoke to find me in a cold bed with the bolster all askew and the eiderdown disgorging duck feathers everywhere.

Having tidied the bed and composed myself for sleep again, I forced my mind to reach for a different dream – the dream I always think of as the nightmare's counterpart. It's a pleasant dream, that one – a brightly lit theatre with ornate boxes and gold and crimson décor, and a bejewelled audience. There's the warm scent of flowers and expensive perfume, and there's a thrum of anticipation.

The memory is my father's final concert at the Mikhailovsky Theatre. I know it is.

He played Paganini's outrageous 'Duetto Amoroso' – once, delicately nurtured ladies were said to swoon at the explicit sounds depicting lovers' groans in that music – and then he played the infamous *Devil's Trill* – the piece that Giuseppe Tartini swore had been vouchsafed to him by Satan himself in a dream in return for his immortal soul.

Maxim was in the theatre that night. If I half close my eyes, I can persuade myself that I see him – the silky dark hair, the long, narrow eyes that could glow with excitement. He was heartbreakingly young then. But to think of him, even after so many years, is deeply dangerous.

Even so, it's the memory of that night that I have preserved. I daresay a pragmatist might remark that memories mellow and become rose-tinged with time, and that I've sprinkled that particular one with stardust. A cynic might even question whether I was actually there at all, since I was only four years old in 1881. But I know I was there – I *know* it and I refuse to consider any other possibility.

Whether it's real or not, it's a good memory – a shining memory – and it's the one I always reach for after the nightmare.

On those nights I catch myself wishing Maxim could still be here, but he cannot, of course. He can never be with me ever again.

TWO

Beatrice still sometimes dreamed she could hear Abigail calling to her. Tonight, she woke shortly after 2 a.m. and sat up in bed, shivering, trying to disentangle the dream from the reality, repeating over and over that she could not possibly have heard Abi's voice. Abi, her bright, lovely daughter, had been dead for two years and she would never call out to Beatrice again.

It was always dangerous to go straight back to sleep after the dream in case it pounced again, so Bea went downstairs to heat some milk, adding a good measure of whisky to it. Niall had drunk whisky, but it had only ever been Irish whiskey. Before Bea had discovered that he was impossibly irresponsible as well as incurably amoral, he used to tell her that Irish whiskey was the finest in the world. *Usquebaugh*, he would say, his voice sliding into the soft caressing Irish inflection that Beatrice always found irresistible. They used to drink the soft, smoky whiskey together, curled up in front of an open fire, becoming pleasantly inebriated, after which Niall would carry her up to bed.

On their first night together, he had read part of Dante's *Divine Comedy* to her – the cantos where Beatrice was Dante's guide through Paradise.

'And now, my darling girl, you're my guide into Paradise,' he said, in his softest, most seductive voice, and Bea, trying to hold on to a sense of self and a modicum of self-respect, had mumbled something fatuous about it being a name for elderly maiden aunts or forgotten Victorian princesses.

It was not until some time later she discovered that the poetry-declaiming skill had allowed Niall to lure a disgracefully high number of other females into his bed. It did not help to remind herself that out of all those females she was the one he had married, because she would not put it past him to have married half a dozen others along the way; in fact she would not be surprised to discover some day that her own marriage had been a fake ceremony.

The dream and the sounds of Abigail's cries had receded, and Bea went back to bed. It felt as if goblin-finger shreds of the nightmare might still be clinging to the room, so she slotted a Mozart concerto into the small bedside CD player. If anything could rout the wizened claws of a nightmare, it was Mozart.

But next morning, even with the kitchen radio tuned to a cheerful bounce of Sixties' pop music and the sunlight laying patterns of bright warmth across the kitchen, she could still hear Abigail's cries in her mind. They were impossibly and heartbreakingly clear, and what if—?

But Bea cut off this thought before it could develop. It was the height of absurdity to imagine she might be receiving a spirit-communication from Abigail. It was an even wilder absurdity to let herself wonder if Abi might not be dead after all and if some kind of telepathy had come into being. And yet Bea could not stop thinking how Abi's body had been so badly burned that identification had been extremely difficult, even with dental records. Was it really so wild to wonder if it had been someone else's body that was found that day? A gypsy, an itinerant, a runaway – somebody who was in the wrong place at the wrong time, and who ended in being buried in Abigail's grave? What if Abi herself had wandered off somewhere, injured, or even suffering loss of memory . . .? With some part of her mind reaching out to her mother for help . . .? Oh, for pity's sake, thought Bea, angrily.

This was simply that grief had not yet run its course. Perhaps it never would. Two years was not all that long, not for the loss of a child. Bea was certainly not going mad in any sense, although it might be a good idea to talk to her GP, even perhaps to ask about some kind of counselling. That was what she should do. What she should not do was to consider, with sudden longing, returning to the place where Abi had died. To Tromloy.

Tromloy. Niall's beloved sanctuary place, their cottage on Ireland's west coast. It had been empty since Abigail's death, and it would be empty now. Would weeds have grown up around it, like the thick thorns in a fairy story? Would tiles have fallen from the roof and windows been smashed? The memories of how Niall and a younger Abigail had enthusiastically searched its gardens for fairy rings came flooding in, and it was suddenly unbearable to think of Tromloy being derelict and forlorn.

It was mad in the extreme to own a house which could only be reached by crossing the Irish Sea, then driving across the width of Ireland, but Bea would never sell Tromloy. She abandoned her half-eaten breakfast, and went in search of the keys. They were pushed to the back of a drawer, and they were heavy keys, slightly old-fashioned, but in a good way – in the good way that Tromloy was old-fashioned. The tiny community of Kilcarne, where Tromloy stood, was old-fashioned as well. The place that Time forgot, Niall used to call it. The place that lay beneath a glaze of amber, caught and held in some gentle era that lay outside the modern world.

What if Abigail was still in Kilcarne, still near Tromloy, caught beneath that amber glaze, not knowing who she really was?

An image of Kilcarne, with the smudge of mountains in the distance and the soft shimmer of a lake in the west, rose up to tantalize Beatrice. It would not matter if Tromloy's gardens were weed-choked or if all the windows had fallen in, or the chimneys were choked with birds' nests. Gardens could be tidied, windows could be replaced, chimneys could be swept. Her own work, illustrating children's books, could be done as well in Kilcarne as anywhere else. She had a new commission for a forthcoming series aimed at twelve-to-fourteen-year-olds, somewhat in the vein of the *Twilight* and *Vampire Diaries* series. 'Full colour jacket, of course, about four full colour interiors and another four halftones for each title,' the editor had said. 'It needs the suggestion of creatures with not-quite-human appetites prowling through misty forests. Exactly your kind of thing, Bea.'

Bea had accepted the commission gratefully, and she was enjoying working on the illustrations. She could perfectly well go on with them in Tromloy. She logged on to a travel website and scanned the ferry schedules and timetables. If she took an evening ferry from Liverpool, she could be in Dublin around

11.30 p.m. on the same night. Before she could change her mind, she clicked on the 'Reserve' button for a ferry leaving Liverpool at 8 p.m. the following day, and typed in her credit card details for payment. She hesitated, then pressed the Confirm button.

After this, she wrestled with the Southern Irish electricity suppliers, who cheerfully agreed that they could switch on the power for her by tomorrow night, and they would see to it there and then. Beatrice, who had had more than one encounter with Tromloy's erratic electricity, was inclined to regard this with suspicion, but the only thing to do with Tromloy's power supply was to hope for the best.

I'm going back, she thought, putting her suitcase in the car next morning, and adding her sketching and painting things and the laptop. I'm going back to confront the memories and the ghosts.

Following the road signs for Liverpool Docks, then joining the queue of cars for the evening ferry, she could still hear Abigail's voice calling to her. She still did not know if she needed a psychiatrist to sort out her mind or a priest to sort out her soul. At least, if it was the latter, once in Ireland she would be in the right country, with priests every ten paces. And perhaps when finally she was in Kilcarne and inside Tromloy, she might be able to finally let go of the dreadful images of Abigail's death.

And to come to terms with the fact that it was Niall who had killed their daughter, before dying himself.

Phineas woke to the strains of his ebullient neighbour singing 'Once I was a Virgin, Now I Am a Whore'. He considered thumping on the wall, but the prospect of a row at seven o'clock in the morning was daunting.

He ate breakfast rather absent-mindedly, because his mind was filled with images of Roman Volf and the possibility of finding descendants.

Roman's name was sprinkled all over the internet, of course – there was even a smudgy representation of his last known concert at the Mikhailovksy Theatre in St Petersburg. Phin studied it, liking the ornate auditorium and the elaborate décor, then began searching for results that might contain the words 'descendants', 'son', or 'daughter'. He was not very hopeful, but after about ten minutes a line of text leapt out at him. The heading, emboldened by the search engine, said, 'Roman Volf, the father I never knew.'

Phin banged the Enter key at once, almost jamming it into the keyboard's base in his haste. Waiting for the page to open, he reminded himself that this might be a false lead – someone making capital out of a similarity of name, or simply trying to cash in on a tenuous connection to a notorious person.

The webpage had a note to say the content was an extract from something written by a music hall performer whose name had been Mortimer Quince, and whose heyday had been the early part of the twentieth century. The article had been found in a bundle of old theatre magazines in a bookshop just off the Charing Cross Road, and some of the magazines' contents had been of use in a thesis on English music halls. So, serendipity being what it was, the author of the thesis thought sections were worth posting for general consumption; they were primary source material that might be of interest to other, like-minded students.

Phin took a deep breath, and began to read.

'One of my favourite memories is the night of my performance at the Shepherd's Bush Empire in 1910. I was billed as "Quality Quince". Theatres like a descriptive name, and I had initially suggested Quattrocento Quince which I thought had a certain alliterative elegance to it. I could, I suggested, sing a selection from the *Italian Girl in Algiers* (dear Rossini), to fit with the billing.

The management was not enthusiastic. They said I didn't look Italian, that people in Shepherd's Bush would not want to hear Rossini, and that most of them would never have heard the word *quattrocento* anyway. Ah me, I thought, such is the lot of a man cast among groundlings, and I wondered what my father would have said to such comments.

Then somebody wondered if Quicksilver Quince might suit the occasion. I rather took to that, but somebody else said there were too many letters in it for the poster; ink was expensive and they were not made of money, so in the end we settled for Quality Quince.

Standing on that stage, facing the packed house, seeing the lights and hearing the buzz of anticipation, I had the strongest feeling that the ghost of Roman Volf – the father I never knew – hovered over me approvingly. Perhaps he was just out of sight in the stage box – the box that in so many theatres is said to be haunted. And perhaps the shades of all the people who attended his final, ill-starred concert at the Mikhailovsky Theatre in St Petersburg, were with him, listening and smiling as I sang.

It's a beautiful theatre, the Shepherd's Bush Empire, with a baroque stage and magnificent porticoes. We had almost a full house, so I expanded my act considerably, both as to volume and expression. I believe there was quite a run on the bar in the interval immediately after my appearance, which speaks for itself.'

Phineas re-read this a second, and then a third time. So Roman Volf had sired a son, and that son had taken to the music halls.

He rather liked the sound of Quince there was a touching, almost childlike vanity in the writing, although Phin smiled rather wryly at the mention of the Shepherd's Bush audience making hastily for the bar after Quince's performance.

There was not much left of the extract, but he read what there was.

'Readers may be interested to know that since coming here to Ireland's west coast, I have been involved in a number of theatrical projects – music festivals and concert parties during the 1940s, staged for the war effort. Even now, in my mature years (I use the word *mature* advisedly, rather than the term *old age,* for I believe I still have a kick or two left in me yet), even in this peaceful backwater of Kilcarne, I believe I can still achieve further successes before I finally retire to create my memoirs.'

Until this last paragraph, Phin had been making notes to follow up the Shepherd's Bush Empire lead, his mind already delightedly remembering its BBC years, thinking it was possible that Quince's appearance there might be documented.

He had not, however, expected to be confronted with the

need to travel to Ireland's west coast. But there it was. Kilcarne, where Quince had spent what he called his mature years, and been involved in wartime entertainments and music festivals.

Had Quince finally created those memoirs? Had they ever been printed? And was there any possibility Quince had married in that peaceful backwater and left a son or daughter – a descendant of Roman Volf?

Mortimer Quince's diary

I am amassing some excellent material for my memoirs. Actually writing them is to be a task for my old age – although I shall never refer to myself as 'old' in the memoirs or, indeed, out of them. The word *old* is much too evocative of senility's more undignified aspects. False teeth and a truss, not to mention rheumatism, and very likely a few other things one would not want known – especially not by the ladies (God bless them).

And so I am making diligent notes. I daresay Sam Pepys did much the same, although I shouldn't think it will ever be necessary for me to bury cheese in the garden to save it from a Great Fire as he did, or be chased round a bedroom by an irate spouse brandishing a cooking pot. If, that is, I had a spouse . . . A gentleman never tells, of course, but I believe there are one or two ladies who would not be unwilling. And cometh the hour, cometh the man . . .

Note to self: Look up that last reference and make sure that (a) it is correctly quoted, (b) that I know who originally said it, and (c) that it is not in any way improper, because it sounds as if it might be very improper indeed in certain contexts.

I've never talked about Roman – although I am hoping I shall be able to do so when I finally embark on creating my memoirs. However, for the moment and in the privacy of these pages I feel it's safe to mention him.

I've always tried to believe that Roman's part in the tsar's assassination sprang from altruism – that it might be interpreted as romantic and even noble. But there is nothing romantic or noble about strangling on the end of a rope in a St Petersburg prison yard, with half the country baying for your blood.

At some scarcely acknowledged level I think there was more

to Roman's death than being hanged – that there was something dark and dreadful. I believe if I could identify that, I could send the wretched nightmare fleeing for its life. But there is no one I can ask about Roman's life or his death, and in any case I dare not let my paternity be known.

This afternoon I spent an hour polishing my renditions of 'Oft in the Stilly Night', and 'Believe Me, If All Those Endearing Young Charms'. I worked hard, so I feel it was unkind of the man in the rooms below to stump up the stairs and hammer crossly on my door. He is a very disagreeable person, and when I refused to open the door, he shouted through the keyhole that my voice resembled the yowling tomcats in the alley below.

Later:

The disagreeable person's rudeness has been somewhat allevi-ated by the lady living in the second floor back, who tapped on my door a few moments ago to invite me to take a glass of port with her after supper. She thought I might also favour her with some of my singing. (Much fluttering of eyelashes at this point, and arch prods in the ribs.)

I do not care overmuch for port, and the lady herself is a little too well-upholstered for my taste. However, it seems discourteous to decline.

Later still:

Port definitely does not agree with me. I gave my hostess a performance of 'Little Rosewood Casket', after which I disported myself to some purpose with her on her chaise longue, since clearly it was expected, and there are times when a man must yield to the inevitable. Regrettably, however, I fell prey to violent and undignified indigestion at what I can only call an unfortunate moment, but thankfully, I regained my own rooms without unseemly incident.

Note: The evening is not one to be included in my memoirs.

THREE

I t had been almost two years since Beatrice had looked inside the folder containing the various documents relating to Abigail's death. She had pushed the file to the back of a shelf and pretended it and its contents did not exist.

But before setting off for Ireland and Tromloy, some impulse had made her reach for the folder and drop it into her suitcase. I'm taking you with me, Abi, she thought, and then was annoyed with herself for such a slushily useless sentiment.

The ferry crossing from Liverpool was calm, the Dublin hotel where she spent that night was comfortable, and driving out of Dublin towards Kilcarne next morning, Bea began to think this had been a good decision. She pulled in to a large supermarket for provisions. Tins and jars and packet soups. Bread and cheese and fruit. Coffee and tea bags and long-life milk, because there was no guarantee that the power would be on by the time she got there, and even if it was it would take a few hours for the elderly fridge to clank its way to a safely cold temperature. On that thought she added candles and matches.

Setting off again, she tuned the car radio to a local, pleasantly chatty station, and smiled to think she would soon be seeing the familiar signs: GALWAY/B. Átha Luain/ATHLONE/ Gaillimh.

Niall used to quote Yeats's famous 'Innisfree' poem on this part of the journey. It was as if the nearer they got to Tromloy, the more he pulled his Irish antecedents around him like a cloak. '*I will arise and go now, and go to Innisfree . . .*' The next verse was something about finding peace, wasn't it? With the thought, the words slid into Bea's mind. '*And I shall have some peace there, for peace comes dropping slow, Dropping from the veils of the morning . . .*'

Bea turned on to the straight run of Ireland's M6 and put her foot down. In the far distance were the misty smudges of the mountains behind Kilcarne. Niall always called them the Mountains of Midnight, with magnificent disregard for their real names. One night he and Bea had walked out to the foothills, taking a bottle of wine with them. They had drunk the wine lying in the deep, soft grass, and Niall had made love to her, with the distant chimes of a church clock sounding midnight. Bea always believed that had been when Abigail was conceived, there in the soft purple twilight, on the exact stroke of twelve. Innisfree: *'There midnight's all a glimmer, and noon a purple glow . . .'*

Niall said it was absurd to fixate on that one night, and hadn't they both been drunk as owls anyway, but Beatrice had always thought of Abi as the child of that soft, enchanted midnight. Was it possible she was out there now, wandering the foothills of her father's Midnight Mountains, not knowing who she was—? Reciting the lyrical, beautiful poetry Niall had taught her . . . She had never understood more than one word in ten, but even as a small girl she had loved the cadences and the rhythms of the words. She had loved pretending she was one of the people from the old tales, as well. 'Today I'm Mab,' she would say. 'I'm an Irish Queen, and I'm going to fight battles so I can get a throne. An' then I'll dance by pale moonshine and hide in an acorn cup an' have a chariot made out of a hazel-nut. Won't I?'

'You might, but you've got a bit of old Bill Shakespeare mixed up in that one,' Niall used to say, indulgent and amused. 'Because that's one of the Queen Mab speeches, but it's *Romeo and Juliet.*' He began the speech, in his soft, caressing voice.

'O, then, I see Queen Mab hath been with you;
'She is the fairies' midwife, and she comes
'In shape no bigger than an agate-stone.

'That's the line for you, Abigail. Because you're not much bigger than an agate-stone.'

Beatrice dashed an angry hand across her eyes, to wipe out the scalding memories.

Here were the uneven crossroads with the lopsided signposts, like two drunken tinkers propping each other up. The road to

Tromloy was the right-hand one; the left led to Kilcarne's small cemetery. Abigail was in that cemetery, and so was Niall. After they died, Bea had initially thought she would bring their bodies back to England, but then she had remembered the big, neatly ordered English cemetery with its uniform rows of graves and memorials, and she had thought Abi would hate it. Abi would rather be here with the midnight mountains and the tanglewood trees, and the lyrical legends all around her. (And her father who had killed her lying in his own grave nearby . . .?) Bea took a deep breath, and swung the car over to the left and the cemetery.

There were no Victorian Gothic iron gates or admonitory notices, or warnings about it being locked at sunset. The cemetery was open to all comers at all hours, because the Irish liked their dead to be accessible. You'd want to be nipping in for a prayer or two for the poor departed souls now and then, they said, practically.

Even though it was two years since she had last been there, Bea went unerringly along the paths to the patch of ground beneath the old beech tree. Abigail would have liked the tree; she would have made up stories about the creatures who might live inside it, and who might come out to dance in the moonlight when the humans were not around. Bea stood for a long time, looking down at the grave. Impossible and unbearable to think of her midnight child down there. She knelt down, and half reached out a hand, then, impatient with herself, stood up and turned away.

Walking back, she saw for the first time that there was an inner garden here. A small wrought-iron gate was set into the old stone wall that ran along one side of the graveyard. Glad of anything that would push the memories away, Bea went over to it. It probably led to the church, or it was the priest's private garden and securely locked. But the gate swung inwards with only a small scrape of old hinges. Bea hesitated, then stepped through.

It was not a garden and it did not lead anywhere. It was a smaller, older cemetery. Most of the graves had memorial stones, and, rather surprisingly, they were all well tended. She walked slowly along them, seeing a few names she half recognized from the little Kilcarne community. O'Brien – that was the family who had owned the local pub ever since Bea could remember. She and Niall had sometimes had a bar meal there. And Cullen – weren't there still Cullens here? Bea had a vague memory of a rather gloomy house, and of two rather timid ladies. There was a pallid look about her picture of them, as if they had been left out in the rain, causing their colours to become diluted.

At the very end, she paused, and as her eyes fell on the inscription of the final grave, the lowering skies seemed to tilt and blur all around her.

The name on the stone was Maxim Volf. The date of his death was 1955.

Maxim Volf. Beatrice had never met Maxim Volf, but she had hated him for two years deeply and bitterly. He had been there when Abigail died – he had seen her die – his evidence had been used at the inquest. Beatrice had been told, later, that he said he had tried to save her. She had not believed it.

But, according to the plaque on that sad, hidden-away ceme-tery, Maxim Volf had died in 1955. More than half a century earlier.

Bea did not remember walking back to her car, but she must have done, because the next thing she knew was that she was sitting inside it with rain spattering the windows.

Maxim Volf. It would be nothing more than a coincidence of names, or someone from the same family – perhaps the father of the man who had been there when Abigail died.

But it was an unusual name. As for family, Maxim Volf had not seemed to have any family or any connection with Kilcarne. One of the newspaper reports had said it was the purest chance that had taken him along that road on that day.

Much later he had sent a message to her through the Garda. He expressed his deepest and most heartfelt sympathies and regret for what had happened, and added his assurance that he had done everything he could to save her daughter and her husband. The message had been forwarded to Beatrice, who had crumpled it up angrily and thrown it away.

The rain was worsening, but she got out of the car and

opened the boot to get the folder she had brought with her.
She knew the contents by heart, but back in the car, she took
out the sheaf of papers, doing so with extreme care, almost
as if, this time, the information might be different.

Death certificates, coroners' reports, police reports, burial
authorities . . . Everything was there. At the bottom was a
newspaper cutting from a local Irish newspaper. Bea smoothed
this out and read it.

Tragedy at Kilcarne – witness finally named

The man who witnessed the tragedy that took place at
Kilcarne in early January, and who tried to save 12-year-old
Abigail Drury and her father, Niall (42), has been named
as Mr Maxim Volf.

We understand Mr Volf suffered a lengthy period of
amnesia immediately after the incident, which prevented
him from being identified. In addition, the injuries
he sustained in his attempt to save Abigail and Niall
Drury made speech difficult, and severe burns to his
hands made it difficult for him even to write information
for the doctors and the Garda.

The inquest brought in a verdict of Death by Mis-
adventure on Abigail and Niall Drury. Mr Volf was being
treated at University Hospital, Galway, at the time, but
was able to dictate a brief statement which was read out
to the coroner and the jury.

Later, the Garda had told Beatrice that Maxim Volf had been
discharged from hospital and presumably had returned to his
own life. Bea had not wanted to know where or what that life
might be. She had a dreadful suspicion that if ever she met
Maxim Volf she might fly at him and try to claw out his eyes,
because she had never managed to rid herself of a conviction
that he had not tried hard enough to save Abigail and Niall,
and she had been left with a disturbing impression of a man
who had materialized almost out of nowhere, played a small
part in a tragedy, then vanished. What she had not been
prepared for was to find a sixty-year old grave with his exact
– and quite unusual – name on it.

She put the cutting back in the folder, and realized with a shock that it was almost four o'clock, and that in another hour it would be practically dark. She had not wanted to reach Tromloy in the dark, but you lost all sense of time when you stepped back into the past.

She drove away from the cemetery, and this time when she reached the drunken signpost, she took the right-hand turn to Tromloy. Here was the five-bar gate that Abi used to swing on, and in the distance were church spires and a few crumbling watchtowers, sharply black against the darkening sky. In a few moments she would see Tromloy. It was starting to feel over-whelmingly right to be driving to Tromloy through the cool dusk, with the after-scent of the rainstorm coming in through the car's open windows.

On the left was the old piece of stone that Niall had found somewhere in the scrubby land surrounding Tromloy, and had engraved with the house's name. It was a bit of the old manor house that had once stood here, he said. Kilcarne Mainéar. He was going to find out more about it one day. He had dented the car's wing on that stone, taking this bend too fast one night because he wanted to get home and make love to her. The mark was still visible on the stone.

Now she had reached the turning on to the path. Thick branches and brambles grew over the path; they whipped across the windscreen, leaving soft green-grey smears so that when Tromloy came at last into view, its outline was blurred.

Bea stopped the car halfway up the track. It was going to be all right. Tromloy still held all of its magic. It was still the serene, forgotten corner that Time had overlooked, the place where peace dropped from the veils of the morning. She engaged a lower gear for the rest of the steep path, and, closer to, a little of the house's enchantment began to dissolve. Even in this half-light she could see that the windows were thick with grime and a section of guttering had worked loose from under the eaves. A few slates were missing from the roof and there were cracks in the paving stones at the house's front. Still, what had she expected after so long? And windows could be cleaned, guttering could be nailed back in place, slates and paths could be repaired, and grass could be mown. She parked on the scrubland at the

house's front, and as she got out of the car the silence and
the twilight closed around her.

Bea left the headlights on to see her way to the front door,
but as she took her case from the boot there was a movement
on the rim of her vision. Her heart jumped. Had a figure darted
across one of the downstairs windows, or had it been her
imagination – or even just the reflection of clouds scudding
across the sky? Bea waited, but the movement did not come
again, and she relaxed. Even so, she would check all the
rooms, and be ready to beat it outside at the speed of light
if she encountered anything suspicious.

The old-fashioned lock turned smoothly, and the door swung
open silently. It's all right, thought Bea. There's no one here.
The house is empty. It's been empty for two years.

She stepped inside.

Jessica Cullen had been interested at first when the aunts talked
about the English lady, Beatrice Drury.

They were having supper, and Aunt Nuala said she had
been surprised to hear that Mrs Drury was coming back to
Kilcarne.

'There must be so many sad memories for her. Her poor
child and her husband killed here.'

Aunt Morna agreed. She said Mrs Drury must be intending
to stay for some time, because the electricity people had been
asked to switch on the power at the cottage.

'Although she'll probably find herself with a series of
hiccupping power cuts for the first week, because Tromloy's
electricity was always a law unto itself.'

Tromloy. Jessica looked up, startled, because the word had
dropped into her mind like a black, dense stone falling into
a deep pool. *Tromloy*. One of the brief, shutter-flash images
darted across her mind – low ceilings and the scent of wood
smoke and peat . . . Firelight on rows of books, lighting up
an old fire screen made by someone who had lived long,
long ago – a screen with old photographs in it . . . And there
was someone in that room who was huddled over and crying
bitterly . . .

But people who saw things that were not there were

sometimes mad, so Jessica pushed the images away, and asked, a bit timidly, what Tromloy was.

There was an odd moment of silence, and Aunt Morna glanced uneasily at Uncle Tormod who was eating his supper in silence, his Bible propped up against the mustard pot. Then, in what Jessica thought of as too careful a voice, Aunt Morna said, 'It's that old cottage just outside the village.'

'Part of an old estate that once stood there,' said Aunt Nuala, briskly. 'Kilcarne Manor, it was. Tormod, have you the salt, please?'

'Tromloy's a bit off the road, Jess,' said Aunt Morna. 'So you might not have noticed it. There's a narrow track leading up to it, although it's very overgrown by now.'

'Still, I believe Mrs Drury always spoke of it as a serene house.'

Serene, thought Jessica. That means quiet. It means safe. The flicker of memory came again, but then Uncle Tormod came up out of the Book of Job to frown at the aunts, and say it did not become them to speculate about their neighbours or criticize the condition of their houses. He who sowed discord among his brethren was one of the things the Lord hateth, said Tormod sternly. His eyes showed angry red flecks for a moment, and the aunts exchanged worried looks.

Uncle Tormod was Nuala and Morna's older brother, which meant he was Jess's uncle, although it was difficult to think of him by that name, because 'uncle' was a warm, cosy kind of word. Tormod Cullen was not warm or cosy in the least. He was humourless and severe, but Jessica tried to think this might be because he could only walk about with a stick, and if he went out he had to be pushed in a wheelchair, which was enough to make anyone humourless and severe.

But the anger faded from Tormod's face and he only said, quite mildly, that none of them should listen to gossip of any kind – Jessica was particularly to mind that, please – and now someone might kindly serve him another spoonful of vegetables.

'I'll do it,' said Nuala quickly, as Jessica reached for the dish. 'That tureen's a bit heavy for you, Jessica.'

The aunts were always stopping Jess from lifting heavy or awkwardly shaped objects, and helping her with things she did not need help with. When she went out with her sketch-book, Aunt Nuala always wanted to sharpen pencils for her. It was as if they did not think she was capable, and sometimes it felt a bit smothering. But tonight Jessica's mind was filled up with Tromloy, so she let Aunt Nuala pick up the large vegetable dish and spoon vegetables on to Uncle Tormod's plate. She said to Tormod that she would not listen to gossip, and did not say she would rather be off in the fields with her sketching things.

The aunts did not really understand about drawing or how you could lose yourself in making a picture, but Donal had given Jess sketching things as a birthday present, and anything Donal did was right. They doted on Donal, who was the son of a distant cousin. They told everyone about the work he did in his parish, whether people wanted to know or not, and how pleased the bishop was with him.

Uncle Tormod said they thought more of Donal than they did of him. Sometimes, when Donal came to stay, Tormod said they were neglecting him and he might as well go into the workhouse and have done, for all the looking-after he got in his own home. When Aunt Morna told him that there were no such things as workhouses any longer and he was living in another century, Tormod brandished his stick at her and recited chunks of the Old Testament at the top of his voice, with what Aunt Nuala thought were bits of Shakespeare thrown in for good measure. Afterwards he demanded to be wheeled over to the church, where they all had to pray for forgiveness, and the aunts put in an extra request for God not to send Tormod another stroke. As Nuala said afterwards, another stroke might be fatal, which would mean they were left on their own, and what would they do then?

The aunts were frightened of Tormod dying and leaving them on their own. Jessica understood that, not especially because she was frightened of Uncle Tormod dying or of being alone, but because she found the world in general frightening and often confusing. She thought there might once have been a time when she was not frightened of anything, but it had been a long time ago. She thought something bad had happened – something that had twisted everything out of shape in her mind – but she could never quite remember what the bad thing had been.

But tonight, listening to the aunts talking about Mrs Drury and Tromloy, she had had the feeling that Tromloy might have something to do with the out-of-shape world. And with that other faint, thin memory – the memory of hands reaching for her – hands with hard, horrid fingers like mutton bones that must be resisted at all costs . . .

FOUR

As soon as Beatrice stepped inside Tromloy, the memories came scudding out of the dimness, strong and insistent and hurting. She pushed them away and went into the long, low-ceilinged sitting room that opened off the hall. Even in the uncertain light she could see the familiar furniture – the button-back sofa, the bookshelves that lined the walls on each side of the hearth. There was even the lingering scent of wood smoke on the air.

The small transom at the top of the main window was partly open – had Niall left it open that last day? Had it been open for two years? A fold of curtain had caught in it, and it stirred gently in the soft evening wind. Immensely relieved to find such a prosaic explanation for the flicker of movement she had seen earlier, Bea closed the window, and went into the kitchen to fill the kettle for a cup of tea. The water ran a bit rustily at first as it always did, then came clear. She filled the kettle, and plugged it in, deliberately not looking at the faint pink stain on the kitchen table, from where she had spilled a glass of wine because Niall was making her laugh about something or other. It had never quite scrubbed out, that stain.

She left the kettle to boil and went out to the car. The box of groceries was set on the kitchen table, and she carried her case upstairs, pausing outside the room that had been Abigail's. The door was closed, but Beatrice laid her hand against its surface for a moment, as if she might be able to draw something of Abi from out of the room. Ridiculous, of course.

She went along to the bedroom that had been hers and Niall's, past the faint outline of the longcase clock that used to stand against the wall. Niall had taken it to a clock-maker in Galway, to have its chiming mechanism repaired. Bea had forgotten about it until now. Was it still in the Galway workshop?

As she unpacked her case, Tromloy's gentle familiarity was

already closing around her. This is what I wanted, thought Beatrice, gratefully, and realized she was even smiling at hearing the soft creakings and rustlings that were part of this house. But as she hung up things in the wardrobe, unease began to seep into her mind. Something within the sounds was different. There was something inside the house that was not part of its normal sounds — or was it something that had once been part of Tromloy but ought no longer to be? The sounds were falling into a recognizable pattern – a soft, steady creaking, almost rhythmic. There would be a perfectly ordinary, unmenacing explanation, of course, but her heart began to race and she felt as if every nerve in her body was being scraped raw.

The sounds were coming from Abigail's room.

For several seconds, Beatrice's mind spiralled crazily out of the realms of the mundane and into the stratosphere of pure joy. The thought of having just one more glimpse of her lost, lovely girl — and it would not matter if that glimpse were only a ten-second one – filled her up like light. But even as the emotion was reaching its zenith, common sense was pulling her back, because of course it was not Abi she was hearing; it was nothing to do with Abi. The darting movement she had seen when she arrived nudged against her mind, but that had been downstairs, and she had identified its cause. These sounds would be a trapped bird, or a rattling window-frame, or even a clanking bit of pipework.

Whatever it was, it would have to be checked. Bea went out to the landing and looked along it, towards the stairs. Then her heart, already skittering nervously, leapt with real fear, because the door of Abigail's room – unquestionably closed earlier – was three-quarters open. She could see the bed with the heaped-up green and bronze cushions, and she could see the bookshelves behind it, and on the wall the old framed photograph of some long-ago actor standing on a stage. Against the hearth was the old fire screen, and facing it was the Victorian rocking chair that Bea and Niall had found in an antiques shop in Galway.

It was the chair that was making the sounds. It was moving

slightly – rocking gently as it always did when someone who had been sitting in it had just stood up. Beatrice stood very still, trying to make sense of this, knowing that of course there would be an ordinary explanation, just as there had been an ordinary explanation for that movement seen downstairs earlier – the movement that had been nothing more sinister than an open window and a flapping curtain.

But there were no windows open here, nothing that could have disturbed the chair, and there was something wrong about the room. For pity's sake, thought Bea exasperatedly, it's been two years – you won't be remembering every detail! But everything about Abi's bedroom was printed on her mind down to the tiniest detail. She knew the furniture, the book titles and the books' exact positions on the shelves; she knew the way the curtains fell, with the faint splash of paint always turned inwards to hide it . . . She knew the way the old wardrobe in the corner cast its shadow on the carpet . . .

The wardrobe's shadow. That was what was wrong – dreadfully and frighteningly wrong. It was not the solid oblong it ought to be – it formed a very specific shape. Or was it just the way the shadows twisted in the half-light? Or a coat hanging from the wardrobe itself? She waited for her mind to make sense of what she was seeing, waiting for the little pulse of nervous fear to disperse and for her brain to say, Stupid! Didn't you realize what you were really seeing? But it did not, and Bea took a step towards the wardrobe. At once the shadow moved, and in that instant Bea had no doubt about what she was seeing. A man-shaped shadow. A shadow cast by someone standing in the narrow space between the wardrobe and the window wall. Someone who had just pressed back against the wall in an attempt to avoid being seen.

For several dreadful seconds sheer terror held Bea helpless. Then some reflex or some instinct – or maybe just panic – kicked in, and she was outside the room before she was aware of having moved, slamming the door on Abi's room, and going down the stairs in a frantic slithering tumble. She retained enough clarity of mind to snatch up her bag containing the phone, then she wrenched open the front door and half fell through it.

The darkness came at her like a wall, but Bea plunged into it gratefully because it was a hiding place, and ran along the broken path that had never been relaid or repaired, praying not to trip on the uneven ground.

She had almost reached the car when she heard soft footsteps coming through the darkness. He – it had to be a 'he' didn't it? – had come out of the house, and he was coming towards her. Bea dived around to the other side of the car, and crouched down. Could she get the door open and drive away before he reached her? The interior light would come on when the door was opened, but the engine was warm and it would fire immediately, and she could be bouncing the car down the lane and out of his reach. If she had the ignition keys ready the minute she was inside—

She could not have the ignition keys ready at all, and she could not bounce the car anywhere, because the keys were not in her bag. There was a brief, infuriating memory of throwing them down on the kitchen table earlier, and leaving them there. But the phone was in her bag, and it was 999 for emergencies in Ireland, like in England, wasn't it? Would he hear her make the phone call? Would he see the light from the keypad? She crouched down, reaching into the side pocket for the phone, trying to switch it on while it was still inside, but her hands were shaking so much she could not find the On switch.

There was a crunch of footsteps close by and Bea gasped and looked up. He was standing on the other side of the car, looking down at her over the bonnet. She flinched, one hand going up in the classic defence gesture, then a man's voice said, quietly and unthreateningly, 'Please don't be frightened. I don't mean to hurt you. I'm going away now.'

The words were gentle and slightly blurred. The voice was hesitant and there was even almost a pleading note to it. It was the last kind of voice Bea had been expecting to hear, and for several incredible seconds she forgot about the need to summon help. Psychopaths probably sounded gentle and polite before they set about butchering their victims, but he did not sound like a psychopath . . .

She said, with a sharpness that surprised her, 'I've called the police – the Garda – they'll be here within minutes.'

She had no idea if he would believe her, but at once he said, 'There's no need for that. I really am very sorry to have frightened you so much.' His voice was still soft and it was also somehow careful, and this time Bea thought she could detect something un-English in it. 'I didn't know you were coming, and when I heard you arrive, I hid in that room. I hoped I could get outside without you knowing.' He seemed to hesitate, then he said, 'That house has helped me. That's why I've been going there sometimes, while it's been empty. It's gentle. Friendly.'

Tromloy, working its charm . . . Bea said, 'You've been in the house before?' and thought this had to be the most bizarre conversation she had ever had.

'I have, but I won't do so again,' he said. 'Not now. You have my promise.'

'How did you get in?'

'There's a broken window catch on a downstairs window.'

Before Bea could say anything else, he was walking away, going towards the path. She drew in a deep, shaky breath, and snatched her phone from her bag because it no longer mattered if he heard or saw. The keypad lit up, and the man turned, as if the sudden tiny radiance had caught his attention. For a split-second the minuscule light fell across his face. He turned away at once, but in that brief moment Beatrice had seen the scarred skin, puckered and ridged. Then he put up a hand to turn up the collar of his coat, in an instinctive concealing gesture, and with an unwilling wrench of pity Bea saw his hand was scarred in the same way. There could not possibly be any connection, of course, but the words of the newspaper article came strongly into her mind.

. . . *sustained injuries in the attempt . . . Hands and face badly burned . . . He was still being treated at University Hospital, Galway at the time of the inquest . . .*

For a moment the moonlight showed up the intruder's hair as well – thick, and grey like the cloth of an expensive coat. Bea had the brief impression that once it had been dark, but that something had drained all its colour.

But he was going away. He was being as good as his word. Beatrice leaned back against the side of the car, then, with an

inexplicable sense of reluctance and almost of guilt, managed
to tap out the three nines that would bring the Garda.

Walking down the hillside, away from Tromloy, it was easy
to melt into the darkness. There had, after all, been years of
doing exactly that. Two years to be precise. You simply thought
yourself into being a shadow – what the Gothic novelists
probably called a 'creature of the night' – and eventually you
became that shadow creature. It was almost a form of method
acting.

Until tonight it had been easy enough to enter Tromloy
through the window with the loose catch, and later to push it
back in place so that no one would notice. Not that anyone
would notice, because no one ever came out here. Except the
man who sought for forgiveness from a dead girl. I failed you,
Abigail Drury. I should have saved you that day – you and
your father – and I failed. And because of that, you both died
a bad death. You're the one who draws me back to Tromloy,
over and over again, Abigail. That's probably the behaviour
of an obsessive or a compulsive or something, but if I can't
allow myself one obsession, it's a sad old life. I can never
forgive myself for letting you die, Abigail. That woman – your
mother – she'll never forgive me, either.

It had seemed almost impossible that Beatrice Drury would
return to Tromloy. But tonight she had, and there had been a
deep sense of loss in walking away, knowing it would never
again be possible to enter the house like a shadow and be greeted
by the scents of wood smoke and old timbers. No longer possible
to reach in that uncertain, fumbling way for the spirit of a dead
girl, who ought not to have died, who ought to have been saved
. . . The nightmare of what had happened had not faded – the
images were as vivid as ever they had been.

There could be no returning to Tromloy. A promise had
been made to a woman with haunted eyes. She had clearly
been frightened, but she had seemed to accept a stranger's
promise. It was a promise that had been made in good faith
and it could not be broken.

Or could it?

*   *   *

The Garda turned up promptly at Tromloy and they were helpful and reassuring. They said to Beatrice didn't you often get vagrants who were after a night's comfortable kipping place, and hadn't Tromloy been empty for so long it would likely be a magnet for all the tramps in Galway County. Bea found this terrifying, until they reminded her that there was a general arrangement with them to just drive out here every few weeks to make sure nobody had broken in. They had done that faithfully, they said, but possibly somebody had just slipped through that net.

'I'd forgotten about that,' said Bea, gratefully.

Back inside the house with the cheerful presence of the Garda, she felt better. Remembering she had plugged in the kettle about a hundred years ago, she offered them a cup of tea. That would be altogether grand they said, and went off to check the house. That was when Bea discovered the kettle was stone cold. Had it boiled and cooled? She pressed the switch again, then tried the light switch, which did not work. When she opened the fridge it was gloomily dark, and the cooker, switched to High, remained obstinately cold, emitting no light, only a faint smell of old grease.

Beatrice explained the problem to the Garda, trying to pretend that the prospect of spending the night in an unlit house with one intruder already to its name did not worry her in the least.

The Garda said you couldn't trust an electricity person from here to the end of the road, and they would phone them on Mrs Drury's behalf first thing tomorrow, pointing out the need for immediate power in the house. In the meantime they would rig up some light so people would know the house was inhabited – they'd a hazard warning cone in the boot of one of the cars, that would be the very thing, and it would shine like a good deed in a naughty world.

Windows and doors were next checked by torchlight, and pronounced secure, with the exception of a loose catch found on a downstairs window. That would be how the man had got in, but they would send someone tomorrow out to deal with that as well. Meantime they would arrange four saucepans and the frying pan across the sill, so that anyone trying to climb in would send them cascading to the floor in a fine old clatter, which would serve as a warning. Beatrice thought that only in Ireland would someone create a security system using saucepans. She thanked the Garda, promised she would phone them if there were any more disturbances, and watched them drive off. Then she went back to the kitchen to see what kind of meal could be put together without electricity.

Dining by candlelight in Tromloy with Niall had been romantic and light-hearted. Doing so alone was dreary and vaguely eerie. Bea set several candles in saucers, then opened a tin of tuna for a sandwich and poured a glass of milk to go with it. At intervals she got up to try the light switches in case the Garda had managed to reach the power company this evening, and somebody had taken pity on her. No one had, of course, so Bea rinsed the plate and knife in cold water, then rather defiantly opened a bottle of wine and took it into the sitting room.

Now that it was dark, the house was starting to feel chilly and unfriendly. Bea glared at the two impotent electric heaters, then knelt down to stack peat turfs in the hearth. At first she thought she had forgotten the trick of making a peat fire, but she persevered, because if she could manage it, it would be warm and comforting, and the glow would chase away the nightmares and the ghosts. Ghosts . . . If ghosts were likely to walk anywhere, they would surely do so in a darkened cottage at the end of a remote lane. Or had she encountered a ghost here already? Bea pushed the thought away. The man who had been in Abigail's room had been real enough. The broken window catch had been real, as well.

It was just on nine o'clock. It would have been companionable to have a workable television or radio, but at least Bea had brought several books with her. She reached for one now – a pleasantly light Agatha Christie. There were worse ways of passing an evening than with a glass of wine – maybe two or three glasses of wine – and a book. Tomorrow the electricity would be on and everything would be normal.

The glow from the candles fell invitingly across the big wing chair by the hearth, and the peat fire was burning up so well it was almost too hot. Bea set down her book, and carrying one of the candles, went up to Abi's room to fetch the old fire screen. It was another of Tromloy's fixtures – it had been in the house ever since Beatrice could remember, and Abi had liked having it in her bedroom. Bea had always meant to trace the screen's origins, but had never got round to it. Perhaps that could be a project while she was here.

She propped the screen across the fire to dilute some of the heat, and returned to Dame Agatha's gentle complexity of suspects. But the screen drew her eye. It was about two feet in height and roughly three feet wide – a hinged structure, with the fold at the centre. Whoever had made it had used a miscellany of photographs and newspaper cuttings, and even what looked like one or two old theatre posters or programmes, all carefully positioned, and glazed. The varnish was yellow with age and in places it had cracked, but most of the scraps were still visible. Abi had liked to lie in bed and look across at the screen. She had made up stories about the photographs and the old newspaper articles.

Most of the females in the photographs had slumberous eyes and faint, enigmatic smiles. It could be immensely sexy, of course, that particular look, even though it probably just meant the subjects had been concentrating on remaining absolutely still for the old-style flash cameras, rather than from any come-to-bed inclination. The men had sleek oiled hair and gentlemanly clothes. They would stand up if a lady came into the room, and hold doors open. Bea had never known who any of the photographed people were, although they all had beautiful complexions and good cheekbones. The man who had been here earlier had had those cheekbones, as well. Or had that simply been the scar tissue distorting his features?

How damaging would it be to chip away the varnish from the screen or steam the photos off to see if anything was written on the back? Probably it would end in ruining the whole thing and destroying any value it might have. Bea would never want to sell it, because it was part of Tromloy and Tromloy's good memories, but that did not mean it would be acceptable to bash it about and spoil it. And, like Abigail, Bea found it intriguing to wonder about the people and the stories behind the photos and the newspaper scraps. What, for instance, had governed the choice of cuttings about somebody's celebration birthday supper, or the inclusion of a half-page of a ragged-edged music score, or a programme from some long-ago musical event in Galway? There were several almost-indecipherable names of people who had apparently performed at that. Bea could make out two or three of the names, but she did not recognize any of them.

Except for one on the very edge of the fragment.

Maxim Volf.

She got up from the chair, and tilted the candle to see the fragment better, but there was nothing more to see. Just that name.

There was, of course, a perfectly simple explanation, although it took her some time to work it out. But in the end she had it. The man who had apparently tried to rescue Abigail that day had not wanted to reveal his real identity or his presence in Kilcarne, so he had borrowed a name seen by chance in an old graveyard. A name that happened to belong to a man who had had some involvement in a long-ago concert in Galway.

Bea was very glad indeed to have thought of this satisfactory solution. As for the man's motives that day, they could be any one of half a dozen. He could have been a glamorous spy or an enterprising burglar on his way to overseeing an international jewel robbery. At the other end of the scale he could be an illegal immigrant or someone engaged in a clandestine love affair.

Could tonight's intruder really have been the same man? It was stretching coincidence, and it was also possible that Bea was getting carried away with the concept of Maxim Volf still being in the area – even that she was dreaming up links where links did not exist. The odds were that Maxim Volf had gone back to his home, wherever that was, and tried to put the tragedy from his mind.

But there had seemed to be links, for all that. The intruder had appeared to know Tromloy – he had talked about finding it gentle and friendly. So how many times had he been in here? Also, Tromloy was not a house you came upon by chance

– you had to look for it. Had the man looked for it? Bea forced herself to examine this possibility in more detail. If it really had been Maxim, was it conceivable that, having failed to save Abigail, he had deliberately searched for her home, and had taken to coming here? But why? As a pilgrimage? As some sort of healing ritual? As a penance, even? The Irish were much given to pilgrimages and penances, although the man had not sounded Irish.

. . . sustained injuries in the attempt . . . Face and hands badly burned . . . He was still being treated at University Hospital, Galway at the time of the inquest . . .

The biggest coincidence of all – the fact that Bea could not stop remembering – was that even in that split-second glimpse, the scars on the intruder's face and hand had looked like the result of burns.

Morna and Nuala Cullen agreed it was unfortunate that they had talked about Tromloy over supper. They had been so careful, always, never to mention the place in front of Jessica.

But it was difficult to find things to talk about at supper-time, with Tormod banning so many subjects. They could not discuss current events, or television programmes containing anything questionable – although, as Morna said, that seemed to rule out practically all the programmes currently on TV. If they did ever stray into dubious conversational waters, Tormod always became agitated; sometimes he silenced them by reading a passage from his Bible aloud. He was particularly partial to the Old Testament, which often seemed to Morna and Nuala a touch dubious on its own account, what with all the begetting that had gone on and the behaviour of jezebels and harlots, not to mention the cavortings in towns which the Lord saw fit to engulf in flames by way of punishment.

Talking about Mrs Drury's return this evening ought not to have been dangerous – they had simply been sharing a piece of local news. Even so, it had been a severe error of judgement to mention it while Nuala was serving the braised brisket, which Tormod liked but nobody else did, and Morna was spooning out cauliflower cheese which none of them liked at all, but which had to be eaten occasionally on account of Mr

O'Brien from the pub in the village giving them cauliflowers from his garden.

The minute Tromloy was mentioned, Morna and Nuala had both seen the sudden bewilderment in Jessica's eyes, the poor child. Tormod had seen it as well, and anger had shown in his face, so they had started straightaway to talk about trivialities, because it was important not to provoke one of Tormod's attacks of rage in case it led to a second stroke.

After the aunts talked about Tromloy, Jessica found the mind-pictures started to come more frequently, and far more vividly. They only ever lasted for a few seconds, but they left a clear print on her vision, like when you looked straight into the sun by mistake and got a dazzling blob of yellow in front of your eyes for ages afterwards.

The hard, insistent hands were there, of course. Sometimes Jessica dreamed about them and woke up shivering and feeling sick.

But now the mind-pictures were filling in all kinds of details. There was a firelit room, with a deep hearth. There was a rocking chair in the room as well, and once somebody had curled up in that rocking chair, and felt safe and happy.

If Jessica managed to keep this image in her mind before it dissolved, she could see an old photograph on the wall – a man in old-fashioned clothes, standing on the stage of an old theatre. It was astonishing how clear the details of that photograph were.

And then something else started to trickle into the pictures. The sound of someone whispering – someone standing very close. Was it the owner of the hands who was whispering? It was a horrid voice, and in a low voice, it said, *'You must never tell about any of this. Never.'*

And then came the really terrible part. The voice said, *'Because if you were to tell, people would think you were making up stories . . . They might say you were mad, Jessica . . . They might even shut you away . . .'*

FIVE

F eofil Markov has come to London!
My bookseller friend had the news this week through one of his numerous exiled acquaintances. A vast number of these exiles seem to be sprinkled across the city (and, I am sure across many cities), but I suppose if a country endures a Revolution, a great many of its people will become displaced. Even after almost three years, the enormity of the Russian Rebellion of 1917 is still reverberating, and one of those reverberations seems to be Feofil Markov's arrival here.

My friend came hotfoot to tell me in company with a bottle of vodka. It would have been churlish not to accept a glass or two and to sit in my rooms with him, drinking it. He says Feofil reached London earlier this year, and added, enigmatically, that it's perhaps better not to question why it was necessary for Feofil to leave Russia in the first place.

'But we should remember how the Romanovs were spectacularly and violently toppled,' he said, refilling our glasses.

'But Feofil couldn't have been involved in the Revolution, surely? He was in St Petersburg in the 1880s – he can't be a very young man these days.'

To this, my friend said Feofil had walked perilous paths in his time, and it would not matter if he was twenty-five or eighty-five or even a hundred and five; he was still likely to be at the heart of any rebellion that was around, and in fact he would probably shout revolutionary slogans on his way to the scaffold, and argue with the executioner when he got there.

For all I care, Feofil can have helped overthrow all the royal houses of Europe one by one, and preached sedition and anarchy in every city of the world. All I am interested in is his memories of my father.

I did not say that to my bookseller friend, of course. I am letting it be thought that I am interested in meeting Feofil purely because I am curious about his memories of Russian theatre and Russian music in the eighties. I shall have to be honest with Feofil, though, because the whole point of meeting him is to talk about Roman, so I shall have to trust him with the truth of who I am.

How likely is it that he will refer to Maxim? I cannot think of any reason why he should, but Maxim's existence was certainly known in St Petersburg in 1881. I believe there was some speculation – journalists were always avid snappers-up of unconsidered trifles of that kind. But if Feofil does talk about Maxim, I shall feign ignorance.

I am not in the least nervous about meeting him. Not the very least bit.

Today I received a booking for two six-minute appearances at an East End theatre. The theatre is small and attached to a slightly sleazy public house, but I shall not let that trouble me, since they will pay me in honest coinage. This means I can assume an air of careless affluence and offer drinks and even supper when I meet Feofil Markov. Also, I will be able to pay my reckoning at the lodgings for another week at least.

I have decided to give the East End audiences 'Little Grey Home in the West', and 'On the Road to Mandalay'. For the second spot, I will sing 'Roses of Picardy'. Even though it's over a year since Armistice, war songs are still in vogue, so the audience can join in the chorus and there will be a splendid atmosphere of bonhomie.

The dream came again last night – probably because I am anticipating the meeting with Feofil, and it's scraping the memories from my deepest mind.

This time the dream went much further than ever before. For the first time I could see that I, and the people surrounding me, were standing in what my grown-up self recognizes as a courtyard. That small child-self had not known the word *court-yard* though, and in the dream I was only aware of being on hard stone flags with high walls on three sides all around us. The sky was the colour of lead, as if the stones of the building had seeped into it, and that hard, cold sky seemed to press down on the courtyard like a monstrous slab of granite.

There were rows of windows set into the stone walls – they were narrow and high up, but most of them had bars, and there was the impression of cramped darkness behind each one. Pallid faces peered down from some of those windows.

At each end of the courtyard were wide stone archways, and beyond one of them was an outline I knew – that of a rearing golden spire towering into the sky. I know now that it's an old and famous landmark, and even in the dream it was unmistakable. It was the spire of the Peter and Paul Cathedral, glittering with unearthly beauty and light against the sky. I recognized the angel-tipped spire of the bell tower – the tower that has, at its base, the imperial tombs with the remains of so many of Russia's tsars. But beyond all of that I recognized it for the cathedral that stands inside the grim Peter and Paul Fortress itself.

I suppose I had always known that the nightmare was set in St Petersburg. But last night I understood that it took place actually inside the prison where my father was executed.

The crowds pressed in on all sides, shouting and making threatening gestures, and it was as if a giant beating heart lay at the core of that courtyard, and as if everyone could hear it and was waiting for it to falter, to slow down, then finally stop.

The people were pushing forward, avid to get as close as they could to what was going to happen, and I was pulled along with them. Then a door set deep into the old stone walls was unlocked and the shouts mounted to a roar. There were jeers, cries of Roman's name, the people calling it out as if it were an insult.

'Hanging's too good for him,' shouted one man close to me, and several people cried out their agreement.

'Oh, my friends, they're doing more than just hanging him,' said another voice, and there was such gloating in that voice that I wanted to fly at the man and beat him with my fists.

It was at that point that I woke up, coming up into my familiar shabby bedroom in the North London lodging house. I was shaking as violently as if I had palsy, and I was hot and cold both at the same time. The anger of the crowd was still echoing inside my head.

*   *   *

And now I am writing this with a thin dawn light trickling through the windows of my lodgings. The dream is still strongly with me, and sleep is impossible. I have applied all the palliatives I usually apply after the dream – a tot of gin, a walk around the room, the reading of a good book . . . None of them has done a scrap of good. As for my shining memory of my father's last concert – that glittering memory of his final performance in the Mikhailovsky Theatre which may only be a chimera – for the first time, that has failed me. All I can see is the ugliness of that courtyard, and all I can think is that I may have witnessed my father's execution and that the dream is an echoing memory of it.

Maxim was in the dream. I heard someone call his name, and I turned, trying to see, but there were only the greedy hating faces, and the smell of sweat and unwashed bodies. But I know Maxim was there, and I know his eyes saw and his ears heard and his mind felt everything that happened that day. It was not until a very long time later that I came to understand how that day must have changed him – how it would have shaped him and perhaps even flawed him.

I miss him, even after all these years.

Tonight's dream has told me – as if I needed telling! – that whatever I do, I can never be rid of the memories of Maxim. And that one day he will find me.

Mortimer Quince's diary

The meeting with Feofil Markov is to be the Pig and Whistle in Islington.

This is not quite the venue I would have chosen for such an important event – the last time I was there, someone made an extremely disparaging remark about a recent performance I had given at the Shoreditch Empire, and when I objected, he brandished a coal shovel and invited me to step outside and settle the matter with fisticuffs. Thankfully, the landlady, an amply proportioned soul, intervened, ordering the miscreant off the premises, and pouring me a large brandy from behind the bar by way of a soothing draught.

I had wanted to arrive just a little late. I wanted to make a

dramatic and memorable entrance and for Feofil to see it. I
think it is true to say I am not unaccustomed to making impres-
sive entrances. I have strode on to many a stage in my time
and silenced an audience solely by my presence. The stalls,
in particular, frequently stop chattering and turn to stare at
me. Often they remain in that transfixed state for a good part
of my performance.

So I planned to make just such an appearance this evening,
although it is perhaps a difficult task to silence a smoke-filled,
ale-smelling pub merely by walking through the door. Still, I
stood in the doorway for a moment, waiting for the people to
sense my presence. It was unfortunate that the coat I had draped
across my shoulders (negligent and nonchalant was the image
I wanted to convey) should choose that moment to slide down
and land in a puddle of spilt beer. By the time I had retrieved it,
the drinkers had gone back to their discussions, and no imposing
Russian-looking gentlemen approached me to enquire if I was
Mr Mortimer Quince. So after allowing sufficient time, I made
my way to a corner table, signalled to the barman to bring a
drink, and set about wiping as much beer as possible off my
coat. (I think it was beer. I hope it was beer.)

That, of course, was the moment when Feofil made his own
entrance, and infuriatingly, the instant he appeared in the
doorway – standing in the *exact* spot where I had stood earlier
– all eyes turned to him. There was one of those brief, but
disconcerting silences that occasionally fall on any group of
people. It was as if the entire pub's attention was drawn to
him, as a magnet draws slivers of steel to its core, and there
was a brief sense of puzzlement, as if they were disconcerted
– as if they were realizing that here was someone they could
not quite classify.

He surveyed the company unhurriedly, as if he had all the
time in the world. I surveyed him, as well. In those first few
moments I was conscious that he was not in the least what I
had expected. He was rather slender, and he had thick, iron-
coloured hair that grew forward and fell over his forehead. I
had been expecting the traditional, recognizable Slav cheekbones, and I had certainly thought he would have compelling
eyes – mesmeric eyes. But although the cheekbones were

there, his eyes were rather small, and even from where I sat I saw that there was a slight cast in one. It's stupid to admit this, but at that first glance those eyes disappointed me. Everyone knows that a cast in a person's eye is unattractive. In some cases it's disfiguring. Was this really the man who had been able to charm his way into the grim Peter and Paul Fortress, and into the cells of the condemned to write his articles?

He looked across at me, his head slightly to one side as if considering me, then he appeared satisfied, walked over to my table and sat down. As soon as he looked directly at me I revised my opinion completely, because the magnetism, the mesmerism, were both there in extraordinary intensity. It was his eyes after all. Those slightly skewed eyes were neither ugly nor a distortion. They were exotic. They were also disconcerting, because they gave the impression that here was a man who might see the world from a slightly different angle to other people – who might even be able to see or sense things other people could not. In that moment, I thought that I should not like to try keeping secrets from this one.

In good, but accented English, he said, 'Mr Quince? Mortimer Quince? I am Feofil Markov. We have a mutual friend, the bookseller from the shop near to St Martin's Lane. He makes this introduction because you want to talk about Roman Volf.'

You have to admire such a direct approach. I said, 'Yes.'

'Roman Volf was your father,' he said, and there was the faintest question mark at the end of those last two words.

In a way it was a relief not to have to launch into one of the careful explanations I had prepared. I have no idea how he knew, though, unless after all the bookseller had guessed and told him. But I only said, 'Yes, he was. Did you know him?'

There was a faint, vague gesture that might have meant anything. 'I had knowledge of him,' said Feofil Markov. 'It is a long time ago. Memory can be erratic.'

'You saw him in theatres?'

'He was a maestro.'

'I know.'

'His final concert at the Mikhailovsky Theatre . . . That was sublime. It was said he had never played so well.'

'"Duetto Amoroso" and the *Devil's Trill*,' I said, as much to show him I knew about Roman's last concert as for any other reason.

'You were there?' A faint surprise showed. 'You could not have been. You would be too young. It would not have been allowed.'

'I think I was there, though.' I tapped my head. 'Memories. I have the images here.'

'But as I have said, memories are not always reliable. Not always to be trusted.'

'I know that.' I paused, then said, 'I have other memories – fragmented ones.'

He leaned forward, the curious eyes intent. 'They are bad memories, those fragments?'

'Some of them.'

'You have the look of someone who has glimpsed darkness,' he said, and incredibly, at the time, the dramatic statement did not sound in the least odd. (Writing it down now it sounds melodramatic, of course – dammit, it *is* melodramatic, and I can revert to my former opinion that he was a poseur.)

I said, very deliberately, 'You have glimpsed darknesses as well, I think.'

'There were darknesses in my country over so many years.' A shrug. 'What is it you want of me, Mortimer Quince?'

'Just Quince.'

'Then, Quince, what do you want? The memories? The fragments you do not have?'

'Yes. Exactly that.'

'Of Roman? Of his life?'

'Of his death.'

'Ah. Do you really want to hear about that, though?' By that time he had summoned a drink. He had requested vodka and incredibly the Pig and Whistle had been able to supply it. I almost feared that Feofil would drink it in one go and hurl the glass into the fireplace with some kind of defiant Russian oath about death to capitalists and damnation to imperialistic tyranny, but the reality was that he drank the vodka in a perfectly ordinary way.

But when he asked me that question, he looked at me over the rim of the glass and there was nothing ordinary about his look.

I was determined not to be intimidated, so I said, challengingly, 'Roman was hanged. Wasn't he? He died.'

Feofil said, 'Yes. Oh, yes, he died. But before the execution I managed to get into the Trubetskoy Bastion where condemned prisoners were held. It was dangerous, but guards could be bribed.' He paused. 'A terrible place, that one – a place that could unfold tales to harrow up the soul. All the time I was there, I expected to feel a hand clutch my shoulder and a rifle thrust into my back.'

'But you saw Roman?'

'For a very short time – perhaps ten minutes. He was not allowed writing materials of any kind, and guards stayed with us. But he had a letter and he wanted me to give it to you – one day somewhere in the future. When I thought it was safe to do so.'

'But that was more than thirty-five years ago,' I said, staring at him.

'Time is relative. And I have only recently been able to come to England.'

I could not think how to respond to that, so I said, 'Why did Roman want me to have this letter?'

Feofil said, very softly, 'Because of Maxim.'

Maxim. The name shivered for a moment in the smoke-filled, beer-scented room, and for a moment the memories of Maxim were strongly with me, bittersweet and stamped for always on my mind.

Eventually, I said, almost in a whisper, 'You know about Maxim?'

'Of course I know. I was there – in St Petersburg. People did know about him.'

'Have you read the letter?'

'I have. It was written in Russian, and I have assumed you have forgotten any Russian you ever knew?'

'Yes. I wasn't much more than four when Roman died.'

'So therefore I have read it and I have written a translation for you. It is in the envelope as well as the letter itself. It will tell you a little – a very little – about Roman. But it will be better than not having anything at all of him.'

'Thank you,' I said, awkwardly.

He nodded in acknowledgement, then put out his hand to clasp mine in a conventional gesture of farewell.

'Do we meet again?' I said.

He did not answer directly. He simply said, 'My address is here,' and put a small handwritten card on the table. It was a part of London I was not familiar with – somewhere near the river, I think.

I said, 'I live in—'

'I know where you live. I know where and how I can find you if I want to.'

I am back in my own lodgings, and my brain is whirling. I have no idea if I shall ever have the courage to seek Feofil out, nor do I know if I want him to visit me here. There was that parting statement that he knew where to find me if he wanted. Do I hope he will want to? Of course I do, although I will admit that I flinch from letting him see these seedy, shabby rooms. That is absurd; Feofil Markov is a man who will have dined in palaces and supped with the great, but I think he could also have known poverty and lived in far less salubrious quarters than these rooms.

I have placed the letter on the bureau by the window, and I am sitting in my usual chair looking across at it. I cannot forget that Feofil said, 'Because of Maxim,' and how, with those words, I felt the pain and the loss of Maxim all over again.

I thought I had initiated the finding of Feofil through my bookseller friend, but I'm now wondering whether it was the other way around. Did Feofil trace *me*? Because he thought that after so many years it was safe to give me Roman's letter?

I have poured a hefty tot of whisky – actually it's the second one I've poured tonight and I suspect there will be a third and then a fourth.

The letter handed to Feofil in the condemned cell is addressed to Roman. It's signed 'Antoinette'. I have no idea who Antoinette is or was, but I have an absurd fear that her words might fade from the pages by daylight, or even that the letter itself – both the original and Feofil's translation – might dissolve like a chimera in sunlight or a cobweb exposed to a candle flame. I do know this is a fantastical idea, but I do not care and I have copied the contents down here.

My very dear Roman

I dare not send this to the Peter & Paul Fortress, but they tell me there is still someone living at your apartment house who can be trusted, and may be able to get messages to you. So I shall send this there, enclosed inside a request that it is delivered to you.

Roman, I shall move the stars in their courses to save you and ensure your release. You cannot have played any part in Alexander's murder. It is impossible. You were with me on the day he was killed – we were in Odessa, in that bedroom with the shades drawn across, shutting out the afternoon, with the bed tumbled, with you making such passionate, such intense love to me I thought I might die from sheer ecstasy.

I bade farewell to you in Odessa that same night with such pain. You know how much I wished I did not have to leave, but I had to do so. You know why. You and I were so close during those days, so much in sympathy, physically, mentally, emotionally . . . To wander round Odessa – to walk through the remains of the burned-out Skomorokh Theatre – to hear you rhapsodizing about how that lost theatre could be rebuilt and restored and how no lost theatre should ever be lost for ever . . . For me, heaven was in all those things.

I did not think that the next time I saw you would be three days later in St Petersburg. I did not think it would be to witness your arrest by the imperial Cossacks.

I saw your arrest from the carriage – did you know I was there? But I was, and I saw everything. We had both been emotional after bidding farewell, and you had walked to the Pevchesky Bridge – it was almost midnight, and the lamps had been lit. They reflected in the waters below the bridge. I watched you and I knew you were seeing those lights as the star studs of musical notes. Do you remember what you once said to me?

'I see music as sprinklings of brilliance on dark water, Antoinette, and each note is a fragment of a diamond, clean and bright and beautiful beyond bearing. That is how music should be played.'

You were recognized by late-night crowds, of course, and they surrounded you, cheering. Someone thrust a violin into your hands – clearly you had no idea who did so or who the instrument belonged to, but you laughed and shook your hair out of your eyes, and in response to the shouts, you started to play. I was not near enough to hear what you played, but I could hear shreds and threads of the music – that night I truly believed I could see them! It was as if fragments of music were streaming from you like stardust, or the diamond sprinklings you had described to me.

It was like something out of commedia dell'arte. The delicate iron tracery of the bridge's railings caught the light from the lamps, showering you with a motley of colours. You were, in truth, the impudent, quicksilver Harlequin that night; you were the fantastical magician-figure wearing the bright silken clothes and the cat-faced mask of the legends. The man who could transform himself into anything or anyone he wanted . . .

But between one heartbeat and the next, the scene changed from fantasy to tragedy. The sounds of marching echoed along the canalside, and the clip of horses' hoofs rang out. Sharply barked orders cut through the night, and a detachment of Cossack guards ran at you. You were halfway across the bridge, the people still following you, and you turned to see what was happening, not understanding. Your followers melted into the shadows – were they genuine, I wonder, or were they theatre-dressing, part of a plot to trap you? The Cossacks fell on you, and I heard shouts of Assassin, and Murderer. Before I could reach you they had dragged you into one of their own carriages.

I tried to follow – did you ever know that? Did you even know I was there? I was too late, though. They had already gone, galloping hard through the city, their carriages jolting

*violently across the ground, taking you into the depths of the
fortress. And I could not reach you.*

*As for that other matter – I shall do what you want. I will
make it all right. I will ensure Maxim's silence, although I do
not think he would speak of it anyway.*

*And I will find a way to clear your name. If I have to force
my way into the courtroom at your trial and tell them you and
I were in Odessa – that I was in your arms and in your bed
when Alexander was killed – then I will do so. They will believe
me, because—*

I dare not write that down, not even to you.

But you know why they will believe me.

Antoinette.

I read Antoinette's letter a second and then a third time,
then I sat back, and watched a smeary dawn break outside my
window.

It is like a knife in my vitals to realize that, whoever
Antoinette was, if she can be believed – and if she can be
trusted! – my father might have been innocent of Alexander
II's murder. He was not in St Petersburg when it actually
happened. I know that doesn't absolve him from all blame,
but I cannot see Roman as a sly, behind-the-scenes, backstreet
plotter. So I am forced to ask a bitter question: Was he hanged
for something he didn't do?

Above and beyond all of that, though, is Antoinette's assurance that she would do what Roman wanted. That she would
ensure Maxim's silence.

Maxim. All the time I was reading Antoinette's letter I had
the strong feeling that Maxim was close to me – as if he might
be standing at my shoulder, so that if I turned my head, even
very slightly, I would see him.

I must never see Maxim again, though. I dare not risk letting
him into my life ever again.

SIX

Phin had studied the photograph of Roman outside the burned Skomorokh Theatre in Odessa from every magnified angle possible. He had checked all the relevant dates half a dozen times at least. And so far he had found nothing that would take him any further. Which left Mortimer Quince.

The idea of investigating Quince was an alluring one, and the prospect of travelling to Ireland, to the place where Quince had lived and organized wartime concerts, and where, presumably, he had died, was attractive. Roman's son, thought Phin. Would he lead me back to Roman? Would it help me to find the truth about his part in the assassination? On a practical note, would the TV people see such a journey as a legitimate, chargeable expense?

These speculations were interrupted by the rugby-playing neighbour who seemed to be dragging furniture around his flat, singing something with a strong Elizabethan flavour as he did so. After two verses, Phin identified the song as one he had found while helping with a compilation of Rabelaisian song cycles the previous year. It was an outrageously bawdy ballad hailing from the sixteenth century; the title was 'Mother Watkins' Ale', and the bawdiness was written with such clever subtlety that it had sneaked its way past several centuries of censors. It was rather unexpected to hear it being sung with such gusto in the middle of present-day Maida Vale.

Phin made a mental effort to shut out the Elizabethan bawdiness, but the sudden flapping of the letterbox pulled him back into the present. He went out to the tiny hall, thinking it was a bit late for the postman.

It was not the post. It was a slightly untidy note from the rugby neighbour, inviting Phin to a party the following evening.

'Nothing grand, just some chaps and a few bottles, and we're going to brew up beer in the bath. That couple from across the landing are coming, but Miss Pringle from the garden flat says she'll go to bed with earplugs and Inspector Barnaby. This is an apology in advance for the noise, and an invitation for you to join us. You'll be very welcome. I daresay it'll go on most of the night, then there'll be a fry-up for brunch tomorrow.'

Phin considered this missive. He was not very good at parties, and he always found it surprising how many parties he was actually asked to. But given the choice between travelling to Ireland to track down Roman Volf's elusive illegitimate son, and spending a night carousing with a roomful of strangers and a bathful of homemade beer, Roman Volf won hands down. He wrote a careful reply, expressing thanks for the invitation and also the apology, but explaining that he was going to be away for a few days, in fact he was leaving quite early tomorrow. As an afterthought he added his mobile phone number in case anything unforeseen occurred while he was away.

He put the note through the neighbour's door, then sat down to wrestle with the intricacies of online air-ticket booking. It appeared that he could fly to Shannon or Galway Airport and, if the map could be trusted, Kilcarne was not much more than an hour's distance from either airport.

Phin booked a ticket for a fairly unearthly hour the following morning, together with a hire car for collection at Galway Airport, and a further booking for what appeared to be Kilcarne's only B&B-cum-pub. It was called O'Brien's and it advertised itself as providing, 'Clean, comfortable accommodation, with great home cooking.'

He emailed his agent and the TV company to explain about the journey, and was considerably relieved to receive a response asking him please to keep full VAT receipts for all the outgoings.

The journey was smooth, and the hire car bucketed its way out of Galway and across extravagantly beautiful countryside. Phin enjoyed the drive, and as he got nearer to Kilcarne he slowed down to look at some of the houses along the way, wondering if Mortimer Quince might have lived in any of them. There had been nothing in the acres of print written about Roman Volf to suggest he had had family here, or even that he had ever been here at all. Why, then, had Quince come here to live? Phin contemplated this intriguing question until he reached Kilcarne. There was a small main street, and O'Brien's was low ceilinged, peat-scented, and comfortably appointed with soft chintzes and oak tables.

Phin unpacked, showered, and went downstairs in search of food and drink. Evening meals could be taken in the minuscule dining room off the bar, and were available from seven o'clock each evening. There was a small menu which offered freshly caught salmon, scallops or prawns, and several kinds of grills. Phin ordered salmon at the bar, and was poured a large glass of wine, which he took through to the dining room. This was furnished with oak tables and window-seats, and the walls were decorated with framed fragments of Kilcarne's past, which were instantly interesting. Phin, sipping his wine with enjoyment, walked slowly along the rows of photographs. Most were views of Kilcarne from the previous century – it did not, in fact, look as if it had altered very much in the last seventy-five years. There were slightly self-conscious rows of cricket teams and school gatherings and outings, and shots of Kilcarne's various war efforts. Phin looked for a mention of Quince, hoping there might be a programme or a poster of one of the concerts Quince had referred to in the article. 'Since coming here to Ireland's west coast,' Quince had written, 'I have been involved in a number of theatrical projects – music festivals and concert parties during the 1940s, staged for the war effort.'

But there was nothing, and Phin, aware of disappointment, sat down to await his meal, which was placed in front of him by a chestnut-haired, grey-eyed waitress who seemed disposed to linger to make sure he had everything he wanted. Another glass of wine? Soda bread to accompany his meal? And was his room all right – he was in the front bedroom, was he? Ah, well now, that was one of the nicest rooms they had. Should she come up later to make sure all was well there? No, it would be no trouble whatsoever, it would be a pleasure.

'Thanks, but I'll be fine,' said Phin.

'If you want anything at all, just ring for me. My name's Grania O'Brien,' she said. 'It's my brother and me who run this place. I'll be around until at least midnight if you want anything. Anything at all.'

Phin hesitated, then said, 'Have you – or your brother – by any chance ever heard of a Mortimer Quince? He lived here in the 1930s and 1940s as far as I know – maybe even a bit earlier. But I think he organized concert parties for war charities, so his name might be remembered.'

'It's all way before my time. I could ask one or two of the older ones, if you like, though. Plenty of them come in here of an evening.'

'Could you do that? Would it be any trouble?'

'It would not.'

Without any real hope, Phin said, 'How about the name Volf? Have you ever heard of anyone with that surname in the area?'

Her eyes widened. 'Volf? As in *Volf*? I have indeed. Is it Maxim Volf you mean?'

'Well, it might be—'

'Because if so, he has a house out on the Galway Road.'

Phin had been reaching for his wine glass. He stopped, his hand suspended midway. 'Someone called Maxim Volf lives here? Actually here in Kilcarne?'

'Yes. He's a strange man if you believe the tales.'

'In what way?'

'Bit of a hermit, so it's said. Still, the poor soul, wasn't he involved in some kind of car crash a few years back, and his face burned, so it's no surprise he hides himself away most of the time.'

'And he lives on the Galway Road? Whereabouts exactly?'

'Not very far. Take the Galway Road, and it's about a mile and a half out, on the right-hand side. Five-minute drive, that's all. The house is on its own, above the road, a bit. Quite a small place, something to do with the church, I think. It's called the Sexton's House. Would he be able to help with your research at all, this Maxim Volf?'

'He might,' said Phin cautiously, but he was already wondering how many people with the surname of Volf you would encounter in the course of a week, a year, even a lifetime, in a place like this. Maxim Volf had to be Roman's descendant. Via the illegitimate son, Mortimer Quince?

'He won't see you,' said Grania. 'He never sees anyone. If you knock on his door he'll ignore you.'

'I could try, though.'

'You could, but I wouldn't bother trying today. He's a great old creature of habit, and he's off into Galway on this day every week for his shopping, regular as the tide.' She leaned over the reception desk. 'Speaking of knocking on doors,' she said, her voice sliding to a softer note, 'if you felt inclined to knock on my door at all, I certainly wouldn't ignore you.'

Phin said, carefully, that he would bear it in mind. He went up to his room, his mind tumbling with this new information. Was it possible that Mortimer Quince had left a son or daughter behind? And was a descendant of that son or daughter – therefore a descendant of Roman – living on the Galway Road, five minutes' drive out of Kilcarne, in a place called the Sexton's House? And if so, what letters and photographs and handed-down memories might that descendant have?

Mortimer Quince's diary

I cannot say whether I had expected to see Feofil again after that meeting in Islington. I will not say whether I had hoped to do so.

I had been appearing at a small playhouse in the East End, and I had returned home, somewhat tired and rather dejected. It's a wearisome business at times to coax appreciation from a moribund audience who cannot see the finer points of fine music and lyrical songs. Ah, the Bard had the right of it when he talked of playing down to the groundlings.

I was slumped in my favourite chair, sipping a glass of gin, and for the first time (no, it was the hundredth time at least), I was questioning whether I wanted to remain in this chancy, unforgiving profession. As I drained the glass, a soft footstep came from the landing outside. At first I thought it was the plump-bosomed lady from the second floor back (I admit my heart sank, for I was in no mind – or, indeed body – to deal with her exigencies). But the tap on my door was certainly not the eager hand of that dear soul. Something hopeful and absurd leapt in my own bosom, although even in those seconds before opening the door I did not dare believe—

But he it was. Feofil. He was leaning with careless elegance against the shabby wall, entirely at ease in the moth-eaten surroundings. His greatcoat swept the floor with arrogant disdain, and as he came into the room he removed the soft-brimmed hat he wore and placed it on the desk, surveying the room with – I could have sworn it! – nothing other than interest.

'You have liquor to offer?' he said, and I was glad that as well as the gin there was a bottle of whisky.

He sat in the most comfortable chair, sipped the whisky with only the faintest raising of one eyebrow at the taste, then said, 'Now I have a proposition.'

I was instantly suspicious. A proposition from Feofil could be anything from an invitation to supper, a booking to sing at a music hall, my help in covering up his involvement in the overthrowing of the Romanovs, or, conversely, my help in restoring a spurious claimant to the toppled Romanov Empire.

It was none of those things. It was a request that we join forces for a journey to the west coast of Ireland.

I stared at him. 'Why?' I said at last. 'I mean – why do you need to leave England, and why Ireland?'

'I do not actually need to leave England,' he said, raising an eyebrow. 'But I have a house in Ireland in a place called Kilcarne. It was bought three years since.'

Three years ago – in 1917 – Russia had been torn apart by the Revolution. People were scattering and fleeing.

I said, 'You've never lived in it, this house?'

'No, nor seen it,' said Feofil. 'Photographs only. But as I get older, I find I should like to see the reality. Someone looks after it for me. A family called . . .' He paused, evidently searching his memory. 'O'Brien,' he said. 'They have a tavern of some kind – for guests and for people to drink. I pay a quarterly sum through the banks to them. There has to be a degree of trust, but I do not think they cheat me. Not any more than most people cheat, you understand. I should like to make sure of that, however.' He drank some more of the whisky. 'The house is called Tromloy. It's small, but I believe it provides a reasonable degree of comfort.'

'Why do you want me to come with you?'

'Oh, because I find you companionable. And perhaps a little for the sake of Roman Volf's memory. For me, he was the maestro.' The enigmatic eyes regarded me. 'Also,' said Feofil, in a more practical voice, 'my English is not yet as perfect as I should wish, and you would be useful on the journey – dealing with money—' A wave of one hand indicated his disdain for, and uninterest in, such a sordid matter.

'And the money itself?' I said. 'The funds for the journey?'

He looked slightly surprised. I suppose if there's money in the bank you don't think about these things, but I've hardly ever had money in the bank, well, I've never actually had a bank – and so I did think about it.

'There is money enough,' said Feofil, as if such things were unimportant.

'We would live in your house?'

'Yes.'

'How long would we be there?'

'I have no idea.' He set down his glass. 'Well? Do you accept my request?'

I have no idea why I said what I said next. I had meant to decline politely, or at the very least to say I would think it over. Then I remembered again my growing dissatisfaction with the stage as a profession and, let us be honest, my continuing lack of real success. So what I said was, 'Yes. I'll come with you to Ireland.'

'I am glad.' But he sounded unsurprised. 'I shall tell you soon when we depart. Somebody – a shipping company or a ferry company or somebody – will arrange it all.' Again there was the uninterest. He would pay somebody else to perform mundane tasks he did not want to do for himself. I was only relieved he had not asked me to handle that part of things, for I had never booked a ferry or made hotel reservations in my life.

Feofil drained his whisky and stood up to take his leave, apparently feeling that no more needed to be said and, I noticed, having consumed most of the bottle of whisky without apparent effect.

In the privacy of these pages, I can admit that the prospect

of going to Ireland in company with Feofil Markov is an
alluring one.

This journey is proving to be an extraordinary experience. We
have used trains and the ferry so far, and when we reach
Ireland we shall cross to its west coast by hired cars with our
own drivers.

Twice so far we have spent the night in luxurious hotels
– Feofil does not appear to think any other kind of hotel
exists. He expects, and unfailingly receives, the best attention
everywhere.

Even on the crossing from Liverpool to Dublin, when I was
ignominiously and disgustingly unwell over the side of the
boat – even then, courteous help was there. Feofil raised a
hand to summon an attendant, and at once I was swathed in
soft rugs and blankets, and fed with warm brandy. 'Do try it,
sir, just a sip. Most of our passengers find it very helpful.'
There was general agreement that the Irish Sea could be as
unruly and turbulent as the Irish themselves, and that 'today
was just one of those days, most unfortunate for you, sir.'

Later, we were served with the lightest and daintiest of repasts.

'I usually find,' said Feofil, surveying his plate with satisfaction, 'that a little caviar with smoked salmon is an excellent
remedy for *mal de mer.* Waiter, do you perhaps have any white
burgundy on ice? Yes, Pouilly-Fumé would be acceptable. We
shall have that, please.'

Incredibly, the caviar and smoked salmon stayed with me.
The wine did nothing worse than give me hiccups, which is
undignified but not, heaven be praised, as disgusting as being
sick over the railings of a ferry.

And now we have reached Kilcarne.

Well, now, Kilcarne. What can I say about it? What is there
to say that won't take all of two minutes? It's tiny – a speck
of a place in the west of Ireland, not on the coast itself, but
near enough to make it possible to go out there if one should
wish. I think I shall wish. A gentle drive of perhaps an hour,
so they tell me (this is if one can find, and drive, a motor car
to convey one, or, of course, a horse and cart). And oh, indeed,

they say, Galway City is a fine old place, and isn't it the most spectacular sight in the world to see the bay at sunset?

Kilcarne itself has a street with three shops, a wine bar called O'Brien's (which becomes the centre of the entire place most evenings), a doctor's surgery, and what I think is a solicitor's office. And there's a minuscule cobblestoned square at one end, and there are houses scattered around. The hills and the fields all around are peppered with farms. And there's a church. Of course there's a church, this is Ireland for pity's sake, with churches every ten paces. But other than that, it's a backwater. The place God forgot and the devil overlooked. I love it.

Because when the sun sets over some mountain range (I haven't yet found out what it's called, that range), there's a soft violet haze everywhere, laced with fiery strings of light so that you feel you're inside a glistening golden cobweb. And when the wind blows in from the Atlantic it's scented with all the perfumes of Arabia, and so achingly sweet you want to reach out and cup it in your hands.

When I commented on this last phenomenon to Feofil a few nights after our arrival (we had been drinking the fiery Irish *usquebaugh*), he said, 'Ah yes, the strange invisible perfume that renders the winds love-sick. Actually, I believe it's salt and fish from Galway Bay, blowing inland, and diluted by the bracken on those hills.'

He can always do that, Feofil. Switch from wild romanticism to disconcerting mundanity in the space of half a heartbeat.

Tromloy is small, spick and span, and very comfortable. My bedroom looks towards the distant, purple-streaked mountains, and there is even a fully equipped bathroom and water closet along the landing.

I have set out my few possessions in the room – the photograph that was taken of me on stage at the Shepherd's Bush Empire is on a small ledge by itself. It makes me look slightly chubby, I think, but I am nevertheless proud of it.

As for Antoinette's letter – the letter that states Roman to have been in Odessa when the tsar was assassinated – that is locked away in a small carved box. Once or twice I have re-read it, lingering on some of the phrases . . . 'I was in your arms and in your bed when Alexander was killed,' Antoinette had written. 'I will tell the truth and I will clear your name . . . They will believe me . . . You know why they will believe me.'

She can't have produced that alibi, of course. Or, if she did, she was not believed. Which leaves me with the question – why was Antoinette so strongly convinced she would be believed? Who was she?

Yesterday I said, 'Why here? I mean, why did you decide to buy a house out here?'

'After the Revolution I wanted to leave Russia. The shape of life had changed for ever.

'It changed with the butchery at Ekaterinburg. The botched, clumsy shootings of the Romanovs. Those young girls – the poor, lame Alexei . . .'

'You were part of the Revolution?' I said.

'I recorded much of it for newspapers,' he said, and brushed a hand across his eyes, although whether to conceal emotion or indicate the skewed eyes I have no idea.

I wanted to ask if the out-of-line eyes were the result of an injury received during the Revolution, but I did not quite have the courage. Instead, I said, again, 'Why here, though?'

'A lady knew of it. A lady whose judgement I trusted. Her family had travelled here – her grandparents, I think. She remembered how they had spoken of it as a place of tranquillity. So, when there came a time when she needed such a place – a place of healing – she came here. The great manor house where her grandparents were once guests was long gone, but she found this remaining fragment. The housekeeper's cottage, I believe. She said it possessed serenity. That it had a feeling of sanctuary.'

'Did she – this lady – did she need sanctuary?'

'For a time,' said Feofil, the shuttered look coming over his face. 'Shall we walk along to O'Brien's for supper later?'

Feofil and I have been in Kilcarne for more than a month now.

I have explored the area – I have particularly explored the land surrounding Tromloy, and it's tantalizing to come across remnants of the vanished Kilcarne Manor. There's a pair of wrought-iron gates that might once have led to it, but that now lead nowhere except to a wild orchard and weed-choked paths. And a tumble of old stones that could have been part of pillars and walls. Traces of servants' quarters, the print on the ground of outbuildings – a buttery or a dairy, perhaps.

I am starting to know the local people as well – there are the O'Briens at the wine bar, of course, and the local doctor, the priest, the schoolmaster and a lawyer. Sometimes we have dinner with them at O'Brien's, and twice Feofil has invited them to Tromloy. On the evenings at O'Brien's the food is very good and the wine flows. After dinner the whiskey flows even more copiously than the wine, and everybody gets very drunk, even the priest – especially the priest, in fact. Feofil, though, remains apparently sober and entirely in control, no matter how much he drinks.

I've never known people like the Irish. They smile at you from the corners of their eyes with a sly charm, and not for nothing are they known as 'silver-tongued'. They will talk fluently and entertainingly about anything under the sun, and they appear to have a relationship with Christ and the saints which is as friendly as if they all had supper together once a week. 'And would you just pass the wine now, Peter, and if it's getting low won't Himself stir up a bit of a miracle anyway.'

On Friday nights in O'Brien's the men solemnly remind one another that isn't it confession tomorrow morning, and even while they're trying to remember that week's tally of sins, they're downing whiskey, and wondering can they get the barmaid into bed. It's fine, you see, to give way to drunkenness and fornication on a Friday night as long as you confess to having done so on Saturday, and then make sure not to commit either of those sins again until after Mass on Sunday.

Feofil is accepted in the community, although it's a cautious kind of acceptance, and I suspect the local people regard him as something of a *rara avis*. He appears to be perfectly content with this life. He is often out – he does not tell me where he goes, so I do not ask. A small motor car has appeared and Feofil sometimes drives it into Galway, bouncing it down the narrow track. I have tried my hand at driving and I believe I am becoming quite adept. It's an exhilarating experience.

Last week I talked to the schoolmaster about helping at the local school and he says wouldn't that be the finest thing ever. We are going to put on simple plays which the children can act out for parents and the surrounding communities. Nativity plays at Christmas, of course.

So far I have no regrets, no longing, for my former life. I do not miss the stage or my raggle-taggle London life the smallest bit. It's good to have the memories of all that, though, and in the intervals between organizing concerts I daresay I shall finally get around to creating my memoirs.

Last night, the nightmare came. And this time it began from the moment when I ran into the corner of the stone courtyard, desperately trying to shut out the sights and the sounds before me.

That was when someone lifted me up and carried me through one of the low archways. I could not see very much, because tears were still clouding my vision, and I was pressed against a soft-scented shoulder. But the air was cooler, and the screams of the crowd were behind us. The woman carrying me murmured something about being safe, about soon being beyond the fortress. Even as she said it, guards sprang forward, barring our way, and I flinched.

But she rapped out a sentence and even in the dream it seemed to be an order and a reproof. The guards hesitated, then stepped back and we were allowed out.

There was a carriage waiting – the fact that it was a carriage, not a motor car, emphasizes for me the passage of the years, for motor vehicles were rare in those days. But a carriage it was, drawn by two horses. I was bundled into it, and something was said – was it in Russian? I don't know, I only know that in the dream I could understand the words.

'We must get the child away.' That was the woman's voice. 'Because now it is over.'

'Roman Volf is dead.' A man's voice, this time.

'Yes. He died inside the fortress.' She half turned her head as if to look back. 'I shall never forget it.'

'You must be so careful.'

'I shall be.'

Then the carriage moved off, and we were jolted across cobbled streets. Night had fallen, and lights reflected in a long, wide river.

The woman looked down at me. She was dark-haired and she had wide, high cheekbones. The child that I was in that dream had no idea of age but, looking at it now, I think she was probably around thirty.

She said, 'I am to make you safe. We go to England, you and I.'

England. The word did not mean very much to me. I rubbed my tears from my eyes with both hands. 'Please – I don't know who you are.'

There was a pause. Then she said, 'It is better – safer for both of us – if you call me Antoinette.'

Antoinette.

I'm wide awake in the bedroom of Tromloy, and the name is still exploding through my brain. *Antoinette.* How reliable was that dream? Had my mind simply remembered Antoinette's letter and woven her into the nightmare? Or had it really been Antoinette who got me away from the Peter and Paul Fortress and to England? Because somebody did do that.

Feofil might know, but I am not sure if I can ask him. We live in the same house with the unavoidable intimacies that involves, but there are times when he retreats behind that invisible barrier.

Despite the nightmare's reappearance, I still believe I can be happy in Kilcarne. If only . . .

If only I did not know with absolute and utter conviction that Maxim will eventually find me.

I lost Maxim on the day Roman was executed. I have always known that, just as I know that one day he will find me. The strands of memory from the past are too strong for there to be any other outcome.

SEVEN

J essica had known, ever since the aunts had said the name of the house – *Tromloy* – that she would have to find it. She needed to see it – to see if it really was the place of those nightmare images, of that firelit room.

Today would be a really good time for her to go out, because Nuala had to be at the dentist in Galway, and Morna would drive her there. Tormod could be left in his study for a couple of hours, although Nuala would put a flask of coffee on his desk, and the phone was at hand if he needed anything. Jess would look in on him, of course.

Jess did not really like being in the small study with Tormod, although she was not sure why this was. So she nodded, and said vaguely that she might take a walk just before lunch. This appeared acceptable, although she was not to go far, said the aunts, and she was to be back for her lunch, was that clear?

After the aunts had set off, Jess put her sketchbook and pencils in her bag, called out a goodbye in the direction of the study, and walked along the little main street. Going past Dunleary's shop, she hesitated, then went inside. They had a small book section, and today there was a new edition of one of Lady Gregory's collections of early Irish myths. It was a paperback so it was not illustrated, but Jess could draw her own illustrations of the stories. And at the end of the week she would have her pocket money, so she might come back then. Mrs Dunleary said she would put the book to one side.

Coming out of the shop, she glanced back to her own house. The postman was just coming out of the gate. Or was it the postman? Wasn't it too tall for him? Jess narrowed her eyes to see better, but the house was just around a slight curve and she could not see properly. But the curious thing was that for a moment the figure had had exactly the same hunched-over stance as her Uncle Tormod. It could not be him, though. He walked around the house with a stick, and outside the house he had to be wheeled everywhere.

As she went past O'Brien's she stopped thinking about Tormod, because she had suddenly realized that she was not having to wonder how to find Tromloy. I know the way, thought Jessica. I'm not even having to stop to think.

Here was the narrow lane, and here were the untidy hedges and the low-hanging branches that had to be pushed aside in places, a bit like the approach to Sleeping Beauty's castle, through the 100-year-old thick thorn and brambles. Jessica knew the path, just as she had known the way here. The dreamlike quality of everything deepened. In another few yards was a chunk of stone by the side of the track, with the single word, *Tromloy*, engraved on it. Yes, there it was, the stone: grey and weather-beaten and old. Recognizable.

And in another moment she would see the house, in just another few steps—

And then it was there. Quite small. A bit neglected, but not so very much so, although a piece of guttering had broken away and hung down over a window, and the grass all round the house was overgrown. Jess would not go any nearer than this, because a car was parked on one side of the house, which meant somebody was likely to be in. But she could stay here, and see if drawing the house would take the flickering images out of her head and trap them on the paper. If she leaned against the piece of stone with the house's name, she would be able to see anyone coming out of the house, and she could be running down the path and out of sight within a minute.

She sat down against the stone, and pulled out her sketchbook. But it was difficult to make the first lines on the page, because the impression that she had seen Tormod walk out of the house unaided was still with her. Supposing he was just pretending to be so helpless, and letting everyone wait on him and push him to places in the wheelchair? Supposing when no one was around, he walked about by himself? It was ridiculous to find this possibility slightly frightening. Jess would not think about it any more, although while she sketched, she would do what she often did when she was worried or confused

– she would whisper her favourite bits of poetry. Poetry was the best company in the whole world.

As Beatrice ate her breakfast in Tromloy's little kitchen, she was deeply grateful that no nightmares had slid through her sleep like sly serpents, and that no mysterious gentlemen had disturbed the makeshift frying-pan security system the Garda had arranged across the broken window catch.

The power was still off, though. In London Bea would have cursed this state of affairs, but, somehow, in Tromloy's otherworldly atmosphere, mundane things such as electricity did not seem to matter very much. She had orange juice and bread and honey, followed by an apple, which was perfectly acceptable and sufficient. After this she phoned the electricity company who assured her the power would be on by mid-afternoon by the latest.

A local builder rang shortly after nine to say he had the Garda's message and he would be at Tromloy by lunchtime. Deal with the troublesome window in a gnat's eye-blink, Mrs Drury.

'That would be fine,' said Bea.

While she was waiting for builders and power suppliers, she could do some work on the commission for the fantasy book illustration. Blue and purple misty forests, the editor had said. Nothing too bland or Victorian Gothic; in fact even a faint flavour of boy-band modernity if that could be managed.

Bea spread out the preliminary sketches she had brought from London, and worked without stopping for an hour, absorbed in the images taking shape on the page. Here were the watchful trees, each with a faint suggestion of a gnarled face within the trunk – spooky but not too macabre – and there was the beckoning woodland path, along which the feckless heroine would trip to her doom. On the right-hand side, far enough down to leave space for the title and any strapline, could be the anti-hero. Bea paused. Did young teenagers like anti-heroes? Should he be Byronic? An American beefcake or cheesecake or a fit, beach-blond boy-babe? She tried several of these out, liking best the image of a brooding, low-browed, dark-haired figure. Not blatantly sinister, but you suspected his grandmama might secretly have harboured a reprehensible taste for human blood, or that great-grandfather, in an absent-minded moment, might sometimes have howled at the moon when it was full. There had better be a smoky-eyed damsel in the picture, as well. Gothic-clad? – no *goth*-clad! But with the suggestion that she probably had a smartphone and tablet in her pocket.

Bea leaned back to stretch her aching neck muscles. She was pleased with what she had done, and she would start to rough out the goth female later. For the moment she would walk down the track as far as the road to clear her head. Perhaps she would meet the builder on his way up to repair the window catch, and perhaps when she got back the electricity would have been switched on and she could cook some lunch.

She pulled on a jacket, dropped her phone into a pocket, and set off. It was a sharp, cold morning; the leaves were crunchily gold, and there was a bite of coldness in the air. Walking down the steep, narrow track, Bea's spirits lifted. Whether it was Tromloy's influence or not, she was deeply grateful that she was able to work properly again, and since she had left London she had not heard Abi's cries.

And then, cruelly and shockingly, out of the bright sharp morning, she did hear them.

It was not Abi's voice exactly, not the way Bea heard it in the nightmares, when Abi called for help. *'Help me . . . Burning . . . Can't get out . . .'*

But there was no panic in the voice she was hearing now – it was quiet and soft. Might it even be a bird calling somewhere? No, it was undoubtedly a human voice, and soft as it was, there was something that brought Abi back. Bea stopped, halfway down the path, listening intently. The sounds came again, and this time she was able to make out the words.

'Her chariot is an empty hazel-nut . . .'

It was as if a giant invisible hand had closed around Bea's body, squeezing all the breath out.

'. . . Made by the joiner squirrel or old grub,
Time out o' mind the fairies' coachmakers.'

It was the Queen Mab speech from *Romeo and Juliet*. Abigail's favourite, the one she had loved to hear Niall reciting, even though she had not really understood it. Bea had drawn for her images of a hazelnut carriage with Mab at the reins, and wild, Rackham-esque fairy creatures streaming along behind. Abi's quick, bright little mind had seized the concept and understood the words, and after that she had sung the speech to herself often, fitting it to snatches of music – different kinds of music, according to her mood and whatever caught her imagination.

And now, within a few yards of Tromloy, someone was half reciting, almost half singing that very speech. It was not quite how Abigail used to chant it, but it was nearly the same – so much so that Beatrice ran down the track and around the sharp curve.

A figure was seated on the ground, leaning against the old stone with Tromloy carved into it, the trees and the thick brambles framing her. Whoever she was, she was very young, and she was absorbed in a sketchpad on her knees. And she was half singing the lines of the speech very softly, as if for company. Exactly as Abigail used to do.

But it could not be Abi, of course it could not. And yet, just supposing—

Just supposing that fantasy Bea had spun turned out to be real? Supposing Abi had escaped in the final moments, that someone else lay in her grave, that Abigail, the real Abigail, had been here all the time, close to the house she had loved, not knowing who she really was?

Don't be ridiculous, Beatrice.

She began to walk towards the figure, trying not to make any noise, fearful of shattering the spell. The chanting came again.

'*And sometime comes she with a tithe-pig's tail . . .*'

The memories stirred afresh. 'What's a tithe pig, Dad? Is it different to an ordinary pig?' And Niall's patient explanation – he had always been so patient with Abi, that was one of the things that had hurt so much afterwards.

'*Sometime she driveth o'er a soldier's neck,*
And then dreams he of cutting foreign throats,
Of breaches, ambuscadoes, Spanish blades . . .'

The chanter seemed to like this last line, because she repeated it, lingering over the words. *Ambuscadoes, Spanish blades . . .* ('What's an ambuscado, Dad . . .?' 'An ambush, Abi . . . And we'll get Mum to draw a brigand with a Spanish blade for you, and he'll have dark flashing eyes and a scarlet sash . . .')

The girl who was singing the lines was slender and small-boned. She looked about fifteen – the age Abi would have been now. This girl had a slightly unruly tumble of hair – was it Abi's bright-leaf hair? Grown over the last two years to an almost pre-Raphaelite cascade?

Bea could see the white oblong of the sketchpad, but she was too far away to make out what the girl was drawing. Would it be the hazelnut chariot of Mab? Or the view of Tromloy from this part of the track?

The girl bent over her sketch, her hair falling forward. She put up a hand, then both hands, to push it back, with a slightly impatient gesture.

It was as if Bea had been dealt a blow across the eyes. In the clear morning light it was possible to see that the girl's hands were badly scarred. The flesh was puckered, the skin drawn into ugly ridges and lumps. It was how hands would look if they had beaten frantically against burning iron, it was how fingers would distort if they had curled around blistering metal . . . Burn scars, thought Bea. Burn-damaged hands. That's what would happen if you were trapped in a lump of burning metal, trying to claw your way out . . .

She was not aware of having made any sound, but she must have done so, because the girl turned suddenly, then scrambled to her feet, hugging the sketchbook to her chest. Her eyes darted down the path, as if about to run for cover.

Bea called out at once. 'Don't be frightened – I heard you reciting and I was interested. I'm . . . I'm Beatrice Drury. I live in Tromloy.'

She spoke instinctively, willing the girl to stay where she was, taking a step nearer.

'Tromloy . . .?' It was a half-question, and Bea said, eagerly, 'Yes. The house just behind us.'

'I came to look at it,' said the girl, a bit uncertainly. 'I was curious. Then I wanted to draw it. Tromloy means *Tromlui*. That's the word for nightmare. But it isn't a nightmare house at all, I don't think.'

'I don't think it is, either.'

'I'm sorry, I'm in your gardens aren't I,' said the girl, suddenly. 'I probably shouldn't be. Is it trespass or something?'

There was a soft Irish lilt overlaying the words. Someone who had lived here for any length of time would pick that up, though. Bea said, 'I didn't know that about Tromloy meaning nightmare.' And please stay where you are, and please let me get a bit nearer so I can see you properly. She took another step, then said, 'I had a daughter who liked that speech you were chanting. She loved it. I used to draw the images for her. The fairies' chariot—'

'And the joiner squirrel and the ambuscado?' There was a sudden rush of eager delight in the soft voice. 'I've tried to draw them as well.'

'Have you? Would you let me see your sketch?' said Bea.

'I would. I don't know if it's any good. Some people say drawing is a waste of time, but it isn't, is it?'

'It certainly isn't,' said Bea at once. The voice was not so much like Abigail's after all. Yes, but voices changed . . . She said, 'I illustrate books – quite a lot of them are children's books. For a living, I mean. It's my job. So I definitely don't think drawing is a waste of time.' She waited to see if this would strike any chord of recognition with the girl, but it did not seem to.

The girl took a step nearer, and held out the sketchbook. Sunlight fell pitilessly across the scarred hands, and Bea suppressed a wince of pain, then put out her hand for the sketchbook.

The moment her fingers brushed against the girl's, she knew with sick despair that it was not Abigail. How could it have been, anyway? There was a strong likeness, though – the colouring, the build. The girl belonged to the same generic type as Abi. It might almost be possible for Bea to have persuaded herself it could actually be Abi, but recognition is a deeper, more primeval emotion, and at that deep level, Bea knew that she had never met this girl before today.

Even so, she was drawn to her – the girl had Abigail's love of that speech and she had tried to capture the images on paper. For that, if nothing else, Bea would have wanted to know her better.

The sketch of Tromloy was immature and the technique was faulty – as it would be if she had never had proper lessons.

But that aside, it was extremely good. Bea turned some of the pages, seeing the other work. It was confident and also very imaginative.

'These are very good indeed,' said Beatrice. 'In fact . . . I'm sorry, I don't know your name?'

'Jessica. Jessica Cullen.'

She sat down again, watching intently as Bea leafed slowly through the sketches again, pausing to smile at a particularly vivid one of a woodland clearing with almost-cartoon faces in the trees and leaves, and a bewildered heroine-figure looking at them.

'Well, Jessica Cullen, I think you're very gifted, and I think if you have the chance to study art properly, you ought to do so.'

'My aunts won't allow that,' said Jessica. 'Uncle Tormod won't let them allow it.'

This struck Bea as a curious statement, but she said, 'You live with them, the aunts and your uncle?'

'I do. It's the house along from the church. It stands behind a brick wall, and it's got those frowny kind of windows under the roof.'

'I think I know the one.' It would be the house where the timid, faded-beige ladies lived. 'Have you always lived there?'

'I don't know. I forget things – I get confused.' She turned to look towards Tromloy, suddenly. 'Mrs Drury—'

'Beatrice. In fact, Bea.'

'Bea, does your house – Tromloy – does it have an old fire screen? About this big . . .' The spoiled hands indicated. 'Stuck all over with bits of old posters and newspaper cuttings and photographs? Faces of people from the past?'

Bea stared at her. Surely no one who had not been inside Tromloy could know about the fire screen? Or could they? The cottage had been empty for two years – anyone could have got in through the faulty window. Someone had actually done just that last night. This girl could certainly have done so, for all her appearance of being disingenuous.

Then Jessica said, 'And there's a room with a fireplace and a rocking chair. It's got bronze and green material on it. There's a picture on the wall . . .' Her eyes narrowed in an effort of memory. 'A man standing on a stage. He's wearing really old-fashioned clothes. And he has woolly hair on each side of his face – like bunches of cotton wool.'

'Mutton-chop whiskers,' said Bea, in a half-whisper.

'Is that what they're called? And a waistcoat with a pattern on it.'

'Yes. Brocade.'

Jessica Cullen was describing the photograph of the unknown performer in Abi's room. It had been there when Bea and Niall bought the house, left behind, maybe simply forgotten, by previous owners. The photo was an old one – early twentieth century – and Bea had never known who the man was. She looked at this girl who might have known about the fire screen in the sitting room, but who could not possibly have known about the photograph unless she had been in Abigail's bedroom.

She said, in a whisper, 'You've been inside Tromloy, haven't you?'

It seemed a long time before Jessica answered, but then she said, 'I think I must have been. But I don't remember when or why I just have pictures of it in my head.' A pause. 'But Mrs Drury – Bea – I think that when I was there something dreadful happened.'

'To you?' This was the most unreal conversation anyone could possibly have. 'Was that when you hurt your hands?' said Bea, carefully.

'I don't remember. They're burns, aren't they?' She looked at her hands as if they did not belong to her. 'I think there was a fire, but I don't know if it was in Tromloy. I can't remember.' She frowned, and a look of fear came into her eyes. 'Sometimes, though, when I do try to remember, I think that something had to be got out of the fire.'

She looked at Bea as if for reassurance. There was no mistaking the panic in her voice, and Bea at once said, 'I didn't mean to pry, or frighten you.'

'No, it's all right. But I must go now. I have to be back for lunch. My cousin Donal's coming to stay, and he'll be here this afternoon, and I'm supposed to help with things. He's a priest, and they're all very proud of him.'

Again, it was a curious way of putting it. Almost as if Jessica wanted to place herself outside the family circle. Bea said,

'Yes, of course you must go back.' She stood up. 'But if you do come out this way again, you could walk up to the house if you felt like it.'

'Come right up to the house? To Tromloy?' Jessica's eyes went beyond Bea to the house.

'If you want to. I'm staying in Kilcarne for a while.' Don't force anything, thought Bea. If there's to be anything else, let it come from her.

And it did. Jessica said, in a rush, 'If I came to see the house, could I see your drawings? The illustrations for the books?'

'Yes, of course. We could talk about your own work as well.'

Jessica thought about this, then said, 'I could come one afternoon. I'd like that.'

'Shall I phone your aunts to – well, to introduce myself to them?' It had occurred to Beatrice that inviting a young girl into her home like this might seem a bit questionable – even slightly sinister. 'Perhaps that would be a good thing to do,' said Bea. 'Give me the number, and I'll call them this evening.'

'No, don't do that. They don't like it when the phone rings, especially in the evening. They say it disturbs my uncle. He's not very well – he hasn't been very well for years. And if he's disturbed there's a row and he shouts, and Aunt Nuala gets upset and Aunt Morna gets cross. I could come tomorrow or the day after, though. The aunts know I go out on most days. Sketching or reading or just walking.'

'No school?'

'I have lessons at home. My uncle was once a teacher, and my cousin Donal's got some kind of qualification. They don't think I should go to an ordinary school.' There was a note of wistfulness in her voice.

Bea said, 'If you can come to Tromloy the day after tomorrow that'll give me time to bake a cake and we'll have it with a cup of tea.'

The girl smiled suddenly, transforming her entire face. 'I will,' she said. 'Thank you.' And then she was gone, running lightly down the uneven ground, her hair lifting as she did so. Bea watched her, seeing her go through the trees. Branches from the trees blew downwards for a moment, partly hiding the small figure, then she was gone altogether.

Bea walked back up to the house. At one level she was not entirely sure she had actually met Jessica Cullen today. Had she somehow entered into a state of mind where she was trying to surround herself with people linked to Abigail's death? Last night there had been a man she had half-believed, half-pretended was Maxim Volf. She still had no idea how much of a wild pretence that had been. And today there was a girl who had sung Abi's poetry. A girl whose hands had been burned as if they had clutched desperately at blazing metal in an effort to escape . . .

Had Jessica been a manifestation of Bea's own wish-fulfilment – formed out of echoes and sadness? Had Bea projected a patchwork of her memories on to the air – getting some of them exactly right, but missing the target with others because the memories had inevitably begun to fade and blur a bit? The psychiatrists would have had a field day with that last theory.

It was all absurd. Maxim Volf had existed and he might even have been the man who had got into Tromloy last night. Jessica Cullen existed as well – Bea even knew, more or less, where she lived. And there were two aunts and an overbearing uncle. So Jessica was real, and she was coming to Tromloy in two days.

Letting herself back into the house, Bea faced the two disconcerting facts about Jessica Cullen. The first was that she had known about Tromloy. She had described the cushions in Abi's room and the fire screen and she had known about the photo of the Victorian actor.

The second fact was a much harder one to face, because it had dug a spike into a wound that was, and probably always would be, raw.

A fire, Jessica had said. A *fire* . . . 'When I do try to remember, I think that something had to be got out of the fire,' she had said, her eyes wide and staring at something terrible.

Was it conceivable that Jessica Cullen had been there when Abi died?

*   *   *

The power had been restored to Tromloy, and Bea made a cup of tea, then heated some soup for an early lunch. After this, she spent a couple of hours adding the smoky-eyed heroine to the book illustration. It was starting to look good, although the heroine had turned out to have tumbling, slightly pre-Raphaelite hair the colour of autumn leaves, long enough to lift in a gentle breeze when she ran . . .

She had no idea whether Jessica would actually turn up as promised, but there was still time this afternoon to drive out to the little market town midway between Kilcarne and Galway City to buy the ingredients for what had been Abigail's favourite chocolate fudge cake.

The road leading out of Kilcarne to the small market town eight miles to the west seldom had much heavy traffic. It was open to rolling countryside for most of the way, and whenever they drove along this road Niall would spin stories about the people in the houses that dotted the roadside. Most were small, the majority had peat turfs stacked against their walls in readiness for the winter, and most were unremarkable. But Niall had conjured up entire and wildly imaginative histories and family lineages for the supposed occupants of these houses. When Abi was a bit older she had joined in, adding her own twists to the stories. Bea could not spin stories out of nothing, but she could spin pictures, and in the evenings in Tromloy, she would draw the characters Niall had conjured up. Abi had loved that – she had given the people names, writing them under the sketches. One day, she said, they would write their own book; she and Dad would make up the story, and Mum could illustrate it. This was one of the things Bea tried not to remember.

The road was the one along which Niall and Abigail had driven on that last day. Had they talked about that pipe-dream book, that castle-in-the-air story they were one day going to write? Had Niall spun more tales about the people in the houses? For a bittersweet moment, Bea could see the two of them together in the car: Niall's dark head occasionally half turning to look at his daughter, his eyes full of that amused indulgence they had once held for Bea. Abi would have been exuberantly pointing things out, her bright hair shiny in the autumn sunlight . . .

Tears blurred Bea's eyes for a moment, but they did not blur the figure outside the greystone cottage that stood by itself on a wedge of land overlooking the road. He was wearing a long dark coat, the collar turned up. The tears had not blurred memory, either. It was the man who had been in Tromloy – the man who had been in Abigail's room. He was bending over the small heap of peat as if adding to it, or perhaps collecting some of it to take indoors.

Without realizing it, Bea slowed down, almost to a stop, and stared up at the house and the figure. She had a sudden picture of the man sitting by a glowing fire in that little cottage, his eyes in the spoiled face unreadable. Would he be reading or listening to music, or watching television? Somehow it was difficult to associate him with anything so prosaic as television. She would allow him a row of well-thumbed books, and music, though. Mozart? No, something much darker. Mahler. Wagner. The books would be what were usually loftily referred to as literary . . .

And this was a ridiculous way to think, because the man probably read whodunits and chick-lit, and listened to heavy metal or rap. Still, if you were going to have an encounter with a real-life *Phantom of the Opera* character, you might as well ascribe to him a few of the more scholarly tastes. If there were to be a villain prowling around, Bea would prefer him to be an erudite villain. Not that the man was a villain. Not that he was likely to prowl into her life a second time, either. And even if he did, she would not want to talk to him. The impulse to attack the man who had failed to save Abi had weakened, but the bitterness was still there. It was just that the man she had met in Tromloy was nothing like she had imagined him.

The cottage was small, but it looked quite solid, and the bit of land around it was well tended. There were curtains at the windows and an impression of warmth and safety in the rooms beyond. It was absurd and illogical to have the sudden thought that none of those rooms would have a mirror, and to find the thought painful.

But at least he's not a complete tramp, thought Bea, accelerating. He lives like an ordinary person in a house with walls and a roof. He might materialize and dematerialize in the night like smoke, but this is an ordinary house.

She glanced in the driving mirror. The man was still standing there, stacking the peat turfs. Bea did not think he had noticed her.

That night, prompted by an impulse that might have come from anywhere, Beatrice decided to sleep in Abigail's bedroom. There was a brief flinching sensation at the memory of the man who had hidden in this room, and how he had been sitting in Abi's rocking chair. 'The house has helped me,' he had said. But how often had he been in here? How often had he been in this room? Slept in the bed even?

It was an absurd notion, of course. If he had indeed been the man who had tried to rescue Abi and Niall, it was possible that he had come out here to find some kind of healing for his failure to save two people from a bad death. It was slightly bizarre, but Bea could believe it.

The bed was perfectly all right – untouched, as far as she could make out. To dispel any disturbing ideas, she got into it and pulled the duvet around her.

In direct sightline of the bed was the old photograph. Studying it in the dimness, Bea thought it looked more as if the setting was a music hall rather than a theatre, and the man looked as if he might be a singer. Whoever and whatever he had been, there was something rather endearing about him; a kind of pleased eagerness, as if he was always expecting life to serve up something wonderful. Niall had always meant to see if the man could be traced – there was a name on the back, he had said – but he had never got round to doing so. This was typical of him. He had been so full of promises and plans and schemes, but none of them had ever been developed or realized.

As she waited for sleep to overtake her, she thought about Jessica Cullen. It was comforting to discover that she was smiling at the prospect of Jessica's visit.

EIGHT

The house that was known locally as the Sexton's House had been home to a series of gentlemen over the years – usually single, seldom very young gentlemen – who had been grateful to be given a house in return for providing simple maintenance of the local church and the cemetery.

Nowadays the strange, reclusive gentleman lived in the cottage – English he was, so the local people believed, and told one another that if that was right it said it all, for the English were a strange, reserved race.

He might be anyone or anything at all, this unknown gentleman who was seldom seen, and only then in the long dark coat with the deep, turned-up collar. He came and went quietly and unobtrusively, mostly after dark, buying his food and provisions the Lord knew where, doing the Lord knew what inside the house. Music, would it be? Playing it? Composing it, even? Sometimes, on that road, it was possible to hear faint music coming from within the house.

He might be a smuggler, or one of those investment people who somehow made pots of money by sitting at computers and switching cash around all over the world – although you'd expect such a one to live in a grander house. Several people thought he could be a writer, for didn't writers shut themselves away in wildernesses for months – years, even – to churn out their work?

It had been a source of wry amusement to the present inhabitant of the Sexton's House to occasionally hear these scraps of speculation. They even provided a degree of reassurance. If you could create a legend around yourself, it might serve to hide you from the whole world. Who had said that? Probably nobody.

This afternoon there had been the most extraordinary mixture of emotions in seeing Beatrice Drury – no, in seeing *Bea*; that was the version of her name he had decided he could use – in seeing Bea slow down her car and look across at the Sexton's

House. Then she had driven off, and the road and the meadows and hedges all returned to their customary quietness.

It was important not to have too much quiet, though, and it was vital not to let quietness into the house any more than could be helped. It was better if music could be played in the rooms – on the radio or the small stereo so patiently saved up for – and if plates and cups could be clattered while making a meal, creating the impression that there were people around, and a meal was being prepared for them. These were normal, comforting sounds. They helped to drive away the memories. Sometimes they almost smothered the sounds of a young girl crying out for help, and the greedy crackle of the flames turning that girl's prison into a burning cage . . .

It had been two years ago, but it was as vivid as ever. So much else had vanished – wiped clean from the mind's surfaces – but that memory had remained.

The afternoon had been sharp and raw, early January at its coldest, with a bite of frost in the air. The car had been bowling along the road just below Tromloy, not going very fast, certainly not exceeding the speed limit. But there had been something on the road's surface – a patch of ice, might it have been? Or had something – someone – darted across the road, causing the driver to swerve violently? The impression that there had been someone had lingered.

The car had been too badly burned for the investigators to establish why it had crashed, though. If any specific conclusions had later been reached, details had not reached the hospital or, much later, the Sexton's House. All that was certain was that at one moment the car had been driving along, the girl in the passenger seat turning to look at the driver, laughing at something that had been said to her. That was another clear memory amidst the confusion.

And the next moment—

The next moment the morning exploded into horror as the car skidded, spun wildly across the road, then smashed into the high, dry-stone wall. Lumps of glass and metal shot upwards, then the car bounced away from the wall and veered back across the road, turning completely over as it did so, the metal scraping sickeningly on the road's surface, a door tearing off. When it came to a stop, it did so resting on the passenger side. If it had not been that side . . . If only it had been the driver's door that had been torn away, it might have been possible to get at the girl. That, too, was a clear, enduring memory.

The boot lid had been torn off, and its contents flung across the road. Two suitcases with Aer Lingus labels on them. A holdall and a box of books. A waterproof jacket and a pair of rubber boots, both of them lying on the road in bizarre symmetry. It had taken several moments to realize that there was a person inside the jacket. The driver, flung from the car? Dead or only knocked unconscious?

The petrol tank exploded then, with a soft whooshing sound, and, as a plume of fire shot upwards, the stench of burning rubber and blistering metal erupted into the morning. Within the spiralling horror was the appalled realization that the bright-haired girl was still in the car, she was trapped on the passenger side, because the car was lying on that side. She was jammed hard against the road, the seat belt cinching her in.

The world whirled in sick confusion and for a moment threatened to plunge into dark unknowing. Then there was the sensation of running hard and fast to get to the girl – nothing else mattered. The man lying in the road did not matter, not for the moment, because the fire was shooting upwards, and in another minute it would engulf the car—

That was when the pain had come, an impossible agony as hands tore at metal and glass burned and scorched. There was the sensation of skin peeling from flesh, as if acid had been thrown on to it, and then of eyes shrivelling and drying. Another layer of panic had slammed in – *are my eyes being burned out . . .?* It could not be given any attention, though, because the world had shrunk to reaching the girl.

But the fire was blazing up, and showers of burning metal fragments and lumps of melting glass were falling on the prone figure of the driver – there was a sudden, sickening stench as his hair and clothes caught fire – that, too, was a memory that had remained.

The images were confused after that. Had he turned his attention to the man lying in the road, his clothes already burning? Had he tried to beat out the flames? There was a blurred memory of having thrown his coat over the man to try to smother the fire. After that, the pictures ran into one another like rain on a greasy windowpane, distorting and deceiving. Or was it only that they were so painful they could not be allowed to take on substance? There was certainly a memory of sinking down on the road in agonized despair, knowing it was too late after all, knowing she must be dead, because no one could be alive inside the blazing conflagration. There had been a spiral of hope, because something was screaming, and if she was still able to do that . . . She was not, of course. The sounds were the sirens of the ambulances and fire engines.

By then the pain of burned hands and face was soaring to levels of agony that surely could not exist, and there were people running everywhere, some of them shouting, others gabbling into phones. Blankets were being unfolded, ice packs were pressed against the burns, a needle was jabbed into one arm . . . Whatever it contained, that needle, it sent the pain spinning and caused the world to expand dizzyingly, and then to shrink. There were reassuring voices close by, but they, too, were distorted, as if people were shouting down a long, echoing tunnel.

'We're looking after you, sir, you're going to be all right.'

The attempt to speak, to ask what was happening, was impossible. Lips could not move sufficiently to form words, and no sound came from a throat that felt as if it had been flayed raw. But he thought he had made some attempt to sit up, to look across to the still-burning car, and the man lying in the road. The paramedics had seemed to understand. They said he was not to worry.

Swimming in and out of awareness on the frantic journey to a small local hospital (University Hospital, Galway, had come later), the voices had repeated the reassurances.

'You're all right, you're safe. We're looking after you.'

And then, as if one of them had understood, one of them said, 'They're both gone, poor souls. No one could have done more. You did all you could.'

But did I, thought the man in the Sexton's House? Did I?

Throughout the agony-filled days that followed, the swirling confusion only cleared fractionally and for brief periods.

Memory was erratic and distorted. Speech was almost impossible.

The doctors were reassuring and patient, both about the physical and the mental condition. There were burns, and there was quite severe smoke damage to the lungs and throat. This last was hindering speech, but that would improve and it could be helped. Plastic surgery could be carried out later, but these things could not be rushed. They had to think in terms of many weeks and probably even months. As for the mind – well, for the moment its memory banks, if they could use that term, had been severely jumbled up. Shaken into the wrong patterns. The extreme horror and pain of the crash had smothered everything else in those memory banks – even down to wiping out name, address, family.

'I had no papers on me? Surely there was something?' The words had been formed with difficulty and pain and they were distorted, but the doctors had been able to understand.

No, they had said, there had been no papers. The firefighters thought a coat had been thrown on to Niall Drury's body – was that possible? Had he any memory of doing that?

'Yes.' There was sudden gratitude at even this fragment of memory, at knowing this small attempt had been made. Speech was still difficult and painful, but it was possible to say, 'I threw my coat on to him – to smother the flames. He was lying in the road – flung clear of the car. I remember that.'

Then, said the doctors, since people seldom went around without some kind of ID, it was likely that anything such as a driving licence, bank card or so on, had been in the pockets of that coat. Which had been burned to a crisp, and any papers with it. And quite aside from the massive tragedy of the whole thing, it was deeply worrying to think there might be a wife, family, friends, who would not know what had happened. Still, the hospital had alerted the Garda and also the English police, so anyone who was missing a husband, son, brother, and who contacted the authorities, could be told about the unknown patient here in Galway. Identification would come along – it usually did. Probably it would come sooner than he expected. Or it might come of its own accord from the traumatized mind.

Later, when it was becoming easier to speak, when the numerous tests for memory loss had been done, it was possible to summon up sufficient courage to ask whether a return of memory could be expected.

There had been a noticeable pause, as if the psychiatric consultant was deciding how far to go, but after a moment he said, 'Our diagnosis is that you have what's called global disso-ciative amnesia. Psychogenic amnesia. It's quite rare, but it can stem from a severe emotional shock – which you certainly had. I'd have to say yours seems to be an extreme case, though. You've lost personal memories and what we call autobiographical information.'

'How long—'

'Will it last? Difficult to say. It can be quite brief.'

'Or it can be long-term.'

'We'll help all we can,' he said, evasively. 'It's been barely two months. There's no magic pill we can give you, but there are various therapies. If we could find someone from your family – or some friends – we'd be able to try what's called reminder therapy. In effect you'd re-learn your life.'

Family. Friends. It was curious – and frightening – how there seemed to be a complete blank surrounding those words. Had I family or friends ever?

'Someone who knows you might still come forward,' said the consultant. 'And your mind could very well heal itself. And on the plus side—'

'Is there a plus side?'

'Well, you don't show any indications of forgetting anything that's happened since the crash – that's something you'll find you're very grateful for. And, generally speaking, with disso-ciative amnesia the actual personality doesn't change. You're the same person you were before it happened.'

'Thank you for being so frank.'

In fact there had been deep, if guilty, thankfulness in accepting the massive blank canvases within the mind. There had even been a sense of liberation in being able to remain in a half-world, partially withdrawn from reality, not really required to cope with the terrifying prospect of returning to the world, maimed and scarred. At some point reality would have to be faced and memory would have to be forced back into the light. But not yet.

Some parts of reality could not be avoided, though. The names of the two people who had died were now known. They had been Niall Drury and Abigail Drury. Father and daughter. They were returning to England – to London – after a brief stay in Kilcarne at their cottage, Tromloy. They had locked it up and before driving out on to the Galway road and to the airport, they had gone into Kilcarne to arrange for one of the local shopkeepers to keep an eye on the cottage. So they were retracing their journey, going past Tromloy's private road when the crash happened.

Both bodies had been too badly burned to establish much at all, but it was thought that Niall Drury had been drinking before the crash. Even after the fire had cooled there had been a strong smell of alcohol on the road, said the doctors, and a pair of driving gloves, flung clear, had had an unmistakable odour of whiskey. The only other person on the scene had been Maxim himself, and since Maxim had certainly not been drinking, it was reasonable to assume that Drury had crashed the car because his driving abilities were impaired from alcohol. It was all circumstantial, of course; nobody could be sure, and as for judging the man, hadn't he gone to a higher judgement, anyway?

A statement had to be made to the Garda, describing, as much as possible, the events of that morning. Of necessity it was a brief and not very detailed statement, put together in a bedside interview. The Garda were patient and sensitive, but there was no doubt that they would like to know when memory returned, and an identity established. Perhaps he would kindly keep in touch, though. Could he leave an address, at all? No, well, there was no cause to worry.

The burned hands and face were starting to heal by then – which was to say as much as they ever would heal. There was more talk of plastic surgery, and also of speech therapy. Speech was improving, though. It was often painful, and it sounded slightly blurred, but it was recognizable as human speech.

NINE

The offer of the Sexton's House had come at the end of a long series of surgical procedures – some had been pronounced a moderate success, others had not made any noticeable difference. But there was starting to be cautious talk of a discharge from the infirmary – of going back out into the world. Had he somewhere he could go? asked the doctors.

'It doesn't seem like it.'

That was when the Sexton's House had been mentioned.

'It's on the edge of Kilcarne, and it's a tiny place and likely to be quite basic,' the consultant had said. 'And you'd need to do a bit of work in return, of course.'

'What kind of work?'

'Looking after the church grounds. Keeping the graveyards tidy. Sweeping up leaves, pruning bushes. The odd bit of maintenance to the church itself – well, two churches, because you'd have a foot in two parishes, as it were. Repairing a broken window, perhaps cleaning out a clogged-up drainpipe or whitewashing a wall. Can you do that kind of thing, d'you think?'

'If I can't, I could learn.'

'And maybe even a bit of cleaning of the church itself as well. Would you mind that?'

'I'll gladly scrub floors and wallow in whitewash if it means I can be independent.'

'Good man. The office of sexton as such doesn't exist any longer, but the work still has to be done, and the church doles out a tiny stipend.'

'Sexton.' The word came out thoughtfully. 'Isn't it from the Latin, *sacristanus*, meaning custodian of sacred objects?'

'You do come up with some unexpected remarks,' said the consultant. 'I'm becoming increasingly curious to find out who and what you really are.'

'So am I.'

'And will you take this sexton's work and the cottage? I'm prepared to stand as guarantor if one's needed. The Irish Church,' he said, a touch caustically, 'likes to cover all bases and safeguard its investments.'

The offer could not be refused. The consultant had become the nearest thing to a friend that had existed during those months.

'I'd be very grateful if you would stand as guarantor.' A pause. 'You do know, I suppose, that beneath all this politeness I'm scoured to the bone with anguish and bitterness, and that I'd sell my soul to the devil if I could have back—'

'For pity's sake don't talk about souls in this country,' said the consultant at once. 'They'll take you literally and you'd never be allowed to be a custodian of sacred objects. And yes, of course I know all that.' He got up to go, then said, 'Listen, don't expect too much of the Sexton's House. It's small and basic, but it would be a roof over your head.'

A roof over my head. It was somehow difficult to mentally slot such a concept into place.

'And certainly don't expect too much when it comes to the money, either,' said the consultant, 'because I think it really will be the tiniest of pittances. But it might be enough to tide you over until . . . well, until you find your place – or *a* place in the world again.'

'It sounds as if my place in the world is going to be that of second grave-digger.'

'So you remember your *Hamlet*, do you?' said the consultant. 'That's interesting.'

Day by day, hour by agonizing hour, a semblance of normality started to return.

The work that was required from the incumbent of the little house was easy enough, and it could be done at chosen times when no one was likely to be around. There was unexpected satisfaction in keeping grass neatly cut, in pruning evergreen bushes, and in buffing up the beautiful old graining of carvings and pews.

As the consultant had said, the Sexton's House was small

and very basic indeed, but it was weatherproof, and there was some furniture in it. The heating was antiquated, but it appeared to work and, even if it did not, there was a brick fireplace, where a peat fire could be kindled. It was unexpectedly attractive to imagine the leaping flames on the old walls. The wiring and plumbing both looked and sounded as if they dated to World War II, but they seemed to work as well. And old-fashioned plumbing and heating and worn furniture did not matter. What mattered – what would continue to matter – were the vast empty chasms where memories should have been.

Then, a few weeks after leaving the hospital, had come the first intrusion into the house called Tromloy.

It had been unforgiveable as well as illegal, of course, and it was prompted by a strange compulsion to see the place where that dead girl, Abigail Drury, had spent her holidays with her parents. What had Abigail's life been? Had she been happy in that house? Had she been loved and cherished? And why was I walking along that road on that day?

Tromloy was on the other side of Kilcarne, at the end of its own unmade road, and it possessed an extraordinary air of beckoning. A feeling that it might be saying, Come inside, because you'll be safe here. Come inside, because there's something in here that will help you. Come inside – there's a way to get in and you'll find it.

There had been a way to get in, although there had been guilt in levering up a loose window catch and climbing through the window. Had Niall Drury meant to have that window catch replaced? Had he been so much in a rush of preparations to get back to his London life and his wife that he had forgotten it?

Once inside, the scents of the house had been strong – peat fires and books and old timbers, all printed on the atmosphere. Had happiness left a print here as well?

Tromloy was empty, but the ghosts of the people who had lived in it and the echoes of their lives lingered. They were in the shadow-outlines on walls where large pieces of furniture had stood, but had been removed. They were in a faint splashy stain on the kitchen table, and they were in the scatter of papers left out on the small dining table, as if somebody had wanted them handy for the next visit.

The ghosts were in the upstairs bedroom as well – in a room with bronze and green cushions piled on a single bed, and with a rocking chair that might still rock if the right person sat in it. And where a benign-looking, slightly portly Victorian performer smiled down from a frame.

Abigail Drury's room. Of course it was. And there was her photograph on the bookshelf. Oh, God, she had been a lovely girl. Bright, intelligent, that wide, generous mouth that would have laughed easily and smiled at the world . . . The pity of it slammed home all over again, and the guilt increased a hundred, a thousandfold. I tried to save you, Abigail, I truly did. But the fire – the blisteringly hot metal—

And yet, despite the deep sense of remorse, there was the feeling that if Abigail Drury's ghost walked here, it did so peacefully. Further along the landing was a big double bedroom, light and clean, a patchwork quilt still lying on the bed, the colours faded and dim, but beautiful. Sunshine would trickle through the small windows and deepen the colours, and glint on the brass bedframe.

There was another bedroom at the back of the house, which looked as if it was used for storage. An old rolltop desk stood by the window, and there were several pieces of old furniture – probably not wanted in the main rooms, but considered too good to throw out.

The feeling of intrusion returned as the burned hands pulled a chair over to the desk, and opened it. There were small drawers inside, and pigeonholes. Were there papers here that would relate to Tromloy's occupants? Even papers that could be used to establish an identity, and that nobody would miss, because Abigail's mother would probably never come here again. Most likely Tromloy would be sold to strangers who would never know anything had been taken.

It was a bit risky to make a light, but the curtains could be closed, and the bedroom was at the back of the house, over-looking open ground. There were candles and matches in a kitchen cupboard.

The guilt had vanished by this time, and the feeling of something beckoning had returned a hundredfold. I think there's something here that will help me. Not anything that will fill in those massive blanks of memory, but something that might give me an identity I can use in the world.

The desk contained old bills and receipts for work and maintenance to the house. A few Christmas cards which had been kept for some reason, and a couple of concert programmes for local events, and for theatres in Galway City. The night wore on, and Tromloy sank into silence, seeming to seal itself off from the rest of the world. Once there was the soft hoot of an owl, and once faint chimes from a distant church clock rippled the quiet. Other than that, there was only the flickering candlelight and the faint rustling of papers.

The faraway church clock had chimed one, then two, and fresh candles had been lit, when the large thick envelope, lying at the very back of a drawer, was uncovered. In a modern-looking hand were the written words, *Old Tromloy*. It was easy to visualize Niall or Bea Drury finding a few old papers relating to the house they had bought, and putting them aside to one day investigate more fully.

The envelope was old, and the flap, once sealed down, had dried and lifted away. There was no longer a sense of intrusion, and the contents of the envelope were removed and spread out on the desk.

And there it was. In the torch's light, there was the thing sought for, hoped for. The identity of a real person. Two things. The first, a letter from The Genesius Theatre in Galway City. Do I know that place? A faint memory of having walked past a tall, stone-fronted building flickered briefly. The letter was short, and confirmed, 'with deepest thanks', receipt of the 'generous donation'. It had been written on an old typewriter, and some of the characters were slightly blurred, making it impossible to tell if the date at the head was 1920 or 1930 or even 1950.

The second scrap was also a printed acknowledgement, this time from a bank in Galway, of a sum of money deposited with them. It was not dated and no amount was shown. An official receipt had apparently been enclosed with the letter, but of this there was no sign.

But even with the smudged old typeface of The Genesius's letter and the somewhat faceless bank communication, the recipient's name on both was clear. Maxim Volf.

Maxim Volf. A man who apparently had had a bank account and who had made a donation to a Galway theatre.

If he had been around in 1930, and sufficiently adult – and sufficiently well off – to be making donations, it was unlikely he was alive now. Dare I take his name? How safe would it be? Might the Garda or the English police – or anyone else – check some kind of database for Maxim Volf? But why would they bother? The inquest was over, Niall and Abigail Drury were buried, and the Garda simply wanted a name for the man who had witnessed the car crash. Just for their records, they had said. And if pressed, wouldn't it be possible to offer a version of the truth? To say, 'I found these, and I think he was my father – or grandfather. So I'm adopting the name.'

It was a name the Garda wanted. And if I'm going to live a life with any degree of normality, it's what I want as well. I can't bear being this nameless, stateless, anonymous being. I want a name, an identity, something to hold on to. Taking this name could not hurt the real Maxim Volf, who was surely long since dead.

But before leaving, it might be as well to make sure there was nothing else in this room, in this house, that could link the newly created persona to Tromloy and therefore give the lie to the fraud. Hunting through the candelit rooms, the guilt and the feeling of intruding returned, but it was something that must be done.

It was not until the church clock had chimed three, and was approaching four, that it felt safe to leave Tromloy, and walk back along the deserted lanes to the Sexton's House.

I am Maxim Volf. I can become a real person again.

It had been a couple of weeks after that night, working in the windswept cemetery on Kilcarne's edge, when a strange discovery had been made. One of the sexton's tasks was to sweep leaves and keep graves tidy. It ought to have been a melancholy job, but the graveyard had a serenity about it; it was even possible to recall fragments of poetry written by the metaphysical poets – the eighteenth- and nineteenth-century young men who had liked to send their heroes and heroines wandering wispily through crumbling churchyards, murmuring elegies and lamenting lost loves. Men who had decorated their desks with skulls and succumbed to romantic deaths from consumption. How do I know any of that? How do I know about that poetry? Was I a teacher? Even a writer on my own account? Working quietly in the cemetery, these thoughts ran back and forth.

Abigail Drury's grave was here. It was under an old beech tree that in autumn would be copper bronze. Would she have liked that? Niall Drury's grave was nearby; a plain stone with nothing more than his name and the dates of his birth and his death. No memorial engraving of any kind. But I'll remember you, Niall Drury. I'll remember you and your daughter, and I'll trim the grass around your graves, and, Niall, I'll never stop regretting that I didn't save you or your girl.

The small inner graveyard was not discovered until the third or fourth visit to the cemetery. It was behind a small iron gate in an old wall – a gate that could easily be overlooked, mainly because it was partly covered with a creeper, almost as if the creeper had deliberately been allowed to grow wild for concealment. But the gate opened easily enough. There was a curious moment when everything seemed to slow down, and there was a sensation of stepping into a different world. Is that my lost memories stirring at last? Or is it simply because I'm about to go through a secret door? Surely all the best fairy stories and fantasies started with a hidden garden gate or a low door in a wall?

But beyond the old gate was only the older part of the cemetery, and at first there did not seem to be any reason for that strange prickle of awareness. There was nothing here, after all . . .

But there was something. A little way along the serried graves was a name that sent the quiet cemetery spinning, and intensified the feeling of having entered a different world.

'Maxim Volf. Died 1955.'

Maxim Volf. The man whose identity I've stolen.

*   *   *

That night, walking again along the dark lanes, slipping through the faulty window into Tromloy, it was almost possible to forget that life from now on must be lived in darkness, because the pity or the revulsion of people could not be endured. Somewhere along the line would have to be acceptance that there would no longer be women who could be wooed or loved or seduced. How much do I mind that? Did I like the company of ladies, in bed and out of it? Did I have a wife, a girlfriend? I have no idea, but if there was someone, she's certainly better off without me now.

Seated in the rocking chair in the bronze and green bedroom, it was easier to put these thoughts aside. Did you sit here, Abigail? Why did you have that old photograph on the wall where you could see it from the bed?

There was no name on the photo, but with care a corner of the brown-paper backing could be peeled back. Beneath, in letters sepia brown from age, were written the words, '*Mortimer Quince on stage at Shepherd's Bush Empire, 1910.*'

The name meant nothing. Probably Abigail, or one of her parents, had found the photograph in an antiques shop or a junk shop, had liked the man's face, and had brought it home to hang here. Or perhaps Mortimer Quince had been an ancestor.

It did not add anything to the curiosity about the dead Abigail. It did not, either, add anything to the occasional flares of memory that were returning – startling, shutter-flash images of that lost life before the car crash. Memory flares, one of the doctors had called them, with typical Irish lyricism. Like the lights you might see on a marsh through fog, he had said, or the lamp-glow of will-o'-the-wisps in the gloaming. Only the Irish could have described the healing of amnesia in such a fashion, but the expression was pleasing.

Sometimes, now, it seemed as if the memory flares might belong to someone else. Was it possible to receive memory flares from another person? Even from someone who was dead? Abigail? It was an oddly comforting thought, even for someone who did not believe or trust in any kind of afterlife.

What was far more disturbing, though, was the suspicion that the flares might belong to – might even be coming from – the dead Niall Drury.

Which was the wildest and most fantastical idea yet.

But sitting quietly in the deserted bedroom of Tromloy, staring at the old photograph of the unknown Mortimer Quince, it did not seem in the least fantastical.

TEN

Phin's dreams had been peopled with fantastical images of Roman Volf and that last extraordinary appearance described by Feofil Markov, when Roman had led a defiant procession along the banks of the Catherine Canal with anarchists and rebels streaming along behind. And the imperial Cossacks in pursuit . . .

Before going down to breakfast, he checked for any voice-mails or emails. There were a few emails that did not need immediate attention, although one was from the Canadian editor who had recommended him to the TV team for the Roman Volf documentary, and who had told his agent he had silver eyes. It was a friendly invitation to have dinner when the editor was in London next month, and Phin typed an immediate acceptance, smiling as he did so. Checking his phone, he found there was a voicemail from his rugby-playing neighbour in London — in fact there were two. They were timed as having been sent the previous day, and Phin listened to them with misgiving.

'Sorry about this, Phin,' said the first message, 'but we had a bit of a calamity just as the party was winding itself down and we were all having breakfast. You'd left for the airport by then, and I suppose you'd switch off your phone during the flight . . .'

Oh God, thought Phin.

'. . . that bloody beer overflowed the bath while we weren't watching and flooded my flat, then sloshed its way down that little flight of stairs into yours. It's not a massive disaster, not as disasters go – good thing you'd left a key with Miss Pringle, though. And it's only the one room of your flat that's affected – the Pringle has had to decamp to her sister's while the builders put in a new ceiling. But if you can possibly remember who supplied your carpet we'll get the fitters in there absolutely first thing tomorrow – we'll make sure to get the exact same carpet, and by the time you get back you won't know anything's even happened . . .'

At this point the five-minute limit, which the mobile phone shop had assured Phin would be plenty for most calls, cut in and truncated the rest of the message. Fortunately, the neighbour had redialled.

'. . . and it's all covered by my insurance, so you won't have to shell out a cent. Pringle's decorators will slosh a tub or two of paint around as well, because beer does soak into walls, doesn't it? Only part of your walls, though. Well, about halfway up from the skirting board, if we're going to be exact. But we'll match the paint up as nearly as possible, and I'll let you know when you can safely come home. Hope you're having a good holiday.'

Phin swore several times, but managed to send a reasonably temperate voicemail back, saying he would be home in about three days, and relaying the name of the carpet store, whose name he fortunately remembered. He added, with as much polite firmness as he could manage, that he hoped everything would have returned to normal by then.

After breakfast he mentioned to Grania O'Brien that he was taking her advice about Maxim Volf and visiting the Sexton's House tomorrow, rather than today. 'This morning I'm going into Galway.'

'It's a beautiful city,' she said. 'Will you be in to dinner tonight?'

'Yes, certainly.'

'Well, they'll look after you from the kitchen. I'm off out to supper at the Cullens' myself. They've their nephew visiting and they like to show him off, so we're usually invited, Rory and me. Bit of a gloomy affair it'll be, what with old Cullen banging on about religion and sin, and his two sisters, poor souls, scared for their lives of him in case he has another stroke and leaves them on their own. Best thing that could happen to them in my opinion, but it doesn't do to say. Still, a good meal they always put on – Nuala Cullen's a great cook, and it does their niece good to have a bit of company, for I doubt she has much of a life, cooped up there, poor child. They say she's not strong enough for ordinary school – lot of rubbish, to my mind, but that's something else that can't be said. Her mother ran away before Jessica was born. Couldn't wait to get away from old Tormod Cullen most like. The Cullen ladies were distraught when they had the news of her death, although thanks be to God, it turned out they were named as guardians for Jess, and it was a great comfort to them when she was brought to Kilcarne. And I'll see if they remember those old wartime concerts you were wanting to know about.'

'I'd appreciate that,' said Phin.

'They'd all have been young children in the forties, of course, but they might remember something. I'll let you know in the morning – unless you'd like me to tap on your door when I get back. We won't be very late.'

'No, please don't bother,' said Phin, hastily.

'Well, if you change your mind, my own room's just along the corridor.'

'Tomorrow will be fine,' said Phin, firmly, and set out for Galway.

It was not a very busy road, and he scanned the houses along the roadside, hoping to identify the Sexton's House. About a mile out of Kilcarne, Grania had said, and set on its own above the road. He passed a few cottages, then thought he identified it, although after the build up he would not have been surprised to see a Gothic pile. In fact it was a small, perfectly ordinary grey-stone cottage, without so much as a leering gargoyle or a sinister chimney pot to its name.

Phin drove on, thinking he would certainly come back out here tomorrow and see if Maxim Volf was inclined to talk to him. Today he would see what Galway City had to offer in the way of theatre memorabilia. He had made notes of several antiquarian bookshops from the phone directory, and once in the city he found a big car park, then began to work through the shops with the aid of a street map. But by lunchtime he had drawn a blank and his feet were aching. He ate a rather despondent lunch at a pub, and considered whether he should switch to visiting the city's theatres. But had Quince ever appeared in any Irish theatre? That article had certainly referred to concert parties for war efforts, but those concerts could have been staged anywhere, from the Irish equivalent of assembly rooms and co-operative halls to the grandest theatres in the entire county. Phin thought he would finish the trawl of the bookshops before making a decision about exploring theatres.

The daylight was starting to fade by the time he reached the shop in a small side street near the river. It was pleasingly cluttered, and on a table near the back were a couple of boxes of theatre memorabilia. Phin knelt down to sift through them.

At first he thought there was not going to be anything relevant, then, near the bottom of the smaller box, he found two old postcards, carefully covered with modern cellophane. They both showed a man standing on a stage – the same man each time. The stage could have been anywhere, but on both of them the name across the top was clear. Mortimer Quince.

Phin lifted the postcards out with care. I've found you, he thought, with delight. This is what you looked like. For the first time, he realized he had been hoping for a younger, slightly more modern version of Roman, but the man in these photographs did not seem to bear any resemblance to Roman. In one postcard Quince was seated on an elaborately carved chair, wearing evening clothes and looking pensive. He was slightly too chubby-faced to achieve the pensive look with complete success, but the general effect was unexpectedly endearing. The legend across the top said, quite simply, 'Mr Mortimer Quince'. In the second shot Quince was standing on a stage, thumbs in waistcoat in the classic late-Victorian stance, looking as if he was preparing to sing to an audience. A curly banner over his head proclaimed him, in elaborate typeface, to be, 'Quality Quince, the Man with the Quicksilver Voice.'

Phin carried both cards to the cash desk to buy them before anyone else could snatch them from his grasp. This done, he returned to investigate the second, larger box. Things often went in threes – was it too much to hope that where there had been two good finds, there might be a third?

This box contained old theatre programmes and posters. It was sad to think these old programmes and tattered posters were all that remained of the hopes and dreams of forgotten performances and vanished performers. Phin pushed this thought aside, and went painstakingly through the contents.

There was nothing more about Quality Quince though, and the hoary old belief about things going in threes was a total fiction after all . . .

Then he found it. At the very bottom of the box, the edges crumbling and the surface badly foxed, was an old poster with lettering, probably originally scarlet, now faded to pale terracotta, advertising the Grand Opening of The Genesius Theatre, Galway City, on 23 November next. 'Come along and bring your friends to a magical night of music. Tickets available at the box office, and small supper bar open for refreshments during the interval.'

There was a list of the entertainment to be provided, and at the foot of the poster was a list of 'Participators, performers, and organizers'. The Genesius Theatre stated its grateful thanks to everyone who had been involved, and to the generous donors who had made it all possible.

And there was Mortimer Quince's name, billed as having directed and arranged the whole thing. Phin smiled at the name, as if greeting an old acquaintance, then scanned the other names listed. Nothing, no one recognizable, probably nothing else to be found here—

Then he saw the name at the very end of the list. It was in exactly the same typeface as the others, but it leapt out at him.

Maxim Volf.

He sat staring at this for so long that the proprietor came worriedly over to ask was he all right.

'I'm fine,' said Phin, coming out of his trance. 'I'd like to take this as well as those postcards, please.'

He watched jealously as the poster was swathed in bubble-wrap and placed inside a stiffened envelope, then carried it back to his car, and laid it with extreme care on the front passenger seat where he could reach it, in case it should jump out of the vehicle of its own accord and be for ever lost. He would like to go in immediate search of The Genesius Theatre, but it was already almost four o'clock, and he did not want to leave the poster and the Quince postcards unattended in a municipal car park while he prowled the city's streets more or less at random. He would try to find an exact address for The Genesius tonight, and he would come back tomorrow . . .

No, tomorrow, he had promised himself that he would check out the present-day Maxim Volf. He would get to grips with The Genesius the day after. The place had most likely long since crumbled to the ground, or been turned into a multiplex or a trendy tapas bar, but fragments of its past might still be found.

He ate a solitary dinner at O'Brien's, wondered if the amiably inclined Grania was enjoying her supper party with the Cullen family, and took himself to his room to re-read The Genesius's poster, in case he had missed any vital nugget of information. He had not, of course, so he finally set it aside, and turned his attention to drafting a possible outline for a scene in which a suitable actor enacted Roman Volf's last defiant performance on the banks of the Catherine Canal. If he could sell this reconstruction idea to the TV company as part of the documentary it would be very good indeed. Hell's teeth, it would be better than good, it would be brilliant and striking and moving. Roman's behaviour that night had been outrageous and foolhardy in the extreme, of course, and ulti-mately it had been tragic, but what a farewell performance! Phin, his mind alive and alight with ideas, drafted out three possible scenarios, after which he drank a large measure of scaldingly potent Irish whiskey, and finally fell asleep trying – and failing – to think of an actor who could believably portray Roman Volf.

Nuala and Morna always enjoyed their preparations for Donal's visit and they liked the buzz of anticipation that seemed to fill up the house before his arrival.

Tormod was looking forward to seeing Donal as well, although he was not best pleased to hear the O'Briens were coming to supper. He said he supposed the invitation could not be withdrawn, but it was to be hoped Rory O'Brien and his sister would not stay late.

Nuala had considered attempting *boeuf en croûte*, but had decided against it because it could so easily go wrong and Tormod would probably sulk or bang the table with his stick if soggy pastry was placed before him. So she was going to play safe with a nice leg of roast pork, with apple sauce. There were some beautiful Bramleys in their own apple tree, and there was no reason why Jessica could not help peel and core them. Morna wondered if it was a good idea to let Jess have the sharp corer, but Nuala said it would be perfectly all right; in any case she would be there in the kitchen with Jess all the time, and it would be good for the child to feel she was joining in the preparations.

It was wonderful to see Donal again, and Rory O'Brien and his sister were always lively company, although Morna and Nuala were rather shocked at Grania O'Brien's outfit which they thought was just a bit too tight and just a bit too short. They themselves had worn their best outfits. Nuala's was cream with coffee-coloured lace, Morna had a powder-blue blouse. Jessica had put on a bronze sweater – it made a lovely splash of colour, said Nuala, and brought out the red glints in her hair.

'Uncle Tormod said I should put something else on,' said Jessica. 'He said something about only harlots having red hair.'

'Oh, your Uncle Tormod gets a bit too caught up with the Old Testament,' said Morna. 'You don't look anything like a harlot, not that I've ever seen such a creature well, I shouldn't think there are any in Kilcarne – but you look great.'

'Just like your mother,' said Nuala, blinking hard, then smiling. 'You always look like that if we mention Catriona. Wistful. No – not that. Hopeful.'

'That's because you hardly ever do mention her. I like hearing about her.'

'It upsets us to remember how she ran away, you see,' said Nuala. 'We were so very fond of her. The baby of the family . . . But when we heard from the hospital where she died – when they wrote to say we were named as your guardians – well, that was wonderful, wasn't it, Morna?'

'It was. Now then, I tell you what, Jess, we'll put you at the corner of the table, by the jar of chrysanthemums I picked this afternoon,' said Morna, who could not be doing with sentiment when there were still tables to be laid and glasses to be polished. 'You'll make an absolute picture there.'

Over supper, Grania told them about somebody who had

come to stay at O'Brien's. 'A music researcher, whatever that might be, and his name's Phineas Fox. Quiet, but very nice looking.' She winked at Jessica when she said this. 'And he's wanting to look into the 1930s and 1940s – he says there were some concerts held hereabouts then, arranged by some old music hall performer who retired to Kilcarne. Mortimer Quince was his name, and this Mr Fox is trying to trace his life – I don't know why, because I don't think Mortimer Quince was anybody very famous. But it'd be useful if Phineas Fox could talk to anyone who might remember the concerts, so I said I'd ask around. Mr Cullen, you'd maybe remember the concerts, perhaps? The later ones, I mean.'

But Tormod could not remember any such thing, and his tone suggested he found the question impertinent.

'Ah well, it's a good few years back,' said Grania, cheerfully, 'and you'd all three have been very young.'

'There might be some old parish records,' said Donal. 'I could ask Father Sullivan has he anything.'

'Could you? That'd be great.'

They had finished their pudding by this time, and Donal had poured a glass of brandy for everyone. Grania had had two glasses; she had had a generous share of the wine earlier as well, and she was starting to sound a bit slurred. She leaned closer to Donal and placed a hand on his arm, saying it was nice to help people, wasn't it? Morna and Nuala hoped they were not heading for an embarrassing incident, and wished they had not seated her next to Donal.

'I've sent this Mr Fox along to see that hermit out at the Sexton's House,' said Grania. 'Something about a name that matched up, he thought.'

Donal did not seem to have noticed Grania's hand. In a suddenly sharp voice, he said, 'What hermit?'

'He's been here for a year or so,' said Rory, 'although a man would have to be desperate to live in such a ramshackle place. Hasn't it been falling down for years? But he looks like a tramp, so I daresay he doesn't notice.'

'A tramp? Who is he?' said Donal, leaning forward.

'I don't think anyone knows,' said Grania. 'The story is that he was injured in a fire – his face scarred quite badly – so he keeps clear of people. Somebody said he was in Kilcarne once before. People would see him wandering around the fields. Bit of a local landmark at one time. Morna, you and Nuala would remember that, surely?'

'I remember,' said Morna, rather shortly. 'I didn't know he was supposed to have come back.'

Jessica, who had not spoken much, but who had listened to the conversation, said, 'People do come back sometimes.'

'Oh, they're saying in the bar that he came back to hide,' said Rory, cheerfully. 'That he returned to the place where his face was ruined. That's one of the stories, at any rate. It's a bit too much like a romantic film or a book for my taste, but people will say anything after a few drinks, isn't that true, Father Donal?'

'Sad but true,' said Donal. 'Tormod, will you have a drop more brandy?'

'I will. Thank you.'

'Probably none of it's true about the hermit,' said Grania, as Donal refilled Tormod's glass. 'Still, Mr Fox might find out a bit more about him. I'll ask him tomorrow.'

'No, don't do that. Best leave it alone,' said Donal.

'Donal's right,' said Morna. 'It's only spreading gossip, and we don't want to do that.'

'We don't like gossip,' said Nuala.

Tormod, drinking the brandy and crumbling cheese on his plate, told them that gossip was an evil and an abomination before the Lord.

'Quite right,' said Grania. 'But I don't suppose Mr Fox will get inside the Sexton's House anyway, for it's said the hermit never opens his door to a single soul. Is there more brandy – well, just a tot to keep out the cold, Father Donal – oh, my word, what a large one you're giving me.' She sent him a look from beneath her lashes that shocked Nuala to her toes.

'That Grania O'Brien is a bold, shameless one,' Morna said later, over the washing-up. 'She flirted – actually *flirted* – with Donal, did you see that?'

'I did. And made some very suggestive remarks, as far as I could tell.' Nuala had not actually understood the majority of Grania O'Brien's saucier comments, but it had been impossible to mistake the tone. 'Tormod was very displeased.'

'I daresay Donal was displeased, as well, but he didn't show it, of course.' They smiled; Donal was unfailingly courteous.

'Jessica was quiet, wasn't she?'

'Yes, but she always is.'

They looked at one another, then Nuala said, 'That man Grania mentioned—'

'The one she called a hermit?'

'Yes. And Rory said looked like a tramp – Morna, it can't be the man who was here before, can it?'

'Not at all,' said Morna, a bit too quickly. 'He won't have come back. We're perfectly safe. It's just people spinning tales in O'Brien's. Still, Rory was right about the Sexton's House falling to pieces. It's a ramshackle old place.'

But they went rather unhappily to bed. It might have been coincidence that made them both wake at the same time – or it might even have been the chiming of the clock in the hall below. One a.m., and that single note was always quite sudden.

But they both knew it had been neither of those things. They both knew it was the sound of footsteps along the landing that had woken them. Soft, slow footsteps going towards Jessica's bedroom.

Morna was out of bed in a minute, dragging on a dressing gown, thrusting her feet into slippers. There would not be anything wrong, of course, and likely as not the steps would be Donal going along to the bathroom. But just in case . . .

As she opened her door, Nuala came out of her room. Neither of them spoke. They did not need to. They could both see the figure outlined against the tall narrow landing window. A figure that dragged one foot only very slightly, and that did not need to hold on to anything for balance as it did in the daytime.

Tormod reached for the handle of Jessica's bedroom and very slowly started to turn it.

The sisters were there at once, Morna taking his arm before the door could be opened, Nuala saying it was cold tonight, and wouldn't he be better in his bed? She would bring him some hot milk with brandy.

For a moment they thought he was going to resist, and they both thought Jessica would wake, but Tormod only stared at them as if he did not recognize them, then allowed himself to be led back to his own room.

Downstairs, heating the milk, Nuala said, 'He didn't know us, did he?'

'No. He was sleepwalking, like – like he was once before. You remember the time when—?'

'Oh, yes,' said Nuala, quickly. 'I didn't think he'd ever do it again, though. I didn't know he could walk as easily as that any longer.'

'Nor did I,' said Morna. 'We'll need to be a bit more watchful. Nuala, did you know Tormod used to go into Catriona's bedroom sometimes? Late at night. Years and years ago, I mean, when we were all young.'

'I did know,' said Nuala, in a voice hardly more than a whisper. 'I saw him once.'

They looked at one another, the knowledge that Jessica slept in the room that had been Catriona's between them.

'He'd stand at the foot of Catriona's bed, looking at her,' said Morna.

'I know. I never dared say anything. There was nothing wrong, of course.'

'Oh no.'

'But, Morna – did you ever think – all those years ago, I mean – that Tormod was – well, a bit too fond of Catriona?'

'She was his sister,' began Morna.

'I know. That's the point. I hardly dare say this, even now, but—'

'But you think Catriona ran away because of Tormod.'

'Yes.'

'So do I.'

ELEVEN

P hin set off for the Sexton's House and the hermit who might be Roman's descendant shortly after breakfast.

Grania O'Brien accorded him a cordial good morning, and seemed disposed to enter into a discussion. She had not found out anything about the wartime concerts at the Cullens' supper party, she said, although there had been a bit of speculation about the man at the Sexton's House. It would be very interesting to hear if Mr Fox found out anything about him.

'Probably he won't want to talk to me,' said Phin, and made good his escape.

He was trying not to hope too much that something would come out of this meeting, but surely this man had to be connected to Roman. The name was too much of a coincidence.

The narrow track that led up to the house was so steep that in the depths of winter it would probably be so iced over it would be impossible to get in or out. But at the top there was an astonishingly beautiful view towards Galway, and Phin suspected Maxim Volf probably did not mind if he was marooned out here for a week or two. There was even a certain attraction about the idea, providing you had sufficient food and drink and warmth. And books, thought Phin. And music, as well, of course, because you wouldn't want to be wrapped in too much silence out here.

As if something had picked up this last thought, as he got out of the car he heard music coming from inside the house. It was Tchaikovsky's *Piano Concerto No. 1* – the piece inspired by the playing of blind beggar-musicians in Kiev. It suddenly seemed very right to Phin that a meeting with Roman Volf's descendant should be to a backdrop of flamboyant music by a Russian composer. He stood for a moment, listening, then took a deep breath and reached for the door knocker.

*   *   *

It was so rare for anyone to knock on the door of the Sexton's House, that it was several moments before the man listening to Tchaikovsky realized what the sound was.

The instinct was, as always, to ignore the knock, to turn up the music's volume and wait for whoever was outside to go away. But the knock came again, slightly louder. Whoever was out there would have heard the music and know someone was inside.

It was possible, from the side window of this room, to see on to the track. If there was no car there, the knock was better ignored, because it would very likely be local children, daring one another to go up to the weird man's house. That had happened once or twice. But if a car was there . . . There was a sudden absurd stab of hope that if a car should be there, it might be the small blue hatchback that Beatrice Drury drove. If so, would I open the door to her? In daylight, with no friendly, concealing darkness?

But the car parked outside was not Beatrice Drury's. It bore the logo of a car-hire firm, which probably meant it was a tourist who had lost his – or her – way. That was relatively safe; the door could be opened, a brief set of directions given from the shadow of the hall, then the world shut out again and Tchaikovsky resumed.

The man standing outside had not the look of a lost traveller. He was in his early or mid-thirties, and he had unremarkable brown hair and an intelligent mouth. He also had extraordinary clear grey eyes, rimmed with black. In a second or two, the eyes would flinch and the sensitive lips would tighten with the blend of pity and repulsion that had become all too familiar over the last two years.

But this did not happen. The stranger said, 'Hello. I'm sorry to turn up unannounced like this.' An English voice, a bit diffident. 'My name's Phineas Fox and – wait a bit, I've got a card . . . Yes, here it is. I'm hoping I've got the right house and that you're Maxim Volf, because I'm researching possible links to the nineteenth-century musician Roman Volf. I think he might have been one of your ancestors.'

The card simply said, 'Phineas Fox, music researcher.' There was a string of letters that probably should have meant something, but did not, and a London address. Clearly this was not something in which to become involved; the man could be sent on his way with curt politeness about never having heard of a nineteenth-century musician called Roman Volf.

Incredibly, the curt politeness did not come. Instead, the admission, 'Yes, I am Maxim Volf,' came out, and once said, could not be called back. But it was possible to dilute it a bit, by saying, firmly, 'I'm not sure about anyone called Roman Volf, though—'

'I'm not sure either,' said Phineas Fox, eagerly. 'But I've been commissioned to dig up material about him, and I've traced a son of his to this part of Ireland.' He spread his hands. 'It's most likely a wild-goose chase and a complete dead-end, but – did you ever hear that you might have a Russian musician in your family? A violinist? The 1870s and early 1880s it would be. He was famous and somewhat scandalous.'

It was the phrase, 'in your family', that tipped the balance. This stranger, this Phineas Fox, was offering a family, ancestors, a history. The deep loneliness of having no one – of being connected to nothing, of knowing that being so disfigured meant there never would be any woman who would want any connection of any kind – was suddenly almost overwhelming. The family Phineas Fox was offering would be a stolen family, just as Maxim Volf's identity had been stolen, but even so . . .

The next words were out before they could be stopped. 'I don't think I can help you, but would you like to come in for a moment anyway?'

The small sitting room had never had two people in it, and it seemed suddenly overcrowded. But Phineas Fox took the deep armchair near the window, and accepted the rather awkwardly made offer of tea or coffee. It felt strange to be putting out two cups and two saucers, to ask about sugar, even to remember a packet of biscuits in a cupboard. Forgotten rituals. Yet I must have done this many times in that other, lost life. And across the coffee cups the atmosphere lightened – it was easy to forget how sharing even the most modest of refreshments broke down barriers.

It was instinctive to sit away from the light, to have a hand ready to shield the more severely scarred side, but Phineas Fox seemed hardly to notice, and he certainly did not seem to find it disconcerting. There was the impression of an eager, inquisitive mind, and of someone to whom outward trappings did not matter very much.

'I'm commissioned to provide background on Roman Volf for a possible TV documentary,' said Phineas Fox. 'And it seems a son of his – illegitimate, apparently – came to this part of Ireland – probably shortly after World War One. That's why I'm here.'

'To find the son? No, to find descendants of the son.'

'Yes. I've also uncovered a Maxim Volf from around the same time, although I haven't been able to link him definitely to Roman yet.'

Maxim Volf. This stranger meant the real Maxim, of course, the man who lay in the small graveyard. It was a curious and unsettling experience to hear the name spoken aloud.

'And since Volf isn't a very common surname,' Phineas Fox was saying, 'I'm making a tentative connection to you. Could I ask if you have any knowledge of your grandparents or great-grandparents? Not everyone does, of course, and people move around so much these days and don't always know their backgrounds. But I wondered if you might know if any of your family were from these parts?'

It would be perfectly possible to deny knowledge of grandparents, to say there was no real Irish connection at all and certainly no connection to Kilcarne.

And yet . . .

And yet here was something to seize and hold on to, something on which, and around which, a spurious reality might be woven. The prospect was as beckoning as the siren song of legend. But it would be necessary to be cautious, to be aware of pitfalls. So—

'I don't know very much about my family at all.'

'Do you have any old photographs, perhaps? Scrapbooks – old newspaper cuttings? Because,' said Phineas Fox, 'it's astonishing how people keep those kind of things, and how they hardly ever throw them away, because – well, I suppose because there's a sentimental streak in most of us that doesn't want to destroy our past.'

Again, it was a surprise to hear the words, 'I believe there's a couple of letters somewhere. I don't know where they came from. Just some old papers that I never threw away, I suppose. I don't recall any mention of your man in them, though. Roman, you said?'

'Roman, yes. Could I . . . Mr Volf, could you—'

'If we're going to be on ancestor-digging terms you'd better make it Maxim.'

'Then, Maxim, could I possibly see those letters? And if they do contain anything relevant could I make some notes? My laptop's in the car. But I promise,' said Phineas very earnestly, 'that I won't use anything you don't want used. And I won't mention any names you don't want mentioning.'

'I'll see if I can find them.' But if only you knew, Phineas Fox, that I don't know any names you could mention. I wish to God that I did.

'Now? Could you do that now?' There, again, was the eagerness.

'Yes, all right. You fetch your laptop while I go up to look for them.'

The letters had been discovered in Tromloy, on the night Maxim Volf's name was found. They had been brought away with the smudgy Genesius letter, and the bank deposit acknowledgement, so there could be no potentially risky traces of the real Maxim. It was probably better to leave the bank and the theatre letter locked upstairs, but there seemed no reason why Phineas Fox could not see the other letters.

'They're both translations, as you can see.' The scarred hand pointed to the brief note written across the top of one of the letters. In slanting writing it said, 'I've translated these for you – Russian to English again! But I thought you should have them. We really will have to work on your language skills!' There was a scribbled initial that might be anything.

'I don't know who wrote that note. Presumably it was the translator.'

'Yes. I wonder who that was,' said Phineas. He spread the letters out carefully, and sat looking at them as if they were the Holy Grail, his grey eyes glowing with fervour. It was almost as if he was absorbing the contents through his eyes, letting them soak deep into his mind. The small sitting room, the entire house, seemed to slide into a different world – a world that belonged to the people who had lived in those letters. It was absurd to suddenly feel as if those shadowy figures had crept closer and were nearby, watching and listening, but the thought formed. It seemed as if Phineas felt the same thing, because he glanced towards the window behind him, as if half expecting to see someone standing there.

Then he said, 'Shall I read them aloud? You said you'd read them already, but—'

'It was a long time ago, and I can't remember much about them. Yes, read them aloud, then we can both hear them.'

Phin spread the letters out carefully, and began to read.

TWELVE

The shorter of the two letters began, quite simply, 'My dearest love.'

My dearest love. I am arranging to transfer the money we discussed into a trust account which I wish to be used for renovating the Skomorokh Theatre in Odessa. I hope it can be done. I will never forget – will you ever forget, either? – how we walked through the burned-out ruins together that first time, and you described to me how the place could be restored and made to live again. At first I could only see the blackened stones and the sad desolation, but you made me see it as it could be – the bright chandeliers, the crimson and gilt, the velvet-padded boxes on each side of the stage . . . It seemed like a wild dream – one of your wildest – but I believe now that your dream could happen. And so quite soon I will be able to send the details of the account that is being created to make your dream a reality. And one day perhaps we shall walk together and openly along Tchaikovsky Street, and enter the glittering portals you summoned out of the ruins.

I am forever yours, as I always was and always will be, Antoinette.

Phineas laid down the letter. 'How extraordinary,' he said, his eyes still on the faded writing. 'I found a photograph of Roman Volf and an unnamed lady standing outside the ruins of that theatre. It's not too much of a leap to think that lady might have been Antoinette. The date was 1881.'

'What was the Skomorokh Theatre?' The name meant nothing, and a long-ago Russian theatre could not hold much relevance, but it was still interesting. 'Did I pronounce that right, Mr Fox?'

'Phin, for heaven's sake. "Mr Fox" sounds like a character from Beatrix Potter, and "Phineas" is out of a nineteenth-century travelogue. You can imagine,' said Phin, his eyes still on the letter, 'the kind of teasing I came in for at school.'

'I can. Names are so important for a child. I remember . . .'
Something darted across the misted surface of memory on
scurrying goblin-feet, then was gone.

'Yes?' Phin looked up.

'Nothing. One of those incomplete thoughts that slides
away.'

'I think your pronunciation was probably fine. I don't know
if I got it right, though. But however it's pronounced, it burned
down in 1878, and three years later there was talk about an
anonymous donor for its rebuilding.'

'And Antoinette was the anonymous donor?'

'I think so.'

'And the man she's writing to? The man she walked with
through the burned-out ruins?'

'Well,' said Phin, 'it's a slightly larger leap, but put together
with the photo I found of the Skomorokh Theatre, I think it
must be Roman Volf.'

'What was that theatre?'

'As far as I've been able to establish, it had been home to
some very illustrious performers. Roman Volf was one of them.
It was named for the *skomorokhs* – maybe that should be
skomorokhi. They were a form of medieval harlequin – itinerant
performers who could sing and dance and play music. They
wrote their own dramas and even their own music.'

'Skomorokh . . . Would the word link to Scaramouche? The
Harlequin figure?'

'Yes, it would,' said Phin, looking up, pleased. 'You can't
imagine how nice it is to meet someone who knows what I'm
talking about – and can make that link. Most people have
heard of Harlequin and Columbine, but Scaramouche isn't
quite as well known.'

'The old traditions of story-telling – of story-performing
– are fascinating, aren't they?' That was another fragmented
thought that might have come from anywhere.

Phin said, 'The *skomorokh* date to around the ninth century,
and . . .' He broke off with an apologetic gesture. 'Sorry, I
get a bit carried away when I'm interested in something.'

'It is interesting. Genuinely.'

'Yes, but I'm still not sure,' said Phin, looking back at the letter, 'if any of it gets me any closer to Roman. Although it gives me a name I didn't have.'

'Antoinette.'

The name lay on the air like a strand of faded silk.

'Yes,' said Phin, and reached for the second of the letters. 'Have you read this as well?'

'Probably. I can't really remember. They've both been stuffed in that envelope for – for longer than I know. It looks like the same handwriting in both, doesn't it, so I'd guess it was the same translator. But read it aloud again, so I can listen.'

'There's no date on either of them, but this one seems to have been written some time after that first one,' said Phin. He began to read.

My love – there is talk of your boy being taken to see the . . . I cannot write that word. Perhaps if I do not write it or say it or even think it, it will not become a reality.

But there is talk of him being taken to watch what they do to you. The people – also the Romanovs – believe Roman Volf's family should know the full punishment their beloved tsar's murderer receives. I will do all I can to prevent him seeing it, though.

I have been able to visit him several times, and he trusts me, I think, although he is clearly frightened and bewildered. I will get him to safety somehow – as far away from St Petersburg as possible. The family are already insisting I leave, because of any repercussions that might follow your execution . . .

Your execution. The two words lay on the air like silt, and the sensation of being pulled into that long-ago world strengthened. For a moment the echoes from that world were so strong it was almost possible to hear – to feel – the padding footsteps of the hangman creeping forward . . . Phin Fox seemed to hear the echoes as well, because he raised his head from the letters, and half looked round.

'Is there someone outside? I thought I heard—'

'Only the ghosts. Sorry, Phin, I didn't mean that literally. I don't think there's anyone there. People don't often come out here, and we'd have heard a car drive up the track.'

'Yes, of course.' Phin glanced over his shoulder at the window again, then resumed reading.

Execution . . . I have written the word. I pray it will not bring the reality into being. I would pawn my soul to save you. No, it is more even than that. I would willingly give my soul to save you – I would seek out the Prince of Darkness myself and barter with him if it would mean you would live.

The writer had begun a second page, and at the head of the second page, had written,

As to Maxim – I think we both know that is a danger of an entirely different kind. And we both know, too, how much I am risking even by committing his name to paper. But I cannot bear to think he will be forgotten completely. So I write his name here, and I give you my word that, in addition to all else, I will do everything I can for Maxim.

And again was the signature:

I am forever yours, as I always was and always will be, Antoinette.

Phin turned the letter over to make sure there was nothing on the back of the page, then said, 'She doesn't say Maxim Volf, not specifically.'

'No.'

Phin looked at the letter again. 'That reference to the execution adds to the likelihood of it being Roman she was writing to.'

'Was Roman Volf executed?'

'Oh, yes. He was convicted of being involved in the assassination of one of the tsars,' said Phin. 'Alexander II in 1881. There was a trial and he was hanged shortly afterwards. There was something of a backlash against his killers – partly by the people, because he had become known as Alexander the Liberator. He was responsible for all kinds of radical changes – reforming the judicial system, and very particularly ending serfdom in the country. I think the new laws weren't quite going to herald the new golden age the people had wanted, but it was a huge step in the direction of freedom and Alexander certainly embraced the concept of what we now call *glasnost*.'

'Openness,' said Maxim, thoughtfully, and Phin shot him a surprised look.

'Yes. So a great many people would have hated Roman for halting Alexander's reform process. But the Romanovs

probably hated him more. The assassination had terrified them
– their power was under threat – and they were ruthless about
hunting down everyone who had the smallest involvement in
the assassination.'

'Including Roman Volf.'

'Yes. But,' said Phin, 'I'm not sure if he was guilty. I've
found one or two discrepancies.'

Maxim glanced at the letters again, then said, 'Who was
the boy Antoinette refers to?'

'I think it's Roman's illegitimate son. The son I traced here.
Without any dates I can't be sure, but it seems to fit. His name
was Mortimer Quince, and he became a music-hall performer
– a singer. I have no idea how or why he ended up in
Ireland – it sounds as if Antoinette was going to smuggle him
out of Russia, though, and he's documented as appearing on
several London stages. But his name appears on a musical event
in a Galway Theatre in 1921 – he was an organizer or a director,
or something. The name of Maxim Volf also appears on it. The
theatre was called The Genesius, and— What have I said?'

'Nothing. Well, except that I think I've seen the place in
Galway. I've never been inside, but I've walked past it.'

'Is it still a theatre?' asked Phin, eagerly.

'I didn't take much notice. It could be. But I just remember
seeing the name over the main door. I wish I could help more.'
And yet a faint memory had stirred at the name of Mortimer
Quince. Have I seen it somewhere? But where?

'Well, it was a very long shot.' Phin reached for the laptop.
'But can I take you up on that agreement to make notes? It
wouldn't take me more than about ten or fifteen minutes to
type those letters into the computer.'

'Yes, certainly. Would it be easier if I read them again, and
you type as I read?'

'Much easier. Thanks.'

This time, with the reading of the words, the emotions
seemed stronger, but the only sound was the swift tapping of
the keyboard on Phin's laptop, and his occasional brusque,
'Yes?' or, 'OK, go on,' as he caught up.

When they finished it took a few moments for the past to
retreat. There was an almost overwhelming compulsion

to continue talking, to keep Phin Fox here longer, but it was a compulsion that must be resisted.

Even so, a huge effort had to be made to say, 'Thank you. I'm only sorry I can't help any more. It's been fascinating, though.'

It was not exactly a dismissal, but Phineas Fox clearly heard it as such, because he stood up and said, 'I've taken up enough of your time. I'm massively grateful to you, though.'

'Will the letters help your research?'

'I don't know yet. There aren't any dates to follow up or verify, and there's only "Antoinette", without a surname. So it might not add much to what I've already got. But you've got my phone number and I'll be here for a few days. I'm staying at O'Brien's. Maybe you'd call me if anything occurs to you, or if you find any other papers.'

'I will. I'd be interested to hear if you turn up anything.'

'I'll let you know. Have you got a phone number I can have?'

As Phin entered the number on his phone – the number of the basic, pay-as-you-go phone, bought for emergencies – the instinct was to shake hands. That was another of the rituals, of course, but you did not offer a hand that had been spoiled.

Phin Fox did not seem aware of that. He held out his own hand, quite naturally. 'I've liked meeting you,' he said. 'I hope we can talk again.'

Impossible to say, 'So do I.' Even more impossible to ask if Phin Fox would like to stay to talk some more about Roman Volf, and about the mysterious Antoinette. And the real Maxim Volf . . . 'A danger of an entirely different kind,' Antoinette had written. 'I cannot bear to think he will be forgotten completely.'

But intriguing as it all was, it was too risky to open a door on to any kind of friendship, however fleeting. It was, though, all right to smile, and to lead Phin to the door and watch him place the laptop carefully on the passenger seat so it would not slide on to the floor, then reverse his car down the narrow track.

And then to go back inside the house, to put the two letters carefully back in the desk, then wash up the coffee cups, and resume listening to Tchaikovsky. Russian music as background for those strange Russian stories. There was a symmetry about that, and, as the music unrolled its sweeping cadences, the images conjured up by Phineas Fox were vivid. A man who had been executed for killing a tsar more than a century earlier, and a woman called Antoinette, who had clearly loved him, who had wanted to renovate a theatre in his name, and who had intended that a child should be protected from the ugly reality of his father's death. And who had not wanted that other Maxim to be forgotten. Curiosity deepened.

But it was better not to become drawn in. It was vaguely sad to hear that Roman Volf might have been wrongly executed, but it could not matter after so many years.

What did matter were those two incomplete thoughts that had darted across the surface of memory. The first had been that sudden awareness of having a liking for the ancient story-telling, story-performing tradition.

The second had been more disturbing and had seemed to come from a much deeper place. It was that strong, clear recognition of the importance of naming a child.

It was growing dark inside the Sexton's House before the other incomplete memory clamoured for attention again. Mortimer Quince. I really have seen that name somewhere. Where?

A thin rain was beating against the windows, and it felt good to go round the little house, closing all the curtains against the cold, spiteful showers. Provisions had been collected the previous day, and although the tiny cash payments from the church authorities did not go very far, with care they went far enough. This week they had stretched as far as a beautifully fresh portion of salmon, which was a rare extravagance and would be tonight's supper.

Mortimer Quince. Where did I see that name?

Looking through the small collection of CDs to see what might provide a pleasurable evening background, that earlier elusive memory slid suddenly into place. Mortimer Quince was the name that had been written on the back of an old photograph. '*Mortimer Quince on stage at Shepherd's Bush*

Empire, 1910.' The photograph had been inside Tromloy, in Abigail Drury's bedroom. Presumably it was still there now.

Could Phin be told about that? It would mean admitting to having been inside Tromloy – it might be better to remain silent. Or—

The thought was shut off abruptly, because there was a sound outside. Had it been footsteps, or was it just an animal scrabbling around for food? But it had sounded too large for an animal, and it also sounded very close to the wall of the cottage – almost as if someone was making a cautious way around the sides. No one could get in – the front door was securely locked; from this fireside chair it was possible to see through to the little hall, and the stout old door with the old-fashioned ring handle and the bolt at the top, drawn across. No one could get in.

Then the door creaked heavily, almost as if something had leaned against it. It was probably just the old timbers contracting in the cold, but only a madman would open the door to find out.

The creak came again, and the edges moved slightly. The door handle moved. Apprehension spiralled into real fear. *There is someone out there. Someone's trying to get in. He won't manage it, though. There's a strong lock on that door. He'll go away in a minute.*

But whoever was out there did not go away. The letterbox moved, then was pushed open. Fingertips appeared, holding the flap open, and eyes stared in through the slit. To move would have attracted attention – all that could be done was remain completely still and pray to be out of direct sightline.

The flap clanged back into place, and the footsteps went away from the door. *It's all right. He's given up.* But even as thankfulness flooded in, a different movement came, this time from the window of the sitting room. *He's still out there. He couldn't get in through the door, so now he's trying the window.* The curtains were closed, but there was a tiny slit halfway up where they did not quite meet. If the prowler stood up against the window, that chink would act like a camera lens. He would be able to see virtually the entire room.

Do I challenge him? Or even call the Garda? The movement

came again, and in the tiny space between the curtain edges, eyes stared into the room. It was instinctive to look round for a makeshift weapon, at the same time reaching for the phone. But how swiftly would the Garda respond to a call from this house?

Then, without warning, anger took over, because how dared some sly Peeping Tom sneak up here and try to get in! In two strides the window was reached, and the curtains jerked open with a furious swish. The prowler was caught in the sudden stream of light from the little sitting room, and it disconcerted him – he stood there motionless, with a rabbit-caught-in-headlights stare. The seconds lengthened, then, incredibly, the phone rang, shrilling through the room, and shattering the strange, frozen moment. The man dodged back from the window, and there was the sound of footsteps again, not fast, making a cautious but unmistakable way across the uneven ground towards the narrow track down to the road.

There was a second's delay while the curtains were swiftly pulled back across, then the phone could be answered.

'Hello? Who's this?'

'Maxim?' It was Phin Fox's voice.

'Phin.' It was a struggle not to say it was very good to hear another voice. 'You startled me.'

'Is anything wrong? You sound a bit breathless.'

'Oh, there was some wretched prowler outside a few moments ago. It happens. I'm the local weirdo, remember. But it's a bit unnerving sometimes, and on a traditionally dark and rainy night . . . Whoever it was rattled the door, and he was standing at the window staring in when you rang. I think the sound of the phone startled him as much as it did me. He's gone now, though.'

'Shall I come out there?' said Phin.

'There's no need.'

'No, but I'd like to talk to you again if you could spare half an hour. About the letters. That's why I'm ringing. I won't interrupt your evening for long. I can be there in ten minutes.'

It would be treacherously easy to give way, to admit that after the prowler the idea of human companionship for half an hour or so was very alluring. But it was probably all right to say, 'I was thinking of phoning you anyway. I've remembered something about that name you asked about. Mortimer Quince.'

Phin Fox responded at once. 'In that case I'll definitely come out. But make the ten minutes nearer twenty, would you?'

'I'll look out for you. But be careful in case the prowler's still around.'

'I will.' A pause. Then Phin said, 'Do you drink wine at all?'

'I do.'

'Then I'll bring a bottle with me, and we can talk over a glass.'

There had been no doubt about the fear in Maxim Volf's voice when he'd answered the phone. Phin had heard it clearly.

He collected a bottle of wine from O'Brien's small bar, then drove away. Accelerating through the thin, misty rain towards the Sexton's House, he was visualizing how it must have felt to sit in that lonely room and see someone pressed up against the window, looking in. Supposing the prowler had actually got inside? How far could Maxim defend himself in a fight? Phin had a sudden dreadful vision of the scarred hands piteously raised to cover the burned face, trying to fight off an attack.

The house had lights in the downstairs windows when he reached it, and as his headlights swept across the door, it opened, and Maxim was there. Phin locked the car and went inside.

'No sign of any prowlers,' he said. 'Are you sure you're all right? Shouldn't you call the Garda?'

'No. Whoever it was didn't get in. I shouldn't think he'll come back, and if he does, I'll be ready.'

'Did you see who it was?'

'I did see him. It wasn't anyone I recognized, but I'd know him again.'

When Phin proferred the wine, Maxim smiled, and fetched a corkscrew and two glasses. Seated near the fire, the wine set on a low table catching the fire's light, the room became unexpectedly companionable.

'You said you were going to phone me about Mortimer Quince,' said Phin.

'Yes. I remembered something about him. A photograph with his name on the back.' He leaned back in his own chair, his fingers curled around the wine glass. 'The photo was in a house called Tromloy,' he said. 'It's on the edge of Kilcarne. Phin, I'm going to tell you something I've never told anyone else. I'm going to trust you. I saw the photo because I broke into Tromloy while it was empty.' He took a defiant drink of his wine. 'Maxim Volf is an identity I stole.'

'Why?' said Phin, after a moment. 'Who are you really?'

'I don't know. I was involved in a car crash two years ago – near Tromloy. A car veered into the roadside, then burst into flames. I tried to get to the two people inside it – to get them out – but I didn't manage it. They burned,' he said expressionlessly.

'And you were burned in the attempt to rescue them,' said Phin, very quietly.

'Yes. As well as having my face and hands burned, my memory got burned, too. I have no idea who I am. Just over a year ago – when I finally got out of the medics' hands – I went to Tromloy because it was where the two people who died in the crash had lived. I can't explain why. Maybe I had some idea of—'

'Asking for forgiveness?'

'I wouldn't,' said Maxim, 'have put it quite so lyrically, but you could be right. I managed to get inside the house using a faulty window catch. The place was closed up – the man's widow had never returned to Ireland – and I went into all the rooms. I'm not proud of it, but I honestly had no sinister intentions. Only then I found a couple of letters – one a bank acknowledgement, the other a note of thanks for a donation to The Genesius Theatre. They were both written to Maxim Volf. I didn't have a name of my own, or any kind of identity, and I saw the name as a ready-made identity. An identity that no one would miss if I took it.'

'Were the letters dated?'

'One was. But it was so smudgy I couldn't tell if it was 1930 or 1950. You can see them if you want, but they won't tell you anything.' He had been staring into the fire, but now he looked across at Phin. 'I do know that what I did was illegal, and I don't know if you can understand. But I couldn't bear being nameless any longer. I took the two letters, and also the ones from Antoinette.'

'Because of that reference to Maxim?'

'Yes. I didn't want to leave anything that might – well, that might give the lie to me being him.' He sat back. 'There you have it. Identity theft.'

'It doesn't seem much of a crime. It's not even as if you hacked into the bank account.' Phin looked up. 'You didn't, did you?'

'The bank,' said Maxim, dryly, 'no longer exists.' As Phin grinned, he said, 'Why did you ring me earlier? I'm extremely glad you did, because it scared off the prowler, but—'

'To ask if you'd come with me into Galway, to The Genesius Theatre.'

'No.' The response was swift and definite.

'I thought you'd say that,' said Phin. 'But listen, I need to find out more about Mortimer Quince and he was connected to that place. So was the real Maxim Volf. And if I'm ever to prove that Roman Volf was innocent of murder, I need to bring all these strands together. Quince and Maxim and Antoinette.'

'Does any of it matter after so long?'

'Yes,' said Phin, very positively. 'I want to clear the name of a brilliant musician.'

'Even so, none of it has anything to do with me.'

'It does,' said Phin. 'Like it or not, you've got entangled in Roman Volf's story.'

'Because I stole Maxim's identity?'

It came out bitterly, and Phin said, 'Yes. And doing that, you found another link between The Genesius and Maxim. You also found Antoinette's letters. Don't you want to know who she was? Or who Maxim was?'

'I admit to a degree of interest,' said Maxim. 'Oh hell, all right, I'm intrigued. Who wouldn't be? But I'm not intrigued enough to come into Galway with you in broad daylight.' He did not say, 'To be stared at,' but Phin heard the thought behind the words. 'Anyway, you don't need me. You can do it on your own.'

'I'd prefer you to come with me. Apart from anything else, I have no idea where the place is. If you like you can just point the way, then stay in the car.'

There was a silence, then Maxim said, 'When would you want to go?'

'Tomorrow morning?'

'I'm making no promise.'

'I'll come to the Sexton's House at half-past ten and we'll argue it out then.'

THIRTEEN

At first Jessica had thought the supper for Donal with Mr O'Brien and his sister there, was all right. She had even quite enjoyed listening to the talk, because Miss O'Brien – Grania – said things that made people laugh. But then had come the mention of a man who lived in the Sexton's House – a hermit – and the atmosphere round the table had changed.

Jessica was not sure if she had ever seen the hermit, but the O'Briens seemed to know about him. Rory O'Brien called him a tramp, and said he had lived here once before. With the words something seemed to drive a hard fist against Jess's mind, and she had had to stare down at her plate, because the mind-pictures were trying to form. Something about the tramp, was it? I know about him, thought Jessica. But what is it I know?

Donal had asked who the man was and where he had come from, but nobody had really known, although Grania said something about him having been injured in a car crash. Then the aunts changed the subject, and supper went on and things were all ordinary again. Or were they?

Next morning, Tormod did not get up for breakfast, and Aunt Morna said he was not feeling very well. They must all be quiet and considerate. Donal came down to breakfast, but he was pale and his eyes were puffy, as if he had not slept. He refused everything except a cup of black coffee, which worried the aunts. Jessica thought they did not know whether to focus on Tormod who was definitely unwell, or on Donal, who might be slightly unwell.

She had hoped she would be able to go to Tromloy this afternoon without anyone bothering or noticing, but after breakfast Aunt Nuala suggested Jessica and Donal went into Galway for the day. Donal always enjoyed visiting the cathedral, and it would be nice for the two of them to be together.

Jess, hating herself for lying and deceiving, said vaguely that she was going to sketch in the fields this afternoon.

'But Donal's not here for long, and he always looks forward to being with you.'

'And he's family,' put in Aunt Nuala. 'His mother was our cousin, and you're like a younger sister to him.'

'I'll only be out for an hour or so,' said Jessica. 'I want to sketch the trees near the beck. I'm going to paint a proper picture at the weekend. But I could go to Galway tomorrow with Donal.'

'We'll do that,' said Donal, and the aunts looked pleased.

After lunch Jess scooted up to her room to put a few of her sketches in an envelope, because Mrs Drury had particularly said she would like to see them. By the time she got out of the house, a pulse of half-fear, half-excitement was beating in her head. Was she really going to go inside Tromloy? Would she see that room with the fire screen, and the window-seat, and the photo of the man on the old stage? But did any of those things exist? Perhaps she really was going mad. With the thought, the words of the soft voice scratched against her mind . . . *'People might say you were mad, Jessica . . . They might even shut you away . . .'*

The nervousness increased as she walked up the rutted track. Jessica realized she was clenching and unclenching her hands, so she dug them in her pockets to stop. She hated her hands. The aunts had bought her several pairs of thin cotton gloves that she could wear all the time, but she hated wearing the gloves even more than she hated her hands.

Tromloy was much nicer than it had looked from the path below. Or was it? Was there something there, waiting . . .? Something that was saying, *Come inside, Jessica, because that's when the nightmare will start . . . Because this is Tromlui, Jess, the nightmare house . . .*

Jess hesitated, but then the door was being opened and Bea Drury was there, smiling and holding out her hand.

'I'm so pleased you've come, Jessica. I've been looking out for you.'

The sitting room was almost exactly as Jessica expected. The low ceiling, the bookshelves on each side of the hearth . . .

Were the rocking chair and the fire screen somewhere in the house, too?

Beatrice Drury had baked the most delicious chocolate cake – 'It was my daughter's favourite cake,' she said. There was tea or Coke or fruit juice, and while they ate and drank, Bea – it was becoming easy to think of her as Bea by now – asked to see Jess's sketches. She studied them all carefully, making comments about each one, then she said Jessica was very gifted.

'Have you ever thought of studying art at university? Or at one of the art colleges? I think the Galway-Mayo Institute has a terrific art and design section.'

Jessica would like nothing more in the world than to be somewhere where you drew and painted all the time, and where people taught you how to do it properly. Uncle Tormod probably would not mind or even care very much if she were to do that – Jess sometimes thought he did not really want her in the house at all – but the aunts would find all kinds of reasons against it. How would she manage in a strange place on her own, they would ask. She was always so nervous with new places and strange people, and she had had so much time off school. They might even tell her that her hands would mean she would not be accepted at an art college anyway.

So Jess said, carefully, that she was not sure if her aunts and her uncle would allow her to go away to study art, and before Bea could say anything else, she asked if she could see some of Bea's own work.

'Of course, if you'd like to.'

Jess wanted to look at Bea Drury's work for ever. She almost forgot her fear that the bad images were crouching in the shadows and that they might suddenly claw their way into her mind. These pictures drew you into marvellous magical worlds – the worlds that existed inside poetry and songs and books. If you saw any of them on a book cover you would want to buy the book at once. One picture was the hazelnut chariot of Mab made by the joiner squirrel, and the wild journeys it had made through people's dreams. It was so beautifully drawn, Jessica wanted to lift it off the page and make it come alive.

'I drew that for my daughter,' said Bea, and she put out a

hand to touch the page as if, Jessica thought, it might bring her daughter back for a moment.

She said, carefully, that she knew some of the words about Mab – and about the joiner squirrel who had been the fairies' coach-maker.

'I know you do. You were reciting it to yourself when we met on the hillside,' said Bea, her eyes still on the picture. But she was smiling. 'Abigail loved the speech, although I'm not sure if she entirely understood it,' she said. '". . . she gallops night by night/Through lovers' brains, and then they dream of love".' She frowned, and looked startled, as if the words had come from someone else, or as if she had forgotten for a moment where she was.

'I'm sorry if I upset you by saying the speech the other afternoon,' said Jessica, hesitantly. 'Because of – um – because of your daughter, I mean.'

'It isn't as upsetting as it used to be. And it's nice to remember things Abigail liked.' A pause, then she said, 'Would you like to see her room? She would have been almost exactly the age you are now, I think. It's not a shrine or anything morbid like that, but some of her things are still there.'

It was impossible to refuse and, in any case, Jess was interested in the girl who had died and about whom Beatrice spoke with such love and sadness. What kind of daughter would someone like Mrs Drury have had? It must have been marvellous for Abigail Drury to have a mother like this, a mother who understood how important painting and drawing were.

But the fear was churning up more strongly. Would Abigail's bedroom be the room with the fireplace? Jess said she would like to see the room, but as she followed Bea out of the sitting room her heart was thudding violently. She had walked up these stairs before. Here was the creaking board that made a sound like gunshot if you trod on it late at night when the house was quiet. And now came the turn of the stairs to the right, with the tiny window that looked across towards trees and fields. There was a small pewter jug on the ledge with dried lavender in it, but the lavender was so old it had faded to a dusty grey. Memories swirled and eddied again. I cut this lavender in the garden beyond that window, and I put it in that jug so that the stairs would be filled with the scent. I really was here, thought Jessica, in frightened bewilderment. But when? Why? And why can't I remember properly?

Bea opened a door, and there was the room. Jessica stood very still.

The rocking chair was in the right place, and the padded window-seat with the green and gold chintz cover was right, as well. And there was the bed with the bright brass frame and the quilt made up of silky squares. In the morning the silk caught the light so that you felt as if you were lying in a marvellous lake of bronze and sunshine. She had wanted to draw the bed and paint it as a coloured river, dreamlike and fantastical, like the death journey of the Lily Maid of Astolat. Had she ever done so? And the shelves of books – I know them, thought Jessica, staring at the rows of titles. I've read them – those very books.

They went back downstairs, and Bea put her sketches away in a big folder.

'I'll put them out of the way for the moment,' she said. 'They can stand in the alcove by the fire if I move the fire screen.'

The fire screen. It was here after all. It was standing in the chimney corner, behind the chair where Jess had been sitting – that was why she had not seen it. As Bea lifted it away from the wall, it was as if a lump of ice had been dropped deep down into Jess's mind, and as if the impact had flung the memories swirling and foaming upwards.

The screen was exactly as she had seen it. There were the pasted-on photos, and the bits of old posters of concerts and musical evenings. It had been dragged across the fire that day to hide something that must not be seen . . .? *Never tell . . . Never tell, Jessica . . .*

Jessica's heart was pounding and the palms of her hands were sticky with sweat, because something inside her mind was struggling to get out, and it was something ugly and frightening and unbearably painful . . .

She thought Bea Drury did not realize there was anything wrong. She thought she managed to go on talking quite ordinarily. About painting, about the things she liked to draw and the places in Kilcarne she went to draw them. Presently, she said she thought she should go.

'They'll want me to help with supper. They always make a bit of a fuss when my cousin Donal's here.'

'Yes, of course. I hope you'll come to see me again,' said Bea. 'We could maybe go off sketching somewhere one afternoon.'

'I'd like that. I'll ask if I can.' Jessica saw that Bea Drury was not used to people having to ask permission for something so ordinary, so she said, 'They fuss such a lot.'

'Yes, of course. I must try to meet them. Ask them if I can call in some time. And you'll always be welcome at Tromloy,' said Bea.

As Jessica walked away from the house, she felt as if something had dug deep into her mind, peeling back layers of thick scar tissue, exposing still-bleeding wounds.

She was feeling dizzy, but she tried to snatch the whirling fragments and pin them down. Tromloy. Abigail Drury's bedroom with the old photograph. The fire screen. And, threading through it all, that dreadful whispering voice, like spiteful scratches against her mind. *'Never tell, Jessica . . . People would think you were making up stories . . . They might shut you away . . .'*

As she reached the stone with *Tromloy* engraved on it, the whirling shards fell into place, and finally Jessica saw and knew and understood what lay at the black core of the memories.

FOURTEEN

S he thought it had been about two years ago – had it been the week after her thirteenth birthday? Two years ago and a bit, then.

It had still been the Christmas school holidays – the few days after Christmas Day before school started again. For a moment the present-day Jessica came up through the memories, to think: how strange to suddenly know she had been at an ordinary school.

But on that day two years ago, the aunts had said Jessica could go out sketching, providing she was warmly wrapped up because it was a sharp, frosty day. She must be sure to be home well before it started to get dark. And Donal was coming today, so Jess must be back to welcome him. It was a long time since he had visited them – almost six months – so there would be a lot of news to hear. And Jessica was not to go along any lonely lanes, or speak to anyone she did not know, was that clear?

Jessica nodded mechanically, but Aunt Morna said, a bit sharply, that she must be extra-careful at the moment, because there had been reports of a tramp wandering around. Mr O'Brien said several people in the bar at O'Brien's had reported seeing the man. A real ruffian he was, often the worse for The Drink. Both the aunts always referred to any kind of alcohol using capital letters, unless it was Uncle Tormod's nightly glass of port and brandy, which he took for medicinal purposes, and for which there was apparently biblical approval.

Jessica did not tell them she had seen the tramp a few times while she was out sketching. People were calling him 'that old tramp', but he was not old at all. He moved quickly, like quite a young man, and he did not seem in the least alarming, in fact he always doffed his hat to Jess if he saw her, causing a thick mop of hair to tumble over his forehead. Once or twice he had called out a greeting, and once, when he had walked along a lane where Jess was sketching, he had said something about her looking like a wood nymph or a dryad, curled up against the old tree. Jessica had smiled and said she would like to be a dryad, and he had nodded to himself, as if pleased with the small exchange, and gone on his way. He had been carrying a bottle of something, swinging it along in rhythm with his steps, then lifting it to his lips.

Jess had thought it was probably unusual for a tramp, no matter how much he might drink, to know about dryads. She would quite like to draw him some time. It would be interesting to see if she could get that careless happiness on paper. This was another thing that could not be said, however, and Aunt Nuala was still tutting about the tramp, what a feckless way for a man to live, it did not bear thinking about. How could such a one get hold of The Drink in the first place, that was what Aunt Nuala would like to know. Aunt Morna said he would have stolen it, of course, wicked shame to him.

They would go on about the tramp and The Drink and the shame for ages, so Jessica put on a thick coat, wrapped a scarf round her neck, and took the opportunity to go out through the kitchen door.

This afternoon she wanted to explore a narrow track that led away from the road. There was a tucked-away house somewhere at the top of the track – Jess had occasionally glimpsed it from the road, and she was intrigued.

She walked through the village, liking that everywhere was still frozen in shades of grey and white, but that there were splashes of colour from where people still had Christmas decorations up. Beyond the village, the road opened on to a main highway into Galway City. Aunt Morna occasionally drove along here if they needed something that could not be got in Kilcarne, and Aunt Nuala generally went with her because Morna did not like driving very much and it was nice to have company in the car. Jess went with them as well, if she could. She would like to go more often, but the aunts said Galway was so busy and loud; you could not hear yourself think, and wasn't it a relief to get back to Kilcarne's peace and quiet. Jess liked the buzz and the people, though. When she left school she would like to go to the GMIT – the Galway-Mayo Institute of Technology, which her art teacher said had a really good art and design course that would end in a Bachelor of Arts degree if Jessica worked hard. From there, the world would be her oyster, said the teacher, who came to the convent school twice a week from Connemara to teach the girls how to draw and paint. She told Jessica that they had a good two years before they needed to plan seriously, but it was something definite and positive to work towards.

Jess was working towards it already, but there was no need to tell the aunts and Uncle Tormod yet, because it would throw them into a twittering state of anxiety, and Uncle Tormod would probably say universities were whited sepulchres and temples of sin, and the end would be that she would not be allowed to go. She was going to work up to it gradually.

The tramp was out and about this morning. As Jess drew level with the five-bar gate, she saw him walking across the scrubland beyond it. He might be going anywhere or nowhere. She watched him, trying to fix in her mind the picture he made, because he was wearing a scarlet muffler today, and against the grey January light it would make a really good picture. He was some way off, but he caught sight of her, and lifted his hat and waved it. Jessica waved back. She knew that if she stopped anywhere to sketch, he would not come over and interrupt her, because he liked being on his own. She watched him for a moment, seeing that he was walking quite jauntily; if he had been at The Drink this morning, it was not making him stumble or miss his steps as Uncle Tormod sometimes did last thing at night when he had had a third glass of port and brandy, telling them that St Paul said a little wine could be taken for the stomach's sake and small infirmities.

Here were the wobbly signposts that had been about to tumble over ever since Jess could remember, and here was the narrow track just beyond them. Now she was here, it looked a bit lonely, and the aunts would have thrown up their hands in horror at the thought of walking up there, but Jess thought it would be all right. She would only go a little way up, and if she heard anyone coming, she could easily whizz back down to the road. If the house looked as if it would make a good picture, she would draw a few rough outlines, then go back home in time for Donal's arrival.

She went up the steep path to the house. There was a chunk of stone on the side of the track with the house's name carved into it. *Tromloy*. There were more bits of old stone in the scrubland on each side of the path – they looked like toy bricks, but immense ones, as if they might be from a giant's toy-store, and as if the giant had become bored with them and tossed them away in a sulk. Moss and lichen grew over some of them, and they might make a good sketch. Jessica would look at the house, then she might come back to these lovely jumbly stones.

The house was a little way above the path. It was not very big, and it, too, had the air of having been dropped carelessly from the sky, and as if it had landed in a place where nobody would expect a house to be. It was just about possible to see the smudge of mountains behind it, like layers of coloured cellophane against the sky.

The house had sloping roof bits, which was really good because the art teacher had set perspectives as a holiday project. Jess thought she would try to get a few of those angles down, and work on them when she got home. She folded up her scarf to sit on, and leaned back against the *Tromloy* stone. It was a bit cold, but she would not be here very long, and after she began to draw she did not notice the cold anyway. She forgot about the time, and she became absorbed with the picture forming under her pencil. It was starting to look really good. She leaned back to consider it, and it was then she heard footsteps coming up the track towards her.

She was not particularly worried, although it was a bit lonely out here. Even the tramp had disappeared. Still, she would rather not meet anyone here on her own, so she closed the sketchbook and wondered if she should go up to the house to see if there was a way of getting back down to the road from there.

The footsteps came around the last part of the track, and a voice that she knew very well indeed, said, 'Jessica. I hoped I'd find you. The aunts thought you were coming out this way to sketch. So you've found Tromloy, have you?'

It was all right. It was Donal. He was a bit flushed from climbing the steep path and his hair was blown about by the wind, but he was smiling, and saying he had told the aunts he would come out to find her.

'And I called into Dunleary's on the way and they said they'd seen you go past. So I thought I'd try to find you. It's bitterly cold, isn't it, but the car's just at the foot of the track, on the roadside.' He was holding out his arms in the way he always did when he came to Kilcarne.

It was silly to take a step back from him – Jessica did not understand why she did that, or why she suddenly did not want to give him a hug or let him kiss her cheek as he always did. It was even sillier to think that when he put his arms around her he held on to her for longer than usual, and that he pressed her against him in a way Jess found embarrassing.

He let her go, but he kept one arm round her, his free hand opening the sketchbook to see what she had been working on.

'It's very good,' he said, looking at it. Jessica did not like to say she hated people to see a half finished sketch, so she closed the book and put it in her pocket. 'You're such a clever girl. I wish I could see you more often – I seem to be missing too much of your growing-up years.' His hand was still around her shoulders, the fingers digging into her skin. Jessica began to feel even more uneasy, and then Donal pulled her against him, so closely she could smell the masculine-skin scent of him. Soap and clean hair. It should have been pleasant and comforting and familiar, but it was none of these things.

'And you're almost grown up now, aren't you,' said Donal, in a strange, whispery voice. 'Thirteen.'

'Yes.'

He smiled down at her. 'That's surely grown up enough to give me a proper kiss.'

The kiss was not what Jessica was expecting. Usually, when Donal came to stay, there was a light kiss on the cheek for each of the aunts, and the same for Jess. But this was full on the lips, and when she gasped and flinched, Donal pulled her back and began to kiss her again. Jess struggled and tried to push him away.

'Don't fight me,' said Donal, in the same muffled throaty

voice. 'It's just a kiss. We're both grown up enough for that. Let me kiss you properly.'

It came again, the hard pressure of a mouth, this time forcing her lips open. Jessica tasted his breath, and gasped, pushing him away, wrapping her arms around her body in defence.

'You're shivering. Oh, don't shiver, Jess. Come up to the house with me now. It's where I'm going anyway. I saw Niall Drury in Dunleary's shop – he's grand company, that one, and we said we'd have a drink in O'Brien's next time he's here and I'm visiting. But he's worried about a loose window catch up at the house, so he lent me a spare key to make sure it was all right until someone can see to it.'

'Let's just go home,' said Jess, uncertainly. 'The aunts will be wondering.'

'I said I'd be a while. And I've always wanted to see Tromloy. It's supposed to stand where the old Kilcarne Manor was, did you know that? Kilcarne Mainéar. I've seen the old parish records – a fine old place it must have been, but this cottage is all that's left of it. I'd like to see it, wouldn't you? And it's perfectly above board – I told you Drury lent me the key, and he's off back to London; he's driving to Galway Airport after he's collected some books for his daughter.' He took her hand and started walking up the last few yards of the track towards the house. Jessica did not want to go with him, but it was difficult not to.

'It'll be an adventure,' said Donal. He smiled at her. 'We'll be looking back at Kilcarne Manor and seeing are there any of its ghosts wandering around. But a secret adventure. Our secret.'

He was already unlocking the front door. He still held Jess's hand, and as he pushed the door open, his other arm came around her waist. His fingers brushed against her small, just-forming breast, and he drew in his breath sharply.

Beyond the door was a small hall, with a carved blanket chest against one wall. The walls were creamy white, and there was a faint scent of peat, mingling pleasantly with the scent of old timbers and polish. Jessica would have liked the house very much if she had not been growing uneasier by the minute. When Donal closed the front door she felt shut in and frightened.

But in a minute he would realize he was behaving strangely, and say he was sorry, and they would go home and everything would be all right.

'I think the window with the loose catch is in here,' said Donal, leading her into a long, low-ceilinged sitting room. There was a deep sofa with buttons, and at the far end was a window with criss-crossed strips of lead on it. A small table held a scattering of papers, as if Mr Drury had not had time, or could not be bothered, to tidy them away before leaving. In the window recess was a deep seat with padded cushions. Jessica had the thought that someone often curled up on the window-seat with a book and felt happy and safe. She did not feel safe, though.

Mr Drury had left a little stack of peat turfs against the chimney breast, as if to have everything ready and welcoming for next time he and his wife were here. There were a few twists of paper and matches, as well. But the room was cold, and Jessica shivered.

'Don't shiver, Jessica. I'll light a fire for us, shall I? Drury won't mind and we'll make sure it's doused when we go.'

'No, don't do that – we'll be going in a minute, won't we—?'

'Oh, yes, but it'd be nice to see the firelight. It's a nice room, isn't it? This was supposed to have been the house-keeper's cottage, I think. Or maybe a bit of the servants' wing. If it wasn't actually attached to the manor, it'd be very close to it.'

Jess was very frightened indeed by now, but Donal had already struck a match and was lighting the peat and the paper twists. At least he had had to let go of her hand to do that. She began to move to the door leading to the hall – in another minute she would pull it open and dart through, and once outside, she would run down the track as fast as she could, and she would not stop running until she was back home. She would be safe there. Donal would not behave so oddly – so frighteningly – in front of the aunts and Uncle Tormod.

But he seized her hand again before she could get the door open, trapping her wrists together, and pulling her back into the room. His hands were hard and bony. Jess sobbed and kicked out, trying to drag her hands away, but he was too strong.

The peat was starting to glow, lighting up the room, the warmth glinting on the windows. Donal's hands were bruising her wrists, making it impossible to break free. He began to drag her closer to him – for a dreadful moment the fire's heat fell on to her face and Jess thought he was pulling her straight on to the flames.

But he pushed her towards the sofa, so forcefully that Jess fell back on to it. At once Donal flung himself down next to her, and began to run his hands up and down her body, sliding them under her sweater, and then up beneath her skirt. Jess thrust his hands away and tried to sit up, stammering that this was all wrong, they should not be doing any of this.

'Please, Donal – please *stop*—'

'I'll stop in a minute,' said Donal, in the same frightening whispery voice. 'But I've wanted to do this for so long . . . And this house was empty and I had the key and the opportunity was too tempting . . . Let me just touch you – let me just feel . . . Oh, Jesus, I'll have to do penance for this afterwards, I know it, but just for a few moments . . . Oh, God, that feels so good . . . I've dreamed of this for so long, Jessica—'

Jess began sending up frantic, scrambled prayers. Please God, make him stop. I'll do anything, God – I'll do all the housework for the aunts, and I won't be impatient with Uncle Tormod, and I'll say my prayers every single night, kneeling down properly, I *promise* . . .

Donal was half sobbing, half panting, and he was writhing against her so that Jess could feel the hard lump between his legs that men had and that must not be mentioned. He was almost crying by now, saying something about it being a mortal sin, but just this once it would be all right, and he would not hurt her.

'It'll be my sin, Jessica, my sin not yours, and I'll do penance for it . . . But you're so lovely, so smooth and innocent and sweet, and those big dark eyes . . . Let me have just this one time—'

The fire was filling up the room with dancing redness – red was the colour of pain and of fear – Jess had not known that until now. But this was Donal, who was a priest, the aunts' beloved Donal, Jess's own cousin . . . Only it was somehow not Donal any longer; it was as if something had taken him over, like in a horror film.

But it was Donal's hands that were thrusting between her legs, the fingers seeking and prodding. Jess fought to push him away, but it only seemed to make it worse, and she began to cry out.

'Don't scream, Jessica. There's no one to hear anyway, no one for at least a mile, and I only want to . . . And you feel so good, and if you knew what it's doing to me—'

He was still holding her, but with his free hand he pulled her clothes away, tearing them in his frenzy, then reached down to the fastening of his trousers. Jessica had only the sketchiest knowledge of what men and women did in bed, other than the giggles and whispers at school, but she could feel something hard and hot thrusting between her legs and she knew Donal was trying to do the forbidden thing, the thing you were not supposed to do until you were married, but that people did anyway . . . But not with a priest, not with someone who was a cousin and who was someone you had known ever since you could remember and seemed like your brother. Not in a strange room with a fire that sent shadows like clutching hands across the walls . . .

Donal began to sob and gasp, saying no one need ever know—

'I'll take the sin on my soul, Jessica . . . Oh Jesus, God—'

The hard stick of hot flesh thrust all the way inside Jessica, impossibly deep, and it hurt, it *hurt*, it was more painful than she had thought anything ever could be. Donal was clutching her and writhing against her, and Jessica cried and struggled to push him away.

'It'll be very quick, Jessica, because I'm so very . . . And I know God will never forgive me, but I can't help it, I can't—'

And then, just as Jessica thought she might faint or be sick, he suddenly cried out, 'Christ, Jesus, I'm going to—' and there was a final frenzied thrusting and a sudden hot wetness. The room spun around her head because the pain was splitting her open, and then incredibly and blessedly, it seemed to be over, and Donal had rolled off.

Jessica lay absolutely still, not daring to move, hardly daring to breathe. She could hear him sobbing and gabbling prayers. When she finally dared to open her eyes she saw he was slumped against the sofa's edge, half kneeling, his hands clasped, his whole body shuddering, rocking back and forwards. Tears streamed down his face.

Jessica lay in a terrified huddle. The world had shrunk to this firelit room, with the glinting windows, and the sound of Donal's sobbing. She did not dare move or make a sound in case he seized her again, but he did not. He stayed where he was, still gasping out prayers, occasionally wiping his eyes with the back of his hand.

In the end, moving very slowly, Jessica risked sitting up, and then she risked getting off the sofa. Donal did not seem to notice her. It took a long time to put her clothes back on because she was trembling so violently. Her under-things were torn because he had ripped them away, and there was a wetness between her legs – she saw with horror that there was blood, but she found her handkerchief and folded it to put there.

It was not until she began to walk shakily to the door that Donal turned his head. He did not look directly at her, but in a low voice – a much more normal voice – he said, 'Jessica, you must promise me you'll never tell anyone about this.'

Jess had no idea how to answer. She did not say the aunts would know something was wrong because she must look dreadful – tear-streaked and shivering, her arms bruised, and her skirt and pants torn. And there was the blood . . .

She said, 'I'm going home.'

'No.' His voice was suddenly sharper. 'You'll help me tidy this room before we leave,' said Donal. 'Drury and his wife won't be back for weeks – Easter, I think he said, and he'll be at the airport by now. But we have to leave everything as we found it—' He broke off, and Jess saw he was staring at the dining table by the window, a startled look on his face. She turned her head to look, and for the first time saw that the papers on the table held two small folders, green and white. There was the outline of a shamrock, and the words *Aer Lingus*.

'The bloody plane tickets back to London,' said Donal, in a half-whisper. 'The eejit's forgotten them. God, he'll have to

come back for them – he could be here any minute.' He
bounded up from the sofa, and grabbed her arms.

'Move fast,' he said. 'Set this room to rights. I'll douse the
fire. Then we'll go home, and when we're there, Jessica, you'll
remain quiet about what happened here, you understand that?
And if you don't remain quiet – if you tell anyone about this
– you'll be very sorry indeed.' The cold frightening note was
there again. 'I could even see that you're shut away,' said
Donal, his face so close that Jess could see the flecks of brown
in his eyes. 'I could do it, Jessica. Your mother wasn't entirely
sane, did you know that? "Oh, Catriona Cullen," people said.
"She was always more than a bit mad." Tormod said it loudest
of all, you know.'

'I don't believe you.' But Jessica was remembering how
Tormod sometimes looked if her mother was ever mentioned. A
shuddering look, as if he might be seeing something repulsive.

'It's true,' said Donal. 'She'd most likely have ended up
being shut away, except she ran away. So no one will be
surprised if you turn out a bit mad. They'll say, "like mother,
like daughter".'

Jessica stared at him, terrified, not knowing how much of
this to believe.

'And remember, as well, that all kinds of unpleasant things
can happen to foolish little girls who talk too much,' said
Donal. He pulled her closer to the glowing fire – so close that
Jess felt the heat brushing her skin – then he pushed her hand
down to the small fireguard. A peat turf broke apart and fierce
heat belched out, searing Jess's hand slightly. She gasped and
managed to snatch her hand back.

'So now, you'll help me to tidy up this place, and you'll
do it very quickly in case Drury comes back for those plane
tickets,' said Donal.

Jess was scared to do anything that might cause him to drag
her over to the fire again so, moving shakily, trying not to
notice the burning pain on her hand, she rearranged the sofa
cushions, and dragged a small rug back into place in front of
the hearth. Donal fetched a cup of water from the kitchen and
flung it on to the peat. There was a hissing, and the warm
glow faded.

'All done. Now we can leave,' said Donal. 'And we'll do so at once, before Drury can come back. I'll drive us.'

'I don't want to be in the car with you. I'll walk home.'

'Not looking like that, you won't. You'll have half the village seeing you. For goodness' sake, will you do something to make yourself a bit tidier. Then I'll drive us back, and we'll tell the aunts you fell over on the icy track. They'll believe that.' It came out sneeringly, and Jessica hated him all over again. 'And remember,' said Donal, 'that if you say anything about what happened here, people will think you're making up stories.' The horrible, cruel other-Donal looked from behind his eyes, and he looked across at the fire. 'Does your hand hurt where it got burned?' he said. 'The fire's died down now, but it's still hot enough to hurt even more than that. So let me hear you promise you won't tell a living soul what happened here, or we'll see just how hot that fire still is.'

The room was silent and still – there was only the faint movement of the dying fire-glow on the white walls. She would have to promise, or he would drag her back to the fire. No one would rescue her – there was no one to hear her scream – that was what Donal had said.

And then, incredibly and startlingly, there was someone. Jess was facing the window, and there was a sudden movement beyond it. A figure. Mr Drury coming back for the plane tickets? No, whoever this was, he was standing up against the window, looking in. The outline was slightly blurred by the old glass and the lead strips, and for a moment Jess could not bring it into focus. And then she saw the cheerful scarlet woollen scarf, and the untidy tumble of hair beneath the brim. The tramp. The man who had said she looked like a dryad under a tree. He had followed her up here. Had he seen what had happened? He had probably seen enough to guess.

She gasped, and Donal whipped round, and saw the tramp also. The man stepped back at once, but Donal was already crossing the room, and dragging open the door. There was fury in his face, and a new terror washed over Jess. She ran after Donal, wanting to stop him, wanting to warn the tramp . . .

But the tramp had already started down the track – Jess could see the flash of scarlet muffler between the hedges. It was all right, he was getting away. She did not want to go out there and risk meeting Donal again, but she could not stay here, so she pulled on her jacket, with the sketchpad still in the pocket, and went out. The door closed smoothly, with a little click as the lock fell into place.

She still felt dizzy and slightly sick, but the cold air helped. Her hand was stinging and red from the fire, but it was not very much. Had the tramp got away? But as she reached the stone with *Tromloy* engraved on it, she saw him. He had almost reached the road, but he kept looking back to see if Donal was following him. Jessica wanted to shout to him not to do that, because it was slowing him down, and in another minute Donal would catch him up. And Donal could not risk the tramp telling anyone what he might have seen in Tromloy.

She began to run. The track was rutted and narrow, and several times her foot slipped on a patch of ice, but each time she managed to keep her balance.

She saw the car before either Donal or the tramp did. It was not coming very fast, and its indicator was flashing to signal that it was going to swing over on to the track. Mr Drury and his daughter coming back for the plane tickets. Donal saw the car, but the tramp did not, because he had turned to look back again. Jess shouted, and ran the rest of the way down the track to the road, but it was too late. The tramp had run straight into the path of the oncoming car. There was a loud screech of tyres as the car swerved violently, and in the same moment, Jess skidded on a patch of ice and fell against the grass verge. The world spun crazily around her, and a sickening pain sliced through her ankle. She bent over, gasping with the pain, aware of confusion and shouting all around her. Then came a soft whooshing sound and a flare of hot, hurting light shot into the air as the car's petrol tank exploded. Jess threw up a hand instinctively to shield her face, and when she looked again, there was the outline of a figure against the sheet of fire, running towards the burning car.

She was dazed and shocked, and the fire was burning up fiercely, but she struggled to her feet, because someone was trapped in the car. Whoever it was, was screaming – dreadful screams – and through the smoke and the belching flames and the sickening smell of petrol, she could see hands beating at the car windows as the flames engulfed it. Terrible. She could no longer see whoever had run towards the car, but she must try to help, she must try to get the person out.

As she struggled to her feet, hands grabbed her, and Donal's voice said, 'No! Don't go any nearer. It's too dangerous and you can't do anything. Not now. Oh God, it's too late now.' It was the real Donal again, the one she had known all her life. His voice was shocked and shaking, but he was saying that help was on the way – he had phoned the emergency services. And this must be true, because already there was the sound of sirens coming towards them.

'We don't need to be involved any more,' said Donal, pulling her towards his own car, parked a little way off. 'It's too late for anyone to help those people, and it's more important that I get you home.' He unlocked the car and half pushed her inside. In the light from the blazing car, his eyes were lit to red. 'No one needs to know we were so close to all this,' he said. 'That we were at Tromloy. But remember, Jess, that what happened in Tromloy must never be spoken of. No one must ever know.'

FIFTEEN

The aunts flew into an instant fuss when Donal helped a limping Jessica into the house. They scurried around fetching bandages for Jess's scraped knees where she had fallen and strapping for her twisted ankle. Aunt Nuala brought warm water and towels for them to wash away the smoke smudges. They both wanted to know exactly what had happened, and it was immediately clear to Jess that Donal had had time to think up a story.

'Jessica was running down the track from Tromloy, and she slipped on a patch of ice and fell on to the side of the road,' he said. 'I had only just got there. And almost immediately a car crashed into the bank, just a couple of hundred yards away. It exploded into flames. A terrible thing.'

The aunts were deeply shocked and distressed. Had people been hurt in the crash? Had the driver been rescued?

'I don't think so,' said Donal. His mouth twisted briefly and Jessica saw that he, too, had the memory of someone screaming from inside the burning car. 'The paramedics were there within minutes, though,' he said. 'And the Garda. They were dealing with it all.'

'Did you go along to help?' asked Aunt Morna, but Donal said they had not, because by the time he had reached Jessica, the ambulances and the firefighters and everyone was already surrounding the car.

'We couldn't have got near it – it was blazing up like an inferno. And Jess was so shaken from falling down that steep track, and from seeing the crash, it seemed more important to get her home as soon as I could.'

'We'd better call the doctor out to her,' said Aunt Nuala.

'Dear goodness, she doesn't need a doctor,' said Donal, forcefully. 'I saw the whole thing. She'll be right as rain in a couple of hours.'

'But the child's in shock.'

'I daresay she is. I daresay I am, as well. Seeing that car burn, knowing there was someone – it looked like two people, in fact – inside it, is more than enough to send anyone into shock,' said Donal.

It was Aunt Morna who suddenly said, 'But why were you both out there? Tromloy isn't far out of Kilcarne, but it's all the way at the top of that track, isn't it?' Neither of the aunts had ever been to Tromloy, but everyone knew about it, of course, and how it was the last fragment of the old Kilcarne Manor.

'Jess was sketching Tromloy,' said Donal, at once. 'She told you about that, she said.'

'Well, not that she was going up to Tromloy exactly—'

'Oh, yes, she was quite clear about having told you,' said Donal, before Aunt Nuala could say any more. 'She told you where she was going, and you said not to go too far off the road, because it was a bit lonely out there.'

'We did say something like that,' said Morna, a bit doubtfully.

'And I was along the road, because I met Niall Drury in Dunleary's, and he was worried about a loose window catch at the cottage, what with him going back to England that very day. So I said I'd try to do a temporary repair job until Oona Dunleary gets someone out there. I'd only just parked the car when Jessica came pelting down the track. Running so fast she skidded.'

'Why were you running, Jess?' asked Aunt Morna. 'That's a steep old path from what I've ever seen, and it'd be icy on a day like this.'

Jess felt Donal turn his head and look directly at her. *Never tell anyone* . . . She shrank back in her chair, pushing her face into a cushion, still aware of the slight burning pain in her hand. *All kinds of unpleasant things can happen* . . .

She said, 'I can't remember.' But she was aware of Donal and she could almost hear his mind working.

Then he said, 'Jess, were you running away from someone? It's all right, you don't need to be afraid to say, if you were. Because there was someone lurking around – I saw him as I got out of the car. A rough-looking man, it was. A vagrant, I'd say.'

'The tramp,' said Nuala, pouncing. 'That'll be who it was. He's been around here a while. Somebody said he'd been sleeping rough at the old Sexton's House, but I wonder if he'd heard Tromloy was to be empty and thought he'd get a more comfortable few nights there instead.'

'And went out to see could he get in?' said Donal. 'I'd say that was entirely likely.' His eyes flickered to Jess again.

'Did you speak to him?' Aunt Morna asked Donal.

'I did. I'd just got out of the car, and he was coming down the track from Tromloy. I nodded to him, then I asked was he here looking for work. He said . . .' Donal frowned, as if trying to remember. 'He said, "Ah, work, there's a thing now, Father. Who'd give work to a rascal like me?"'

'The impudence,' said Morna.

'I said I thought he looked perfectly capable, and he said, "Father, I'm capable of anything in God's world or the devil's. I know that today".' Donal looked across at Jessica again. '"Capable of God's work or the devil's," those were the words.'

Jessica knew Donal had not spoken to the tramp. She knew those words about God's work or the devil's were Donal's own.

She also knew that she would never tell anyone what Donal had done to her. Donal had said people would think she was mad and she might be shut away. That terrified her. The thought of what Donal might do to her if she told what had happened terrified her even more.

She would never dare to be alone with Donal again.

The memories were still spinning in a sick confusion as Jessica went down the track, turning to wave to Bea Drury halfway down.

She felt as if huge invisible hands had snatched her up and shaken her until she could hardly breathe, and then had dropped her with a painful thud on the hard ground.

Donal. Two years ago he had done that to her, there in that warm, welcoming house. Even now she could remember the sudden pain when he had pulled her hand close to the fire. She looked down at her hands, at the twisted scar tissue across the fingers and palms of both hands. Those scars had been caused by something far worse than the tiny burn that day. How had they happened? Had she told someone what Donal had done, and had he found it and punished her as he had threatened? If so, she had no memory of it.

There's something more, thought Jessica. There's another memory as well as the one I've found today. There must be. But whatever it is, it's buried so deeply I can't reach it. Then, with sudden determination – but I will reach it, she thought. Somehow I'll find out what did that to my hands.

Bea had watched the small, strange figure, so like Abigail in so many ways, and yet so unlike her in others, walk down Tromloy's track. Jessica seemed to hesitate at the curve in the path, then half turned, as if unsure of something. She's coming back, thought Bea. Or is there someone there who's meeting her? She leaned forward, thinking she had seen a figure come up the track towards Jessica, but after all it had only been the movement of a tree. Jessica had turned back, though, and she waved. Bea smiled and waved back, not knowing whether Jess could see her at the window, but doing so anyway.

It had been a curious afternoon. It had been clear that the sight of the fire screen had upset Jessica – she had tried to hide it, but she had recognized it and been disturbed by it. Bea sat down, staring at the screen, remembering how Jessica had asked about it when they first met. Was there an old fire screen at Tromloy, she had said. A screen with old posters and faces of people from the past. She had known about the photo in Abi's bedroom, as well. A man on a stage, she had said. Old-fashioned clothes, and woolly hair like cotton wool on each side of his face. How had she known about that? How could she have known?

But the fire screen and the photo had both been at Tromloy for years – they had been there when Bea and Niall bought the house – and Tromloy was empty for long stretches at a time. Might Jessica have come up here sketching, and looked through a window and seen the screen? No, she could not have done. The screen had always – *always* – been upstairs in Abi's room. It had never been in this room until three nights ago, the night of her arrival, when Bea had made that peat fire and it had got too hot. The photograph of the music-hall performer had always been in Abi's room, as well. No one could possibly have seen them from the ground.

They had not been mentioned today – Bea had deliberately avoided doing so and Jessica had not referred to them at all – but it had been clear that the sight of them had disturbed her. Why?

It had grown dark, and Bea got up to switch on the lights. The small wall light on the side of the chimney breast fell directly on to the fire screen, lighting up the fragment of the theatre programme, with Maxim Volf's name showing clearly on it. Maxim . . . She looked at it for a long time. She had not thought she would ever risk damaging the screen, but she suddenly wanted to know if that scrap of paper had any more to tell – if anything might be hidden under it. Before she could change her mind, she fetched a handful of DIY implements from the cupboard next to the garden door. There was a thin-edged chisel and a flat-bladed scraper that Niall had used for wallpapering, although he had been apt to get bored halfway through any kind of decorating job and give it up.

She unfolded the screen and laid it flat on the carpet, then began to chip at the old dry vanish. The scraper worked best; its edges dug into the surface, and praying not to cause any major damage, Bea began to edge the programme cover away from the base. It resisted, and she thought it was going to disintegrate, but then a corner came free, and within five minutes she was able to lift it out. It came up with only the smallest tear on one corner.

It was absurd to suddenly feel excited. There would not be anything on the back of the programme that would give any more details about the enigmatic Maxim Volf. But someone called Maxim Volf had tried to save Abigail that day and he was still living here.

The programme cover was not a single sheet after all. Whoever had incorporated it into the screen had folded it in half. The folds had split, of course, but Bea spread it carefully on the dining table, placing the edges together. Some of the corners were missing and some of the lettering was faded beyond legibility, but she was able to read the majority of it.

*'Grand opening of the splendid new Genesius Theatre on
23 November 1921. A wonderful programme of music, arranged
and directed by the famous English music-hall performer,
Mortimer Quince – known to audiences as "Quality Quince,
the man with the Quicksilver voice". National favourites of
song and music performing on stage. Concert commences at
7.30 p.m. Supper bar open during interval for refreshments.'*

The Genesius. Bea and Niall had been to that theatre several
times over the years – it was a lovely, beautifully restored old
place and it staged some very good plays and concerts. Niall
had taken Abi to a pantomime matinée there on the day before
they died. They had had lunch beforehand, and Abi had phoned
Bea that night, describing it all. It had been brilliant, she had
said. And she and Dad would be home tomorrow night, and she
would tell Mum all about it then, and Mum could draw the
people from the pantomime. 'You can do that, can't you? Aladdin
and the cave and the genie coming out of a lamp?'

Bea had laughed, and when she put the phone down she
had already been reaching for her sketchpad to rough out a
few of the images Abi wanted so they could discuss them
when she was home. Only Abi had never come home. Bea
had found the sketches weeks later, and burned them.

It was ridiculous to be so suddenly knocked out by a wave
of grief after two years, but grief did that. It ambushed you
when you were least expecting it. Bea took a deep breath,
dashed the tears away impatiently, and studied the programme
again, trying to be dispassionate.

After Mortimer Quince's name was a list of the people who
had been involved in The Genesius's opening night. She did
not recognize any of the names, except for Maxim Volf's.
There was no indication anywhere to suggest what part he had
played in the evening – he might have been a performer, an
organizer, or a sponsor. He might even have sold programmes,
or served behind the bar at the interval.

But there was one thing that did give a clue. The programme
was decorated with one of the elaborate vine-leaf, curlicue
borders so typical of the era. At the top of the page, set into
the centre, was a small oval photograph. It was smudgily
reproduced, and it had faded considerably, but when Beatrice

took it over to the main light, she recognized it. It was the same photograph hanging on the wall of Abi's bedroom.

She ran back upstairs again, and unhooked the photo, turning it over. The backing had come loose already, probably from age, and it was easy to peel it back. On the reverse of the photograph, in old, spidery writing, were the words, *"Mortimer Quince on stage at Shepherd's Bush Empire, 1910."*

It was impossible to know what connection there might have been between Mortimer Quince and Maxim Volf. But to add to The Genesius and the 1921 concert, Bea now had a second date and a place: 1910 in London, and the Shepherd's Bush Empire. Was that a line of enquiry she might follow when she was back in London?

But for the moment, another theatre was closer. The Genesius in Galway. A theatre she knew and had visited. Could she bear to go inside that theatre again? Would there be any point? Would it bring her any nearer to the truth about the chimera that was Maxim Volf?

SIXTEEN

Mortimer Quince's diary

I'm becoming aware that Maxim is getting closer. It's difficult to describe how I know this, but it's as if the knowledge is trickling into my mind in tiny threads and whispers. As if Maxim is saying, *I will soon be with you again . . . I am not very far away . . .*

This looks completely mad, written down, but this is my private diary, so I don't see that it matters if I sound like a raving idiot at times, babbling, like Lear, of green fields. I have no idea what to do about this feeling regarding Maxim. I don't know if there is actually anything I *can* do about it.

Feofil has never mentioned Maxim since that day he said I should be out of his reach in Ireland. But I am very aware that the knowledge of Maxim – of what he was – is strongly between us.

Dare I write how much I still miss Maxim? It's something I've never admitted or acknowledged to myself. I do miss him, though.

Today I have had a request to undertake some very prestigious and interesting work!

It came in a letter, couched in flattering terms, sent by the director of a theatre in Galway City. He was sure I had a very busy life, he said, but he and his fellow directors wondered whether I might see my way to the organizing and presenting of a musical concert at a newly restored theatre. They had heard of my London successes and also the work I had done with the children in Kilcarne, and were very much hoping I could accept the commission.

(I feel that 'successes' is something of an exaggeration, but I shall not correct it.)

Feofil says the offer is no more than I deserve.

'The Kilcarne school work you have done has been excellent and professional. I should not have expected anything less of you, though.'

'But this is a big professional theatre. A newly launched concern. Am I equal to it?'

'I'm surprised you even ask the question,' said Feofil. 'Do not forget who you are.'

It's sometimes difficult to live up to being Roman Volf's son.

I shall chronicle the Galway theatre exploits in these pages, in as much detail as possible, since it is certainly something that must form part of my memoirs – if ever I have time to create them!

This Galway theatre has an unusual history. It was originally a church, but it has been falling to pieces for centuries – all the way back to the seventeenth century to be precise, because, like Marie Lloyd's song, it was one of the ruins that Cromwell knocked about a bit.

Dear Marie. We were once on the same hill. Foresters Music Hall, in the Mile End Road, it was. She sang an extraordinary version of Lord Tennyson's drawing-room ballad, 'Come into the Garden, Maud,' making it so risqué and suggestive I'm surprised Tennyson didn't rear up from the grave in horror. The management was stunned. I was stunned. The audience decamped, as a man, to the bar in disgust, which was a pity since I was next on the bill, and I had to perform to a virtually empty house. But these are the slings and arrows of outrageous fortune, or, in this case, of outrageous misfortune, and in Miss Lloyd's defence I have to say she stood me a large port and lemon afterwards by way of apology; well, actually she stood me three.

But to return to the Galway City venture. It appears that Cromwell's men spent a couple of rumbustious weeks in the old church, stabling their horses in the nave, using stained-glass windows for archery practice, and, for all I know, carousing with ladies in the crypt. What they didn't damage or destroy, the weather and local vandals did in succeeding centuries.

Then, a couple of years ago, a committee was formed to

raise funds to renovate the place. The money seems to have come partly from a grant made by the Dáil Éireann, partly from private sponsorship (I suspect this provided the lion's share), and also from smaller donations made by the public. So now the church has been deconsecrated (I think this is the right term), and fitted out for use as a theatre and what they are calling a cultural centre. The letter is careful to explain that it is fairly small, and that the main area – which used to be the nave – seats only 350 people. To me, this is not so very small. I would not say this in public, but I've played to a lot fewer than 350 in my time.

It's to be called The Genesius. A quick forage of the dictionary (together with a consultation with Feofil), reveals that St Genesius is regarded as the patron saint of actors. I have committed this information to memory, so as not to be caught out, and I said to Feofil that I thought it a very nicely judged and well-chosen name for a church-turned-theatre.

Feofil, deadpan, said, 'Genesius is also supposed to be the patron saint of clowns and lawyers.'

The Genesius is to open on 23 November, which is St Cecilia's Day and, typically Irish, it's thought it would be a fine fitting thing to make the first performance a musical concert.

Why The Genesius directors should ask a has-been music-hall performer to organize such an important event, I have no idea, but I shall accept.

I have begun work compiling a suitable musical programme for The Genesius opening. So far I have tracked down two choral societies, one in Galway and one in Connemara, and I shall take the motor and drive there to listen to them next week. I shouldn't think it's important that the furthest distance I have so far driven is along Kilcarne's narrow main street. I daresay there won't be many motor cars on the road between Kilcarne and Galway, anyway.

It's remarkable that I, who once quaked at attending auditions and hung on the every word of directors and producers, am now on the other side of the footlights, so to speak. I am resolved to be kindly and tactful with everyone, though.

*   *   *

The choirs are splendid and this week I found some excellent folk groups – the Irish love their own music, they're proud of it and rightly so, for it's stirring and lively. We can have a medley of Irish songs – most probably the audience will join in.

I am exercised in my mind as to whether I should sing something on my own account. It's very tempting, but on consideration I don't think it would be right. I would, though, love to find a really strong female singer to perform Marie Lloyd's famous song – 'One of the Ruins That Cromwell Knocked About a Bit'. This is a tricky one, however. The Irish will tell extravagant stories of Oliver's rampage across Ireland, and how his Ironsides roasted men alive and ate them, or beat Royalist leaders to death with their own wooden legs. They'll relate it with complete sincerity, saying a shocking old time it was. But they can be unpredictable, and there's no knowing how they might react to a British music-hall song about Cromwell. Even if it were being sung in a former ruin that Cromwell really did knock about.

I've played in many a theatre in my time, and it's fair to say I've probably seen every kind there is. From the spit-and-sawdust pub rooms, to the Italianate halls with frescoes – the pretentious Pavilions and the tawdry Tivolis . . . To the saloons where the floors are awash with ale and other unmentionable fluids as well, and the cellars where sometimes the audience sing along with the performer, and sometimes pelt him or her with rotten fruit . . . And even the dubious gaffs near Leicester Square where infamous *'poses plastiques'* are offered.

So I think I can regard myself as a reasonable judge of theatres, and I think I can say with authority that The Genesius Theatre is beautiful. There's been no attempt to conceal the religious origins, and the stone arches and hammer beams are all still in place, as well as some of the marvellous rood screens with their intricate tracery. The story is that these screens were hastily smuggled into the crypt and hidden when Cromwell's Ironsides marched in, and that they never found them.

The stage is small as stages go – there's no apron, but a proscenium arch has been created, with ornate, gilt-tipped curlicues and scrolls across the top. There are deep red velvet curtains, which open and close with a satisfying swish, and the auditorium seats have red velvet padding, as well.

The directors want to engage a particular Irish pianist for the centrepiece of the evening. He is well known and much loved – also immensely gifted – and we have agreed that he will play two solos. Tchaikovsky's *Piano Concerto No. 1 in B-flat minor*, which is a splendid dramatic composition, and a Mozart. We have yet to decide which Mozart. The pianist has accepted the request, and everyone is extremely pleased.

The nightmare came last night. It's been absent for so long I was almost starting to believe it had gone for good.

I could blame a great many things for its reappearance – the large supper eaten in company with several convivial locals; my slight concern for Feofil who I notice is looking somewhat haggard recently (he brushes aside any concern, and says he is perfectly all right); even a small contretemps with the motor car when I drove to Galway yesterday. I daresay they will manage to replant the hedge, however, and the punctured tyre has already been replaced.

But that very afternoon I had been listening to one of the Irish pianist's gramophone records in preparation for meeting him. Feofil recently bought a splendid gramophone and some records. He is very critical of the recorded performances, and listening to him I remember that this is a man who met Prokofiev and knew Rimsky-Korsakov (he memorably said that Rimsky-Korsakov might 'one day amount to something'), and who wrote that Tchaikovsky's work was 'intensely expressive', but then observed that the Romantics were 'never natural melodists'.

This, too, is the man who was in the Mikhailovsky Theatre on that last night, and who later described Roman's execution so vividly. 'Roman Volf faced Death as if he was auditioning it to provide accompaniment for one of his concert hall performances.' Later, in the Russian magazine, *Golos*, Feofil said, 'A dark and suffocating web of tragedy wove itself around the last months of Roman Volf's life, and it was believed by some that his descendants would be trapped in the spider-strands of that dark web for many years into the future . . .'

Inevitably, listening to the gramophone records stirred the thready spider-web memories.

In the dream, I was – as always – hemmed in by the screaming, jeering crowd in the prison's courtyard. And this time the dream did not cheat. This time I saw everything. I saw the faces of the people, eager and avid and howling for blood. Roman Volf's blood. They hated him. I understand that now. They hated the man who had been one of the glittering idols and icons of his era, who had charmed and seduced from concert platforms and sumptuous stages, and wrung out the souls from his listeners with his genius. But who had then been convicted of a squalid murder – that of the Tsar Alexander, known to thousands as the Liberator, the liberal, the reforming emperor. After the assassination, they forgot – or perhaps had never cared anyway – that he was also a man who, as well as fathering eight children inside his marriage, had had at least seven illegitimate children by several mistresses. All they could think was that their tsar's body was torn into bloodied fragments by the assassins' bomb, and to them it made him almost a martyr. As somebody (who?) once sagely observed, there is no hatred so great as the hatred that replaces adoration.

In the dream, I could again see the pallid faces looking out of the tiny, barred windows high up in the stone walls – the other prisoners, and probably also guards waiting and wanting to see the execution. Uniformed guards lined the square, rifles at the ready, bayonets glinting as spears of sun came in and out of the clouds.

Then a massive dull crash echoed through the square, reverberating deafeningly. Showers of brick and stone dust and splinters cascaded on to the heads of the crowds, and there were startled cries, because most people had been watching the main door through which the guards had come, expecting the condemned man to appear there. But he did not. The crash was from a square platform that had been lowered from a window halfway up the wall. It jutted at right angles from the wall itself – there was a narrow ledge all round it, and over it was the grim outline of a gallows, with the hangman's rope in place.

People pointed and shouted, and a man standing near to me called out an explanation.

'See that inner trapdoor at the centre of the platform,' he said. 'That's where they'll make him stand. And soon as the noose is round his murdering neck, they'll release that inner trap and down he'll go.'

Recording these details, I am aware that in the dream I could again understand everything that was being said. And yet why would I not? If I was born in Russia, I would have spent those years speaking it. What I don't understand is why I remember virtually nothing of the language now.

The guards were starting to lower something over the edge of the massive trapdoor, by means of thick, ugly chains, and a ripple of puzzlement went through the crowd. Then there was an ugly clanging sound, and the strange structure fell down into place.

It was a cage. A cage made from thick black iron bars, so small in comparison to its surroundings that it should have been insignificant. But it was not. Once you had seen it, you did not really see anything else. And in last night's dream, for the first time I saw it clearly. It was oblong in shape, perhaps four feet across each of the sides and six feet from the base to the top. It hung from the iron chains hooked on to the underside of the trapdoor, and the guards pulled it this way and that, until it rested directly beneath the inner trap – the trap through which the hanged man would drop. He would go down through the trap and so into the cage.

The child that I was in the dream did not fully understand the cage's purpose, but the people around me did. They began to shout.

'The cage! The burning cage! He'll hang, then he'll burn inside the cage!'

As the shouts intensified, filling up the courtyard with sound and fury, there was a stir of movement from the room beyond the trapdoor, and the condemned man was brought out.

I don't think he struggled – his hands were bound behind his back, and he was wearing a deep blindfold, so that the guards had to guide him to stand on the waiting flap. Could he sense the presence of the rope directly over his head? He could certainly hear the crowds screaming below him, for at one moment he tilted his head, as if to catch every nuance of sound. I remember I let out a sob at this point, and that I wanted to press my hands over my eyes to shut out the sight. But I did not. He could not see what was happening, so I would see for him.

The rope was slipped over his head, and the man next to me, who had pointed out the inner trapdoor, said, 'They're being quick.'

'Merciful,' said another voice.

'Wasn't merciful what happened to the tsar. Torn to bloody gobbets, he was.'

'They say hanging's a quick death, though. Eight seconds, isn't it?'

'If they get it right.'

'If not—?'

A shrug. 'Slow strangulation.'

But it seemed to me, still huddled in miserable terror, unnoticed by most of the crowd, that the men on the trapdoor were going to be very quick indeed. For a brief time I thought I heard and felt, once again, that pulsing heart Roman's heart, racing too quickly, to meet its final beat of his life.

The noose was put in place, tightened, adjusted – the seconds stretched out – then at last the rapped out command was given. For a split-second everything in that square seemed to stop, as if Time's mechanism had frozen. Then the trap opened, and the condemned man dropped straight down with a sickening jerk into the cage's confines directly beneath.

At once an immense roar came from the watchers.

'Cut him down!'

'Light the fire!'

'The burning cage – now, *now,* NOW!'

The guards were already kneeling at the edge of the open, inner trapdoor, and two of them held aloft flaring torches. Using extreme care, they threw the flares down into the cage. The fire caught at once, and the guards stepped back, slamming down the inner, smaller trap that formed the cage's roof, then going back inside the building.

Leaving the man in the cage to burn.

The stench of burning began to fill up the square, and the flames licked greedily around the bars, vivid and shocking against the dull grey stones and the leaden sky. Sparks showered down on to the crowd, who dodged back, but they did not move very far; they were still shouting, and they were so angry, those people, that they seemed hardly to care if they were scorched by the burning fragments raining down. They jeered and yelled, raising their fists in fury.

'Burn him! Nothing to be left of him!'

'Burn every bit of skin and flesh and bone and hair!'

'Murderer! Assassin!'

That was when arms came round me, and held me warmly and strongly, and Antoinette's voice said, 'I have been searching for you – searching the crowd – thank heaven I have found you at last. My dear boy, you must not be here. Come now with me.'

I could not see her very clearly – either because the dream was blurring everything, or because the smoke from the cage was filling up the courtyard, or perhaps simply because my own eyes were misted with tears and fear. But I could hear her, and I clutched at her hands.

I said, 'He's dead. Isn't he dead?'

Antoinette seemed to take a long time to answer. Then she said, 'Yes. Yes, he's dead.'

I rubbed my eyes with my fists, trying to scrub the tears away. Then I said, 'Maxim . . .'

I stopped, but Antoinette seemed to understand. She said, 'It's all right. Maxim will be safe. I promise you.'

The dream ended there. I suppose Roman's story could be said to have ended there, as well.

There was the carriage journey then – the remembered lights reflecting on the river – what river was it? – and the sense of urgency; the impression that we must get away as quickly as possible. But I was encased in fear and bewilderment and exhaustion, and I can only remember parts of the journey.

What I do remember is the ache of loss for Roman.

And the deeper ache because that was the day I knew I had lost Maxim.

SEVENTEEN

Mortimer Quince's diary

S ome really exciting news has come today. The Genesius concert is to be recorded on cine film. The film will be shown in cinemas as part of newsreels of current events. This is immensely gratifying.

'We like to include one or two light-hearted items to follow all the gloom of the week's news,' said the willowy young man from the film company who came to look at the theatre.

He and his assistants have spent two afternoons calculating where the camera – there may be a plurality of cameras for all I know – should best be positioned. There were earnest discussions as to light and sound and acoustics. It's important, they explained, not to distract the soloists by their activities. It's fairly clear that by 'soloists' they mean the famous Irish pianist, and that he's the real reason they're making the cine film. But I don't care, because this is all marvellous publicity for The Genesius.

They're going to set up the camera and its accoutrements halfway along the central aisle, so that it's directly aimed at the dais and the piano itself. I pointed out, as politely as possible, that this meant people in the end aisle seats would not have a clear sightline to the pianist, but they said you could not have everything in life.

Even with these disruptions and the probable annoyance of the people in those particular seats (who I suppose can be offered their money back if they complain), I am more delighted than I can say that the concert will be recorded for posterity.

A disaster has struck.

The Irish pianist has had to cancel his appearance. This is dreadful. It cannot be helped – the poor man has succumbed to appendicitis, and although the troublesome organ has been summarily removed, it will be some time before he can contemplate any public appearance. He is desolated. His agent is desolated. I am desolated. The entire Genesius Theatre group is aghast, and panic has engulfed the board of directors.

We still have a wonderful concert, but the glittering heart – the pianist – has been torn out of it. Feofil says this is being melodramatic which, coming from Feofil, is a bit rich, since he is one of the most melodramatic people I have ever met. When I said so, he merely gave one of his philosophical shrugs and said life had a way of dealing blows, and blows had to be accepted.

This is quite true, but Feofil does not have to placate printers, who will have to be told that the wording for the programme covers and posters must be changed at what's almost the eleventh hour. As I write this, I have no idea what the programmes and posters will be changed to.

I dare not even think how I am to tell the cine film people.

There was no particular reason for me to go to The Genesius today. I had intended to spend the time in Galway engaging battle with the printers, but the theatre draws me, so, when I alighted from the omnibus (Feofil having gone off with the motor earlier in the morning), I walked past the printers' offices, and went along to The Genesius. It's a little removed from the main thoroughfare, within sight of a glint of the river, and the street is one of those unexpected pockets you find in almost any city – a place where you can believe that any footsteps you might hear are not completely your own, but might be footsteps of people long since dead, or even not yet born. Today I had the feeling more strongly than usual, that those long-ago footsteps walked with me. Twice, I even found myself trying to get into exact step with them.

The theatre was not locked – the directors have employed a caretaker, a slightly raffish but apparently reliable man – and he would doubtless be wandering around somewhere. I paused in the main doorway, which is at the head of a short flight of stone steps, then went inside. Even after so many years of performing, I still feel a *frisson* when I enter a theatre – any theatre. I am a man of theatre, after all, no matter how fifth-rate some of those theatres have been. (Not all. I still cherish the Shepherd's Bush Empire appearance.)

The curious, hybrid atmosphere of The Genesius fell softly around me the minute I was inside. Most actors will tell you – with various degrees of dramatic emphasis – that all theatres have ghosts, starting with Drury Lane's famous 'Man in Grey' and its capering Regency comedian Joe Grimaldi, all the way down to the humbler levels of spectral chars eternally trying to scrub out fake blood after Macbeth's death, or phantom stagehands who obligingly pass you a stage brace, then vanish in a puff of thespian-tinged vapour.

But The Genesius isn't haunted. It's still evolving as a theatre, and it hasn't had time to acquire any ghosts. Memories do cling to its stones, but mostly they're the memories of its former incarnation – soft echoes of prayer, of confessions whispered behind screens, of penances dutifully chanted, and of supplications tremblingly offered. Of marriages and funerals and christenings.

I make no apology for succumbing to such an outburst; this, after all, is my private record, and none of it will find its way into my memoirs. (Although possibly that last part about memories and ghosts could be incorporated somewhere. Just in case, I have underlined both paragraphs.)

I walked quietly down the central aisle, and sat down in one of the red velvet seats halfway along. There was some kind of rehearsal or practice going on somewhere – I could hear music from behind the stage. I listened, trying to identify it, but I was unable to pinpoint its place in the programme. In any case, it was fragmented, a series of cascading scales, then several bars played over and over again.

It was difficult not to yield to despair at the sight of the gleaming concert grand that had already been carried on to the stage, and that was awaiting tuning to concert pitch. A fall of curtain to one side cast a shadow along the side of the piano – a shadow that almost made it look as if someone was standing in the wings. I watched the shadow for a while, because it was exactly how and where a performer would stand, waiting for the cue to make an entrance. The music had ceased, and the old building settled into its own brand of silence. There are different qualities and different depths of silence, and this was a very deep silence.

Then the silence broke apart. From the shadows that wreathed the stage, a voice said, 'I've been waiting for you. Where on earth have you been?'

I gasped, and started up.

'And why,' said Feofil, appearing from the wings as casually as if he had walked into the sitting room at Tromloy, 'are you sitting in the dark down there, as if you're waiting for a ghost to appear?'

'I'm gathering courage to face the printers,' I said. 'I didn't know you were here.' He came lightly down the stairs at the side of the stage, and sat in the chair next to me.

'Ah, those printers. You have not yet been to see them?'

'No.'

'Good. I hoped to see you before you did. I have something to suggest.'

'What is it?'

Feofil said, 'You have put your name to the event and it will be on all the programmes and posters. Yes?'

'Yes, certainly. Well, you know I have. You saw the designs. "Arranged and directed by" that's what they'll say.'

Feofil turned to face me. In the dim light his expression was unreadable. 'For me,' he said, 'and for no other reason, will you let your real name be printed?'

Something seemed to shiver and half form on the air – something I thought I had suppressed, something I thought had died quietly and obediently after I left St Petersburg and changed my name. I stared straight ahead, not daring to look at Feofil. Then, as if from a long distance away, as if his voice was coming down a long dark tunnel, Feofil said, 'Will you do that for me, Maxim?'

Light years seemed to pass, and several worlds might have been born and died before I was able to answer. At last, in a voice that was barely more than a whisper, I said, 'You knew.'

'My dear boy, I was there – in St Petersburg. Of course I knew. I have always known.'

I said, 'Fair enough.' I frowned, and this time got my emotions into a semblance of order. 'I can't see the point of what you're asking,' I said. It came out more sharply than I had intended, so I said, 'Even if there is a point, I won't do it. I can't. I can't let anyone know who I am. Maxim – Roman Volf's son – that person, that child, had to vanish all those years ago.'

'Maxim . . .' His voice lingered on the name, 'Maxim, listen to me,' said Feofil, and there was a gentleness in his tone I had never heard before. 'It's been a very long time. So many years. Here, now, in this place, in this newly created theatre, you can be your real self again. After such a long time you would be safe.'

'I'll never be safe. Maxim Volf had to vanish. Antoinette told me that. He could never be in the world again. I could never be Maxim again, not ever. I had to forget him. I did forget him.'

But the words held no conviction, because of course I had never forgotten that child I had been. He had been with me all the time, a shadow self, a dark alter ego. And when Feofil called me by that name – the first time anyone had used it for almost forty years – it was as if time was dissolving all around me, and as if I could see all the way through the mists to that fragment of my life I had striven to forget. To the time when I was Maxim.

It had been Antoinette – always Antoinette, of course – who had tried to explain it to me, in terms a four-year-old could understand.

'Russia is in turmoil after the tsar's murder,' she had said; there had been tears in her voice and in her eyes. 'Your father was convicted of being one of the killers, and as his son you are at a great risk.' She did not use the word danger – dear generous, intuitive, Antoinette. She tried not to frighten me. It did not make any difference, though. I had already seen and felt the anger and the bitterness against my father – it had been like a choking, blinding cloud in the courtyard that day. Even at such a young age I understood that such bitter fury might be turned on to Roman Volf's son.

And so, as Antoinette's carriage bounded and bounced across open countryside, leaving Russia behind, the plan had been created.

'You have to become a different person,' said Antoinette. 'A different name, a different country. Maxim Volf is to vanish.'

'For ever,' I said, half to myself.

'Maxim, I am so sorry. You should not have to endure any of this.'

'Why are you helping me?' I said. 'I don't understand.'

'I help you because . . .' This time the tears spilled over. 'I do it for your father,' she said. 'For Roman. But also I do it for you. We are going to England, you and I.'

'Together?'

'Yes. There is a man here whom I wish to leave behind – a man I married and should not have done. People make mistakes, you see. I have made so many,' said Antoinette, smiling down at me. 'But when we are in England, everything will be all right. I cannot look after you myself – I dare not – but I will make sure you are safe. And you must remember – always remember – that Maxim must be forgotten. You must never let Maxim come back. Promise me that. Promise it for Roman's sake.'

I had promised, and I had pretended Maxim was a separate person, that the forgotten child who had been smuggled away from a gruesome execution and taken on that frantic pelting journey across Russia to England no longer existed. I had understood he could not exist, because he was in danger from the people who had hounded his father. Maxim Volf must never appear in the world again. As Antoinette had said, Maxim must never come back.

'I could never let Maxim come back,' I said to Feofil. 'I promised Antoinette.'

'Antoinette kept you safe,' he said.

'Yes. There was a family in North London – I lived with them for a long time, but I don't think I ever knew exactly who they were. They were kind. Generous. I tried to be part of that family, but we had little in common. I grew up—'

'Homesick?'

'Yes. Incomplete, even. As if I knew I was in the wrong place. So, when I was seventeen, I left,' I said.

'Your father's influence finally drew you to the theatre.'

'Yes.' I hesitated, then said, 'All the time I kept my promise to Antoinette. I kept Maxim out.'

'I think at times you found it hard to do that.'

'He was always there, you see,' I said. 'A secret self. I'm sorry, that sounds like a twopenny romance novel, doesn't it? But it's what it felt like. A dark alter ego, stalking me all through my life. I fought him, but he followed me.'

'A *doppelgänger*,' said Feofil, half to himself. 'Literally translated as a "double-goer". In some cultures, regarded even as an evil twin.'

An evil twin. Had Maxim been that? The feeling of loss swept over me again, and Feofil, who is nothing if not intuitive, went on talking.

'The concept of the *doppelgänger* is also sometimes known as a spirit double,' he said, as if we were discussing an academic point. 'I have read of it. The phenomenon is almost certainly due to hallucination, but it's something that crops up with remarkable regularity in legend and literature. The English poet Shelley related how once he saw his own other-self, did you know that? He described it – I think it was in *Prometheus Unbound*. A character meets his own image walking in a garden.'

'But,' I said, 'if one actually meets that counterpart self, that death-persona, one is said to be certainly doomed. I read about it as well. I do know,' I said, earnestly, 'that it's just a legend. But I still don't think I dare let Maxim come back.'

'Because you fear you will be recognized as the son of the man hated by so many Russian people? By the Romanovs themselves? Or because you believe the legend?'

'Either. Both.'

'But you can let him back,' said Feofil, his strange eyes never leaving my face. 'The Romanovs are dead – their reign ended in 1917. Please, Maxim, do this. Let your name be seen as part of this new theatre venture.' I did not speak, and he said, 'If for no other reason, do it for the man who died in that St Petersburg courtyard.'

The man who died . . . We stared at one another.

'All right,' I said at last. And then, with a sudden surge of spirit, 'But if the legend is true, and I do meet some dreadful fate—'

'Then,' said Feofil, straight-faced, 'it will be entirely my fault. But you won't meet with any dreadful fate. The only dreadful fate you'll meet is if you don't find a replacement for the Irish soloist.'

I looked at him for a long moment. 'Well?' I said. 'What are we going to do about that?'

Something deep and strange – something I did not dare put a name to – flickered between us. Old memories and new ghosts whispered their way nearer.

Then Feofil said, quietly, 'I think we both know already what we are going to do.'

EIGHTEEN

Mortimer Quince's diary

Even though it is long after midnight, I am seated at my desk in the little upstairs room of Tromloy, trying to write down all that happened this evening. I cannot go to my bed until I have set it all down, not because I fear I shall ever forget any of it – I shall not – but because I want to trap the emotions and the memories for ever. Tonight has been a night when secrets were broken open, when legends lived, when ghosts walked, and when past and present merged.

The Genesius Theatre glittered and coruscated tonight. Even before the concert started I was full of pride to be part of – to have helped bring about – such an evening. The newly fitted lights, polished to diamond-brilliance, shone on beautiful old stones, once despoiled, now restored. The lights glinted on the gilt-tipped paintwork and on the four theatre boxes, two on each side of the stage. The cameras and their sound machines were all in place. From my unobtrusive seat I looked at those cameras and thought: they will capture everything that happens tonight.

The audience were clearly in a mood to be pleased, delighted to be part of this event, for wasn't it the finest thing to see the terrible old ruin of a church brought to life, and didn't this augur well for a splendid new era.

The performances were polished and seamless, and everything was exactly as I and the directors had planned and hoped. If there were any backstage problems or hitches or delays, they did not show. The choirs and the lovely orchestral suite were applauded, the comedy turns were greeted with huge delighted cheers, and everyone joined in the choruses of the rousing folk music.

At the interval the audience thronged happily into the supper bar. I went, as well, listening to the praise, hearing people saying what a marvellous evening, wasn't it all splendid. And the main event was still to come. The soloist had still to perform.

The soloist.

As people resumed their seats, the small orchestra filed back into their places on the stage. The conductor made his appearance to a polite spatter of applause, and bowed to the house. He waited for the murmurs and the throat-clearings to die down, then he turned and made a gesture to the wings – a gesture that was halfway between a beckoning and a welcome. My heart began to thump and race erratically, and the silence stretched out and out. I dug my fingernails into the palms of my hands, feeling the tension mounting.

And then, in the flicker of an eyelid, he was there. Standing on the stage with all the arrogance for which he had once been famous, the violin held loosely, almost negligently in his hands. His disconcerting eyes swept the rows of the audience, as if assessing their worthiness to be present and, incredibly, I had the feeling that anyone found wanting would be requested to leave.

I did not move, but he looked around the audience, and found me, of course. His head inclined in a small bow of acknowledgement towards me, and I lifted one hand to sketch a half-salute. I thought: I must take hold of this moment and keep it safe, and I must never let it go. Because never in the whole of my life, not if I live to be a hundred, will I ever experience any emotion that will match this.

The silence lengthened. He was making them wait. Of course he was. Then, when he was satisfied that the attention had been wound up as near to snapping point as possible, he turned to the conductor, raised the gleaming violin to his chin, and positioned the bow. The conductor lifted his baton, and it began. Music flooded that beautiful theatre – Paganini's infamous 'Duetto Amoroso'. Disturbingly sensual, but evocative and exquisite. Afterwards would come Guiseppe Tartini's intense and intricate 'Violin Sonata in G minor' – famously known as the *Devil's Trill.*

Before an enthralled and half-mesmerized audience, in a renovated former church on Ireland's west coast, Roman Volf played the music he had last played in the Mikhailovsky Theatre at St Petersburg, almost forty years earlier.

*   *   *

It was approaching midnight when at last I, and the man I was still addressing as Feofil, reached Tromloy.

He slumped in a deep armchair in the main sitting room. His face was pale and there was a transparent look to his skin, as if it had been stretched across the bones. But his eyes burned with fervour, as if all the lamps of the world were glowing in his mind. I understood. Even from my own humble theatrical level, I understood that playing in public after so long had ignited the deep and intense flame of genius that had burned all those years ago in Russia.

And now, at last, we faced each other with the acknowledgement – the admission – of who he really was. I had not dared speak of it during the days that had followed our conversation in The Genesius. He had not spoken of it, either, and I had been afraid to risk shattering the still-fragile understanding that was forming between us. I had known, as well, that once we began to talk, there would be too many questions I would ask, and that he might not have the answers to all of them – even that he might not want to give those answers. I had no idea whether I would dare to ask him about the tsar's murder – whether he really had been implicated in it – or about Antoinette and who she was, or about who my mother might have been.

And so I had let him leave Kilcarne each morning, and return late each afternoon, and I had known – of course I had known! – that he was painstakingly rehearsing those two iconic pieces of music with The Genesius's orchestra, that he was doing so as Feofil Markov, because even after so long he dared not let his real identity be known. But knowing, too, that all the time he was forcing his extraordinary talent into life again.

I cannot say, even in these private pages, how long it was since I had realized the truth. Perhaps at some unacknowledged level I had known it from that first meeting.

We sat together in the firelit room, and neither of us spoke until, at last, he said, 'Is there brandy in that decanter? Thank you.' I heard that even though those lights still burned, his voice was thready, exhausted.

I poured the brandy and one for myself, and sat down opposite him. My first question might have been anything.

What I said, of course, was, 'Why didn't you tell me who you were at the start?'

'I needed to get to know you,' he said. 'I needed to be sure you would not reject me. Also,' said the man whose musical gift had mesmerized thousands, 'I like to make the dramatic gesture. Tonight I did so.' He drank the brandy gratefully, and a little colour came back into his face.

'Why didn't you come to England until now? Why didn't you get in touch with me before this?'

He took a few moments to answer, as if he was choosing the words, or as if this was something he needed to get right.

'For a very long time I couldn't risk being recognized,' he said, at last. 'For my sake but also for yours. The Romanovs never forgot what was done to Alexander – they never stopped hunting his killers. If they had realized I had escaped the gallows . . . As for travelling – the passport system at that time was complex. Even when Feofil Markov's identity was established, I couldn't draw official attention to myself. Feofil didn't exist, you see. There was no record of him anywhere. It wasn't until after 1917, when the Romanovs were all dead, and the system for travelling was made easier, that it was finally safe to come to England to find you. The tragedies and the injuries the Revolution inflicted were over. History had been made, and I believed I was safe – and that you were safe, too. But the cost had been a high one.'

'You said injuries . . .'

It was not quite a question, but he said, 'There was so much fighting – rioting – I was recording it all for several newspapers, and it was impossible to avoid some of the violence.' That gesture came again, not quite touching his eyes. 'Much later – when I had recovered – when it was known my sight was safe – I came to realize it was increasingly unlikely that I would be recognized. There were photographs of me, of course, from concerts and performances, but photographs were not as widely circulated then as they've since become. As Feofil, no photos were ever taken. And even if anyone had seen a resemblance between the two and wondered, Roman was not known to have had a disfigurement.' That brief gesture to his eyes again. 'In any case,' he said, 'everyone believed

Roman to be dead.' He smiled, then said suddenly, 'Did you recognise me?'

'Yes, but I'm not sure when I did so. Or if it was even visual recognition. I had only really seen you once, remember.'

'At the Mikhailovsky Theatre when you were four.'

'Yes.' Before he could say anything else, I said, 'How did you get out of the burning cage?'

He smiled. 'I was never in it.'

'But Antoinette's letter – the letter you gave me. You said . . .' I hesitated, then said, 'You told me Roman gave it to you in the condemned cell. Before he died.'

'I was in the condemned cell for a time,' said my father. 'And Roman did die that day in St Petersburg. Feofil Markov took his place. Just as Maxim died for you on that day. I hoped that one day I should be able to give you that letter. That one day it would be safe to have the truth between us.'

'And that wild march along the Catherine Canal? Did that happen?'

'It did,' he said. 'But when I wrote those articles about it, I exaggerated it. It made better reading. Also, I wanted to impress a lady,' he said.

'Antoinette?'

'Yes.'

'I wondered—' I stopped, then said with determination, 'I wondered once or twice if Antoinette might be my mother.'

'No, she was not.'

'I didn't really think she was,' I said. 'It was just an occasional, romantic daydream I sometimes had.'

'Your mother was a very dear and charming lady who died when you were born. I do not forget her, though.'

Then he put out a hand and took mine. In a voice I had never heard him use, a voice that thrummed with emotion, he said, 'Oh, Maxim, I'm so glad I found you.'

He smiled at me, then he leaned back and closed his eyes. The glass slipped from his hands, and shattered on the hearth.

At first I did not realize. I thought that the exhaustion and the emotion of the evening had taken over. But then – it's difficult to describe this – suddenly I did know. Perhaps an instinct comes into force – perhaps there's something deep in the mind that recognizes the difference between a living body that is only asleep, and one that has fallen into the final sleep of all.

The shattered glass lay in splinters on the floor, and my heart felt as if it, too, had smashed and was lying in splinters . . . That is a melodramatic, even pretentious sentence, but I shall let it stand. I don't care how melodramatic or pretentious – or even hysterical – it looks. Because Roman Volf was dead. I had found him – or had he found me? – only to lose him so soon afterwards.

I knew there was no point in calling for help. This time, my father had gone, irrevocably and for always. I sat in the chair, looking at him. He was perfectly tranquil, and I was deeply grateful for that. His life had been turbulent – I did not know the extent of that turbulence, and probably I never would know it – but when it came to the end, he had made his exit as swiftly and smoothly as if he had simply stepped out of the lights.

But he had left behind a wealth of unanswered questions. This, of course, was typical of him. As I write this, with dawn creeping across the skies of Kilcarne and the candles guttered in their holders, I still have no idea what happened that day in St Petersburg. If he really was inside that fortress – inside the condemned cell – I have no idea how he got out, and became the journalist, Feofil Markov. And I still have no idea who Antoinette was.

There are traditions attached to death, and there is certainly a tradition – somewhat Victorian in flavour – attached to the reading of a will. The grieving and greedy relatives grouped around a table, the desiccated figure of the solicitor, pince-nez in place, mumbling legal phrases in which no one has any interest because everyone wants to know how much money there is, and who inherits it.

The reality, for me, was that I walked along to the small, pleasantly untidy, office of Kilcarne's only solicitor, was given a cup of morning coffee, and told that there were two simple provisions of my father's will.

'There is a bequest to The Genesius Theatre,' said the

solicitors. 'With a request, not a stipulation, that you continue to act in a management capacity.'

'I hope that can be possible,' I said.

'The other bequest,' said the solicitor, 'is to you.'

'Tromloy?' I said, hardly daring to hope.

'Yes. Mr Markov has left it to you for your lifetime – a new lease will be created. If you wish to buy the place outright, the monetary bequest he has also left you will be sufficient for you to do so. If you do not wish that, after your death the house is to be sold and the proceeds are to go to The Genesius Theatre.'

The strange thing is that there is no sense of emptiness in Tromloy. It is, as it always has been, a place of welcome. Today I walked round the rooms, and I thought: I can live here on my own. I can continue the work at The Genesius – I think they will agree to that – and I can create my memoirs. I have all the notes I have made over the years, and I even have my box of old posters and programmes and photographs. There is a small package of papers that were Roman's, as well. I have not looked at those yet. They might contain everything about him – the answers to all the mysteries surrounding his life – or they might contain nothing at all. Either way, I think it will be a long time before I can face knowing.

I do not think I shall buy Tromloy. When you have had so very little for most of your life – when there have been times when you have not known whether you will be able to eat tomorrow, or whether you can afford the rent of your room for another week – well, you value money in the bank very much. So I shall leave that money in the bank, and I shall ensure that after I die the house will be sold, and, as my father wished, the proceeds will go to The Genesius.

I shall live and work here, and one day – please God a very long way ahead – I shall die here, and I shall ensure that I am buried in the old, peaceful cemetery with the friendly trees. And I shall also ensure beforehand that my grave bears my real name – the name Roman wanted me to finally acknowledge.

I will acknowledge it. I will be buried as Maxim Volf.

NINETEEN

Jessica had not been able to eat any supper when she got home from visiting Bea Drury. All through the meal she kept her eyes on her plate, not daring to look at Donal, not wanting to look into the eyes of the creature who had done that to her – that painful, ugly, *intimate* thing – and who had collapsed sobbing on the floor afterwards. And then had made those threats.

Never tell, Jessica . . . Because all kinds of unpleasant things can happen to foolish girls who talk too much . . .

What of the tramp? Donal had run after him with that vicious fury in his face. Had Donal caught him – had he pushed him into the oncoming car, or into the burst of flame? But, when Jessica tried to pin down that part of the memory, all she could see was the sheet of roaring flame and the outline of someone – the tramp? Donal himself? – silhouetted in front of it. Grania O'Brien had said it was thought the tramp had returned – that he was living at the Sexton's House, his face scarred by burns. Was it the same man? If so, might Donal go after him again?

Several times during supper, Donal brought Jessica into the conversation – teasing her gently for being such a quiet little mouse, asking was anything wrong, and wanting to know about her sketching and painting. Each time he did this Jess managed to mumble a reply.

'Oona Dunleary at the shop was saying she saw you out sketching yesterday, Jess,' said Morna. 'She said it looked as if you were walking out to – to Mrs Drury's house.' Jess felt her heart skip a beat and she saw Donal look up sharply.

'That's rather a lonely part of Kilcarne,' said Donal. 'I wouldn't have thought there was much out there to sketch.'

Tormod, who had been eating his supper in a mumbly kind of way, said that was the part of Kilcarne where the old manor house had once stood.

'Kilcarne Mainéar,' he said. 'A godless family it was who

lived there. Worshippers of Mammon, such greed. It was fitting that the line should die and the place fall into ruin.'

The aunts exchanged glances, because if Tormod got started about Mammon and the sinful cities of the plain, there would be no stopping him.

But Donal intervened, asking Jess where she had been going. Jess found herself looking up at him without wanting to, almost as if a string in her mind had been pulled.

She said, vaguely, 'I was just exploring different bits of Kilcarne for a sketch.' Donal continued to look at her, and Jess began to feel a bit panicky, because it was there again, that look, cold and cruel, just as it had been that long-ago day in Tromloy. He knows, she thought. He knows I went out to Tromloy yesterday, and he thinks I might have remembered what happened two years ago.

But Donal did not say any more, and somehow Jess got through the rest of the meal and the hours that followed. There was a television programme, and a crossword Aunt Nuala was trying to complete, then it was just about late enough for Jessica to go to bed without causing comment. She put a chair across her bedroom door, but although no one disturbed her, she did not sleep very much. Every time she closed her eyes she saw Donal in the firelit room at Tromloy, and she felt his greedy clutching hands and the hard insistent thrusting of his body.

Next morning, Donal insisted on cooking scrambled eggs for breakfast, making the aunts sit down so he could wait on them, and telling them he was famous for his scrambled eggs in the parish – he always prepared a large panful when they had one of their breakfast prayer meetings. His parishioners said no one could cook scrambled eggs like Father Donal Cullen.

'And this morning,' he said, having spooned the eggs on to everyone's plates, 'straight after breakfast Jessica and I are going into Galway City. Remember, Jess, we said we'd do that today? I've been looking forward to it.' His eyes – the cruel hard eyes of the real Donal – flickered over her. 'We'll go to the cathedral, and we might have some lunch. You wouldn't mind if we didn't get back until later, would you?' he said to the aunts.

The aunts would not mind in the least. They were delighted to think of their beloved Donal taking Jessica out for the day.

'We won't look for you until late afternoon,' said Aunt Nuala.

Jess was appalled. She went up to her room and sat on the bed, and tried to think how she could get out of going to Galway. Even if she could slip out of the house unnoticed, she had no idea where she would go. The thought of Bea Drury and Tromloy flickered on her mind, but she hardly knew Bea, and she could not turn up on the doorstep and ask to be hidden because she thought her cousin was going to do something dreadful to her. Bea would think she was mad.

No one will be surprised if you turn out a bit mad, Donal had said. *Like mother, like daughter . . .*

Aunt Morna rapped cheerfully on the bedroom door and called out that Donal was ready, and not to keep him waiting. And since there did not seem to be anything else to do, Jessica put on a coat and scarf and went out to the car.

As she got in, Donal said, 'You've remembered, haven't you?'

'Remembered what?'

'Don't pretend. You were silent as the grave last night, but every time you looked at me . . . And then the aunts said the Dunleary female had seen you going out to Tromloy. What were you doing there?'

He had started the car's engine, but he did not put it into gear. Jess did not dare tell him about meeting Bea Drury, so she said, 'Somebody mentioned the place, and I was curious.'

'And you saw it, and it woke the memory,' said Donal. 'That house. That bloody house and all its secrets. Did you go in there? Because that woman – Beatrice Drury – is back, isn't she?'

'No. I don't know.'

'You such a liar, Jessica. I can see you've remembered. But do you also remember that you promised never to tell anyone what we did that day. Did you keep that promise?'

The cold anger was strongly in his voice, and Jess shivered. 'I haven't told anyone anything,' she said.

'Haven't you? Perhaps I'd better make sure you don't,' said Donal, in a dreadful gentle voice. 'Perhaps I'd better remind you of the things that can happen to silly little girls who talk about things best left secret. Oh, Jessica, you really shouldn't have gone to Tromloy.'

Jess turned her head away and pretended to be looking out of the car window. 'I told you, someone mentioned it,' she said. 'I was interested. That's all.'

'You recognized it, didn't you?' He snatched her hand and his fingers closed tightly around it, dragging at the scarred flesh. Jessica cried out with the pain. 'Tell me the truth,' said Donal, and his fingernails dug into the vulnerable scars even deeper. Tiny pinpoints of blood stood out.

'Yes. Yes, I did remember,' said Jess on a sob. 'I went inside Tromloy and Beatrice Drury was there and she was very nice to me, and I remembered what you did to me.' Donal's hand relaxed its hold, and Jess was so grateful for this, she said, 'But I don't know everything. I still don't understand—'

'What?' He sounded distant, as if he was working something out.

'I don't understand what stopped me remembering it,' said Jess, almost to herself. 'It was two years ago. What you did and then the car crash—' She broke off, and turned to look at him. 'Why did I forget those two things so – so completely?' She stared at him, and as he did not speak, she said in a whisper, 'There's something else, isn't there? Something I still don't know – something I still need to remember. It's about my hands – it's about what happened to my hands.'

Donal reached for her hands, gently this time, turning them over, as if examining the scars. Jessica pulled her hands away from him abruptly. 'Did you do that to my hands?'

'Don't you know? Don't you really know?'

'No.'

Donal put the car into gear and drove away from the house. The aunts were at the window, waving and smiling, and he put up his hand to wave back. As he turned on to the road, he said, very softly, 'You talked to Beatrice Drury, didn't you? You told her.'

'No . . . Donal, I didn't tell anyone!'

'I don't believe you.'

He drove through Kilcarne's little main street, beyond

O'Brien's and Dunleary's shop and on to the wider road beyond that led to the main Galway road. But Donal was indicating a turn right, and alarm signals started to beat against Jess's mind all over again.

'Where are we going? Donal – we don't turn off here—'

'Oh, but we do,' said Donal. 'We aren't going to Galway, Jess. We never were. We're going to Tromloy.'

Phin had intended to set off at ten o'clock for the Sexton's House. He was, however, slightly delayed by a new voicemail message from the rugby-playing neighbour, who appeared to have phoned him around one a.m. to the background of a rousing chorus of 'My God, How the Money Rolls In'. Phin was deeply relieved he had remembered to switch off his phone when he went to bed.

He listened to the sound of the neighbour shouting exasperatedly to the singers to 'bloody shut up, I'm trying to make a phone call', then the neighbour's voice came back on with a robust account of how the redecoration to Phin's flat was getting on.

'They're making a really good job of it, and the paint matches up so well you'd never know the difference. Well, not much, anyway. Hardly at all. And it's as well the carpet people couldn't supply the new carpet until Thursday, because of the painter falling off his ladder. He wasn't hurt, but it was a bit unfortunate that he tipped over the tub of paint in the process, well, it was more than a bit unfortunate, because then he had to walk across the floor to get his phone to call for help, which meant a trail of painty footprints all along your hall. But there's no need to worry, because I've told the carpet people to bring an extra section to replace it. All on the insurance, dear boy. We'll have a couple of drinks together when you get back; in fact the chaps thought we'd better have another party since the last one got a bit spoiled by the beer disaster. But we'll wait until you're back for that, so we can cheer you up. Enjoy the rest of your holiday.'

Phin did not know whether to laugh or throw the phone across the room. In the end, he sent a fairly temperate message back, saying the planned party should on no account be delayed until after his, Phin's, return; that he was snowed under with work and would probably be too busy to attend any parties of any kind for several months, and that in any case he might be in Ireland for a while yet. They should, he said firmly, go ahead and hold the party without him. He then sent an email to the estate agents who managed the flat, asking if they might have on their books any other, similar properties, but with good solid walls, and – if at all possible – restrictive clauses in the lease regarding music, parties, home-made beer, and the loud performing of bawdy songs at unsociable hours.

After this he set off for the Sexton's House. He had no idea whether Maxim would come with him to The Genesius, nor did he have any idea if it had been a good idea to suggest it. He would like to have Maxim's company, but he would not push it.

But Maxim opened the door as soon as Phin drove up the track, and he was wearing a long dark coat with a deep collar. Phin guessed he would turn up the collar as soon as they were among people. He got into the car with a cursory nod, and he was outwardly perfectly composed, but Phin could feel the apprehension in him. With the idea of dispelling this a bit, he told him about the flat and the exploding home made beer.

Maxim seemed to enjoy the story. He smiled, and said, 'God, that reminds me of—'

'Yes?' Phin glanced across at him, and saw that he was frowning.

'I don't know. Another of those infuriating half-glimpses of a memory. It's gone now. But if it involved a party and home-brewed beer that went wrong, it'd probably have been something studenty.'

'We've all been there,' said Phin, grinning, and let the subject drop.

They reached the centre of Galway shortly after eleven, and Phin identified a large car park and managed to find a space.

'Is this the nearest we can get?'

'I don't know.' Maxim looked out of the window. 'I've never driven here – at least, not as far as I know. I don't know if I can even drive. But I think this is reasonably close to the theatre. If you go through that walkway over there – between those two buildings – then bear left, I think you'll see it ahead of you.'

Phin turned to look at him. 'Are you coming in there with me?' he said.

'I'm not sure. Why d'you want me to?'

'Lots of reasons. For moral support. Because two pairs of eyes are better than one. Because I might not recognize the place, even if it rears up in the middle of the road and gibbers at me. Because if there's anything to be found about the real Maxim Volf, you might want to know it. Because—'

'You've made your point,' said Maxim, dryly, but Phin saw him look around the car park. He's checking how many people are around, he thought. Then Maxim turned up the deep collar of his coat, hunched his shoulders and shrugged. 'All right. But a brief visit.'

'Probably it'll be closed at this time of day and we won't be able to get in.'

But they did get in. The main doors stood half open, and there was a large A-frame sign advertising an exhibition of The Genesius's past. 'Its history, its emergence from the ruins, and its successes,' said the sign. 'A pictorial journey into bygone eras.'

'Now that,' said Phin, 'could be very helpful indeed. We'll take the pictorial journey, shall we? Is that all right?'

'Phin, for God's sake stop asking me if things are all right! If I don't want to go in, I won't. But let's try, and if I want to beat it out of the nearest exit, I'll meet you back at the car.'

'Fair enough.'

Beneath the sign about the exhibition, in modest and almost apologetic typeface, was a small and courteous placard. 'We do not make any charge for entrance to the exhibition, but hope that visitors may feel able to leave a donation.' On a small shelf was a large box with slots for coins and notes.

'Very trusting of them,' said Phin, fishing for his wallet. 'Anyone could dash in here, scoop up that box and be off down the road before they were spotted.'

'It's chained to the wall,' said Maxim.

'Oh, yes, so it is. I hadn't noticed that, but then I have this beautiful trusting nature.'

'And I have a cynic's outlook. In fact—' Maxim stopped, and looked about him, and Phin saw that the pupils of his eyes had contracted to pinpoints.

'What?'

Maxim said, 'I have a feeling I'm recognizing this place. Or am I? No, I think it's just that I've walked past it. And theatres have such strong atmospheres, don't they? Let's look at the exhibition and the bygone era.'

The exhibition was in the auditorium, and as they walked towards the display boards and the printed legends about the theatre's past, Maxim said, 'Tell me again what we're hoping to find.'

'Photos of Maxim – the other Maxim, I mean. And Mortimer Quince, of course. Roman's son. Hell's teeth,' said Phin, forcefully, 'they were both part of that inaugural concert – their names were on that poster I found, advertising its Grand Opening. So if one or both of them aren't somewhere in this display, there's no justice in the world.'

'But if they were behind the scenes I mean, won't it just be the actual performers in the photos?'

'I hope not. But I'm not leaving this stone unturned,' said Phin,

It was very quiet in the theatre. Phin supposed it was rather early for most people to be wandering around, and The Genesius was a bit off the tourist/visitor track as well. He glanced back at Maxim, hoping he had not been too forceful with him. But Maxim was walking slowly along the displays, clearly interested, occasionally pausing to examine something more closely. He's all right as long as there aren't people around who might stare at him, thought Phin. Or pity him, of course – yes, that's what he hates the most. I'd love it if one of us were suddenly to shout, 'I've found something,' but it's starting to look a bit unlikely. Damn, this seemed like such a good lead.

And then it did happen. Maxim, who had been studying one of the smaller displays, said, 'Phin. Come and look at this.'

'What?' His voice is completely controlled, thought Phin. So it can't be anything very much that he's found.

Maxim indicated the board. There were four photographs, all black and white, and two slightly fuzzy. Above them was a printed note, saying that they were shots taken during rehearsals for The Genesius's opening night in November 1921, and immediately after the performance.

The largest photo was of a small orchestra, most of them in shirtsleeves, with a man who was clearly their leader standing on a podium. Next to it was a group of singers, with someone talking to them. Even though it was grainy and badly focused, it was possible to see the eagerness of the man's demeanour.

'He's so keen on what he's doing, isn't he?' said Maxim, echoing Phin's thoughts.

'Yes.' Phin peered more closely at the photo. 'It's Mortimer Quince,' he said, suddenly.

'Are you sure? I don't remember the photo at Tromloy very clearly, so—'

'It is him,' said Phin. 'Slightly older than the man on the postcards I found, but it's the same man all right.'

The third photo was another anonymous group – the people might have been anyone, but the fourth—

'Dear God,' said Phin, staring at the single figure in evening dress, standing as if he had deliberately arranged it so, in a spotlight. A violin was held loosely in the man's hands, and he had turned his head, as if slightly impatient with the photographer.

This photograph was labelled. The small printed note said, 'Taken immediately after the performance, and showing the Russian journalist, Feofil Markov, who took part in the 1921 concert at very short notice, and received a standing ovation.'

'Feofil Markov,' said Maxim. 'That's who you thought had translated Antoinette's letters.'

'I still think he did. But that isn't Feofil,' said Phin.

'Who is it?'

In a voice he hardly recognized as belonging to him, Phin said, 'It's Roman Volf.'

'Good God. Are you sure?'

'I've studied too many photographs of Roman in the last couple of weeks not to know him. He's a lot older, but it's unmistakably Roman,' said Phin. 'God alone knows what he was doing performing on a stage in an Irish theatre – under an assumed name – when the world believed him to have been hanged in Russia forty years earlier.'

Maxim said, 'Look at that.'

'What? Where?' And then Phin saw that along the bottom edge of the display board was a note that said, 'Photographic stills reproduced by kind permission of the Irish Film Society, affiliated to the Irish Film Institute and Irish Film Archive, Dublin. Taken from the cine film of the concert on the night of 23 November 1921.'

'Which means . . .' said Maxim, and then stopped.

'Which means,' said Phin slowly, 'if that reel of film is still in existence, that somewhere on a dusty shelf is a can of film containing a live recording of what was probably Roman Volf's final performance.' He sat down on a low window ledge, still staring at the photograph. 'I can't take this in. I wanted to find proof that Roman was innocent. I didn't expect to find that he escaped execution and ended up here. And that there might be old film footage of him performing.'

'What do we do now?'

'What I think we do,' said Phin, reaching for his phone, 'is furtively photograph that shot – keep watch, will you, because I'm probably about to infringe half a dozen copyright laws.'

There was a brief interval, then Phin pocketed his phone. 'Good,' he said. 'Let's get out before someone comes boiling out of a security office and confiscates the phone.'

As they came out of The Genesius and headed for the car park, Maxim said, 'What next?'

'Next, I need to see if the lady at Tromloy—'

'Beatrice Drury.'

'Yes. I need to see the photo of Mortimer Quince that you found. I need to ask her where it came from and whether she has any more.' As he unlocked the car, he said, 'I can easily drop you off at your house on the way back.' He paused. 'Unless you feel you could come with me.'

'To Tromloy?'

'Yes.'

Maxim got into the car. As he reached for the seat belt, he said, 'All right.'

'All right, what?'

'All right, I'll come with you to Tromloy.'

Phin stared at him. 'Now you really have surprised me,' he said.

'I really have surprised myself. Let's do it before I succumb to stage fright and change my mind.'

TWENTY

Since she had found Maxim Volf's name on The Genesius programme, Bea had been trying to make up her mind to go to the theatre to see if she could find out any more about him.

It was ridiculous to feel so apprehensive about this. There was probably nothing to find, but in order to be sure you were facing a cul-de-sac, you had to go into it. She ate breakfast, checked emails on the slightly erratic internet connection, then worked for a while on the half-completed illustration for the teen fantasy book.

Perhaps she could time the journey to have lunch in Galway. There used to be a nice pub near The Genesius itself – she and Niall had sometimes had a late supper there after seeing a show. She put the illustration away, and went upstairs to get a coat before she could change her mind. She would not let the memories stop her from tracking down Mortimer Quince and Maxim Volf.

It was not quite raining, but there was a thin, light mist everywhere. Bea stood at the bedroom window for a moment, enjoying the way the mist gave everything a layered appearance, like the pop-ups in a child's book. The mist transformed Tromloy's gardens into an eerie enchanted tanglewood, and she wondered how massive a task it would be to have the land tidied up. It would spoil Tromloy's charm to have any kind of formal landscaping or patio-laying, but it might be a good idea to have the thrusting rosebay willow cut back, and the trees pruned. Then she remembered the parlous state of her bank balance, and thought Tromloy could be left to its wildwood for a bit longer.

But she would take some photos of the garden looking like this, because it might make a good base for an illustration, or even a full-blown painting sometime. She went downstairs to hunt out the camera, left her coat and bag on the kitchen table

ready to leave, and ran back up to the bedroom before the
marvellous mistiness vanished.

She was just squaring up the camera and trying to remember
how the zoom operated when there was a movement on the
edge of the scrubland, in between the old trees. Was someone
out there? Bea clicked the camera anyway, the automatic flash
activating itself in the dull morning light, and took several
more angles. Then she leaned closer to the window, because
there really was something moving out there. Was it a cat, or
even a fox prowling through the long grass in search of prey?
No, too large. She waited for a few more moments, and just
as she was thinking she really would set off for The Genesius,
the movement came again, and this time there could be no
doubt. It was not an animal – it was a person, in fact it was
two people. A youngish-looking man, rather thin, with dark
brown hair. With him was a figure Bea recognized. Jessica
Cullen.

For a moment she thought they were coming up to the house
– that perhaps Jessica had brought the cousin she had mentioned
to meet Bea, which would be a friendly, normal thing to do.
But almost immediately it was clear that the two figures were
not approaching the house; they were walking through the
trees. Bea, slightly puzzled, began to have the impression that
there was something wrong about them. Was the man half
pulling Jessica along? Forcing her? Surely that could not be
happening. Or could it?

She had no idea whether she should go out and challenge
them. Tromloy's boundaries, like everything else about it, were
a bit vague. They had never been delineated or fenced or
walled, because it had never mattered. It might well be that
Jessica and the man were walking on the common land beyond
Tromloy's lawful precincts. He might be helping her over a
bit of uneven ground. As Bea watched, the figures vanished
from sight. Where? But the ground out there dipped unevenly,
and they had probably stepped into one of those dips. Or
should she walk out there anywhere, and appear to meet them
by chance? Just in case . . . It was at this point that the man
appeared again, but this time without Jessica. His coat collar
was turned up and his shoulders were hunched, and it was

impossible to avoid thinking this was the classic furtive, I-don't-want-to-be-seen demeanour.

Bea was still holding the camera, and almost as a reflex action, she flipped it back to *zoom* and focused it on the figure, because if there really was something wrong about this, she would at least have a record of the man. The flash fired once, then twice, glinting on the window both times, and it must have caught the man's attention, because he turned sharply to look across at the house. Bea clicked the camera again, and this time he looked about him, then began to half run towards the house.

Bea stepped back from the window at once. She was not exactly frightened, but she was starting to feel uneasy. She reminded herself that she was in her own house and that she had a perfect right to photograph anything she wanted. She had been doing just that, in fact, wanting to capture the lovely mistiness of the day so she could paint it. Yes, but whoever this was — Jessica's cousin, Donal? — he had seemed to be taking Jessica somewhere she did not want to go, and now he was on his own and there was no sign of Jessica. Bea dropped the camera on the bed, and ran down the stairs to make sure the front door and also the little garden door were locked. It was all right. The garden door that led off the kitchen was not only locked, it was bolted, top and bottom, and it had only the tiniest pane of glass at the top. The faulty window catch that Maxim Volf had used to get in had been repaired. And the front door was locked. If the man knocked on the door, Bea did not have to open it. If necessary she could call out to ask what he wanted. But probably he had gone away by now. She went back upstairs to look out of the bedroom window again. There was no sign of him, or of Jessica. The chances were that she had misunderstood or misjudged the situation.

Then, from downstairs, from the front of the house, came a sound that made her freeze with terror. It was a sound she had not heard for two years, but it was unmistakable. The sound of a key turning in the lock. And of the door opening, and footsteps coming along the hall.

Once beyond Kilcarne's main street and beyond sight of the houses, Donal had pulled the car off the road, far enough into

the trees for it not to be seen. The track to Tromloy was only
a few yards beyond them, and, before Jess could scramble out
of the car, he had already got out of the driver's seat and come
around to the passenger side. His hands, pulling her out of
the car, were strong and hard – the hands she remembered.

He said, 'If you scream, I'll say you've succumbed to one
of your mad fits and I'm trying to get you home.' His face
swam closer. 'I mean it, Jessica.'

'I'd tell people the truth,' said Jessica, sobbing angrily, and
fighting to get away.

'And given the choice, who would people believe?' said
Donal, pushing her on to a very narrow footpath, so overgrown
with thrusting bushes and trees it was barely visible. 'Would
they believe a girl who's been strange for at least two years
– they all say that about you, you know – or would they believe
an honest, hardworking parish priest? The girl's cousin who's
trying to help her and is so distressed by her condition. And
don't look at me like a frightened rabbit, because I'm not
going to kill you.'

'What then?'

'I'm just going to show you what might happen if you ever
break that promise you made not to tell.'

'I won't,' cried Jessica. 'Truly, I won't.'

'Let's make assurance doubly sure though, shall we?'

He took her along the footpath. Brambles and low branches
whipped into her face, but Donal pushed them back impatiently. It was like a dream where things started out normal
and pleasant, but gradually slid down into something very
frightening indeed.

They must be quite near to Tromloy – Jess glimpsed it several
times through the overgrown bushes and tried desperately to
see if Bea Drury was there, or if her car was. If she could get
free of Donal she could run to the house, and she would not
care if Bea thought she was mad; she would beg to be taken
into the house, to be safe.

Once she thought Donal hesitated, as if unsure where he
was, and Jess managed to say, 'Where are we going?'

'We're almost there. It's not far, in fact if the plans are
accurate—'

'What plans? Donal, please let me go. I promise I'll never say anything.'

He did not seem to hear the last part of this. He said, 'The plans of the old Kilcarne Mainéar. The ones Father Sullivan has. You really can be unbelievably stupid at times, can't you? Don't you know anything about the place where you live? I've seen those plans, and they show the layout of the manor and all the small buildings around it. In the finest detail. The buildings have all gone now, of course – well, except for Tromloy – but once upon a time—' He broke off, and gave a small, satisfied nod. 'I thought so,' he said. 'It's here, exactly where the plans said. Exactly where I thought it would be. And this is where you're going, Jessica.'

Jess stared in horror at the small trapdoor set deep into the ground. There was a ring handle, and although the wood was almost rotten, beneath it was something black and hard – something that looked as if would never rot away.

Donal did not let go of her hand, but he kicked at the weeds that had grown across the trapdoor.

'It was part of the scullery wing of the manor,' he said. 'It's the old ice pit – where the cook would store blocks of ice, wrapped in straw, for the cold desserts at their grand parties. There's a metal lining under the actual trap, to keep the place cold.' He turned to look at her. 'And for the next few hours it's going to be your prison.'

As Jessica stared at him, sick with fear and panic, he said, 'I'll come back for you, of course. At least – I'll come back for you this time. But if there has to be a second time, then I won't. And make no mistake about this, Jessica, this is a place where no one will ever find you.'

'Wait,' said Jessica. 'Someone does know about that day. When you raped me. I did tell, after all.'

'Who?' Then, as she hesitated, frantically searching her mind for a name Donal would believe, he said, 'It's Beatrice Drury, isn't it? You told her while you were there?'

'Yes,' said Jess, desperately. 'Yes, I did tell her. So you see, if you throw me into that place – if I'm missing – she'll guess it might be your fault. She'll tell the Garda, and they'll arrest you – at least, they'll question you. And they'll search everywhere for me.'

He stared at her for a moment, and Jess held his look. Inside, she was thinking, I'm sorry to be telling this lie, Bea, but it can't matter, and if Donal thinks you know, he won't dare do anything to me.

But Donal said, very softly, 'You bitch. I knew it. As soon as I heard you were at Tromloy, I was afraid you'd told her.' He kicked against the ring handle with his foot, to lift it from its embedded position. It did not move, and Jessica felt a lurch of hope that Donal's plan was not going to work. But he kicked it again, much harder, and this time, with a dreadful creaking sound, as if old, cracked bones were trying to move, the ring handle came free. Donal reached down with his left hand and pulled at the trapdoor. It resisted, but then it came up, clanging back on to the ground. Ancient, sour breath gusted out, and Jessica flinched, but Donal seized her from behind, pinioning her arms to her sides, and forcing her towards the yawning blackness. Jessica struggled and kicked out, but he was holding her too tightly. She drew in breath to scream properly, but Donal was already clamping one hand over her mouth. As he forced her to the edge of the ice pit, Jessica sobbed and fought for all she was worth, not really believing he meant any of this. He could not possibly mean to put her in that black underground cavern; he would just be giving her a warning to keep quiet, in the way that small burn on her hand in Tromloy had been a warning two years ago.

But Donal did mean it. He pushed her on to the black rim, then gave her a vicious push, sending her tumbling forward. The mist-shrouded morning whirled around Jessica and she struggled in panic to keep her balance, but the push had been too strong. With a sickening jolting feeling, she fell into the yawning blackness.

She hit solid ground almost at once, the impact knocking the breath out of her. Cold dankness, foul smelling and thick, was all around her, but there was still a square of light overhead, from the open trapdoor. Jessica struggled to her feet, and saw the pit was not in fact so very deep after all. If she stood on tiptoe she might just about reach the edge and grasp it to pull herself out. Out to where Donal would be waiting for her, to throw her back down? She hesitated, and his head and shoulders appeared in the opening above her.

'Three hours,' he said. 'That'll be long enough for the aunts to believe we've been into Galway and had lunch. I'll be back for you then, and we'll go home as if nothing's happened. But until I do come back, think about what it would be like if you were down there for ever. I can make sure Beatrice Drury doesn't squeal, and that's what I'm going to do now, while you're down there. But after that, if ever you tell anyone else what I did to you that day, by God, Jess, I'll shut you down there again, and that time I won't come back to let you out. I mean it.'

The wizened creak of the old hinges came again, and the trapdoor crashed down. The light shut off and Jessica was in the worst and densest darkness she had ever known.

Three hours, he had said. How far could that be trusted? Was there any other way she could get out? But the blackness was so absolute it was like a wall in front of her eyes – it was like being blind. Even so, she tried again to reach up to the trapdoor. If she could just feel the outline of it, she might manage to dislodge it. Her fingers brushed against hard-packed earth and roots – horrid! – then there was the feeling of the black steel sheet that lined the underside of the pit's lid. But even by stretching up as high as she could, she could make no impression on the trapdoor, because it was designed to lift outwards, not to drop down. After what felt like an hour, but was probably only a few minutes, Jess gave up, and sat down in a frightened huddle, wrapping her arms around her bent knees in an effort to keep warm.

Three hours. All right, somehow she would get through those hours. She would not think about what might be all around her – or about what creatures might slither or scuttle in a place like this. Probably it was too cold for most of them anyway. Her eyes were starting to ache from staring into the blackness. Once she thought that coloured lights, like the shredded strings of a rainbow, were floating past her, and she made a grabbing movement to try to trap them. Stupid. There was nothing there.

Three hours. She would do what she always did when she was frightened or unhappy – she would pull around her the poetry and the stories. All the poetry she had ever learned at school, paragraphs from favourite books. She would see in her mind her bookshelves in her bedroom at home, and look along them, as if she could pull one of the books out.

Bookshelves . . . Abigail Drury's bedroom had bookshelves. Jessica could remember them from when Bea Drury had taken her there. She could remember, as well, that she had recognized the books – not just as titles she had read somewhere, but as the actual book she had read, right down to a splodge of paint on the cover of one, right down to the inscriptions in some of them.

Jessica pushed away the horrid darkness and the thought of three hours still to be got through – although probably it was only about two now – and concentrated on Abigail's books. There had been a volume of Shakespeare's speeches and sonnets, and inside it was written: 'To Abigail, with the promise that one day we'll ride together in Mab's empty hazel-nut chariot, and that we'll pluck the wings from painted butterflies to fan the moonbeams . . . From Dad, with love.' She could see the writing quite clearly in her mind.

Next to the sonnets was a book of Irish poetry – W. B. Yeats. She remembered that one particularly, because they had been studying Yeats's work at school. Inside, in the same writing, it said, 'One day we will go to the Lake Isle of Innisfree – and you'll see for yourself that midnight's all a-glimmer, that noon's a purple glow, and that the evening is full of the linnet's wings . . . All my love, always, Abi, darling . . . Dad.'

Jessica could even remember how she had felt sad to think of those two people being dead. It helped in the cold, dark ice pit to think about the unknown Abigail, whose father had known about Queen Mab's hazel-nut chariot, and the purple glow over Innisfree and who had wanted his daughter to see those magical things for herself.

She had been chanting the Queen Mab speech to herself the day she met Bea Drury.

'Her chariot is an empty hazel-nut
'Made by the joiner squirrel or old grub,

'Time out of mind the fairies' coachmakers.'

Time out of mind . . . Her mind felt as if it was slipping out of time now. That was only the darkness, though, and being so frightened. Or was it? *Think* Jessica. Don't notice the darkness, think about Abigail Drury and her bedroom. When did you read her books? It must have been after that day in Tromloy with Donal. What had happened after that day?

And then, from out of nowhere, came a single piece of knowledge, startling in its clarity and stunning in its certainty.

Soon after that day with Donal she had started to be ill.

She had started to be sick.

The sickness had become a regular occurrence; it had happened almost every morning, and it meant Jessica missed school on quite a number of days. Delayed shock, said the aunts, as Jess retched miserably over the lavatory each morning. And not to be wondered at. Aunt Nuala, her kind face creased with worry, said, a bit too quickly, that people were often sick after a shock, it was well known. They sent a note to the nuns at Jess's school, explaining about her seeing the dreadful car crash. Jessica would make up any work she missed, they said, and the nuns, distressed to think of one of their girls witnessing such a dreadful event, were sympathetic. They sent notes on the lessons Jess had missed, and Jess worked on these at home.

The aunts were starting to watch her by then. They had either written or phoned Donal, who had apparently been reassuring, and said they were to leave Jessica to recover in her own good time and God's.

'And he's sent some herbal tea for you, Jess,' said Aunt Nuala. 'One of his parishioners makes it. You just pour hot water on to it, and it's very soothing.'

The herbal tea tasted horrible, but Jess drank it obediently. Easter came and went, and she stopped being sick. But other things were happening. Skirt bands started to be tight. Her breasts, which had been small and light, felt swollen and tender.

Aunt Morna drove into Galway to buy new, larger-sized skirts. She wanted Jess to go with her, but Jessica would not. Both the aunts suggested timidly that she went along to see the doctor, just for a general check-up – they would come with her. Jess said she was quite all right and she did not need to see a doctor. When they tried to insist, she cried and shut herself in her room.

After that, they left her alone, until the day near the end of May when they confronted her with considerable awkwardness and embarrassment. Faced with direct questions, Jessica gave in, and finally admitted that the monthly bleeding which, for her, had begun a year and a half earlier, had not happened for the past four months.

The memories, once started, unrolled with increasing speed, cascading around Jessica as she sat huddled and shivering in the cold, bad-smelling ice pit of the vanished Kilcarne Manor.

TWENTY-ONE

J ess had known, of course, long before the aunts began to suspect, that she was probably going to have a baby as a result of what Donal had done to her. But every morning she woke up hoping that this would be the day when she would discover she had been wrong – that the monthly bleeding, usually a bit of a nuisance, at times vaguely uncomfortable, would appear. But the days and then the weeks slid by and it did not, and panic swept regularly over Jess in sickening waves.

She had no idea what to do. People in Kilcarne did not get pregnant without being married, or at the very least being engaged, and they certainly did not get pregnant when they were only thirteen. She was terrified of anyone knowing, even a doctor, because it might mean the truth would come out. *No one would believe you*, Donal had said. *They might even shut you away.* And then had come that meaningful look at the fire burning in the hearth, and the hard insistent hands pushing her too close to the heat. And the words about how unpleasant things could happen.

Jessica tried to push the memory away. She tried to think herself into a world where Donal's threats could not reach her. When she could reach that world – and it became easier after the first few attempts – she could walk through forests and meadows and draw and paint everything she saw. It was a world where hands did not force her on to a sofa, or where someone did not sob uncontrollably and pray for forgiveness on his knees while she was bleeding on to her handkerchief.

Once or twice she was aware of a feeling of disappointment, because presumably that was the being-in-love act that people raved over and that songs were written about. But all it had seemed to be was the pain of having a thick hard stick thrust into you and jabbing into your body over and over.

*   *   *

'Yes, there was a man,' said Jessica, eventually forced into admitting this to the aunts, trying to give them a story that would be believable and that would not be dangerous. 'He was near Tromloy. And he forced me to—' She shivered, and huddled back in the chair.

Morna and Nuala looked at each other in horror, but Jessica saw that they had already half guessed the truth.

'He raped you.' Aunt Morna whispered the word, but it still lay on the air like a bruise.

'Yes, but I don't know who he was,' said Jessica, in a hard, desperate voice, because it was vital they did not find out the truth. *Never tell, Jessica . . . Because all kinds of unpleasant things can happen to foolish girls who talk too much . . .*

'It was like being in a nightmare,' said Jess. 'It was a blur of . . . of pain and being terrified. Then afterwards I ran away, and I fell down the track because it was all iced over, and then there was the car crash. But I can't remember anything else.'

'And now,' said Aunt Nuala, her face white, her eyes wide with horror, 'and now you're having a baby. You are, aren't you?'

'Yes. No. I don't know. I wish I was dead. Leave me alone.'

She ran up to her bedroom and slammed the door, throwing herself on the bed and sobbing. But later, she heard the aunts talking, trying to think what to do. It was almost inevitable that they should light on the tramp, and blame him.

'Donal saw him,' said Nuala. 'He was out there at Tromloy that day. Donal told us, remember. That'll be who did that to her, the black-hearted villain.'

'He'd attacked her before Donal got there,' agreed Morna. 'Capable of anything in God's world or the devil's, that's what he told Donal. That's the next best thing to a confession in my mind.'

Jessica hated letting them think it had been the tramp, but she was afraid that if she said it was not, they would go on asking questions. Then Donal would get involved, and he would think Jess had talked after all. Also, people were saying the tramp had left the district, and no one had ever known his name, so it could not really hurt him if the aunts blamed him.

The aunts wanted her to see the doctor, and they wanted to report the attack to the Garda, or talk to Father Sullivan. Jessica refused, and started crying again. This time she cried so hard she made herself sick, which sent them into a new panic.

'Jess, you must see the doctor, you really must.'

'I won't. If you try to make me I'll run away. I mean it.' She had no idea where she would run to, but she did mean it.

They were dreadfully upset at this. Aunt Nuala said all over again that Jessica was so like her mother, their dear, dead Catriona, and they could not bear to think of losing her as they had lost Catriona. Aunt Morna said they would find a way of dealing with things, and Jess must trust them. Jess had no idea if she could trust them or not. She had no idea how it could be dealt with, and she did not think Aunt Morna had, either.

Uncle Tormod had to know. Jess had to be there when they told him – she did not know if this was because there might be questions to be answered, or whether they were frightened to face Tormod on their own. When she refused and shut herself in her bedroom, Aunt Nuala cried and begged her to come with them, so in the end Jess gave in.

She sat in a miserable huddle while Morna and Nuala explained as well as they could what had happened – at least, what they believed had happened – and what it seemed was going to happen now.

Tormod listened, his lips thinning, his face hardening into a dreadful stony mask. The aunts talked too much from sheer nervousness; Nuala, embarrassed and stumbling over her words, said apologetically that they were not entirely sure of all the facts, and Morna instantly supported this, saying Mother had never explained the exact mechanics of pregnancy to them. Mother, said Morna, would have been shocked to her toes to think of young girls being told before marriage about the prac-ticalities of pregnancy and how it came about. Why, said Morna, it was questionable whether Mother had even understood those details herself. Shockingly old-fashioned all of it, of course, and when people said Kilcarne had never really moved out of the mid-twentieth century, they were probably right.

When they finally stammered themselves into silence, Tormod leaned forward, and his face was no longer a stone mask, it was flooded with ugly, angry crimson. Red flecks showed in his eyes, and Jessica thought it was as if something had flung a lump of blood in his face, and some of the specks of the blood had clung to his eyes.

In a terrible hissing, hating voice, Tormod said, 'Like mother, like daughter.'

The aunts flinched as if he had struck them. Catriona was hardly ever mentioned, but on the rare occasion when the aunts said anything about her, they always told how it had been the worst day of their lives when Catriona ran away. 'But then,' Nuala always said, 'we had you, Jess. Catriona was lost for ever – dead in childbirth – but the doctors told us she had wanted us to have you – her dying wish – and you made it better for us.'

Tormod was gripping the arms of his chair with clenched hands, and he was not looking at Jessica. It was as if he could no longer bear to see her.

'She must go,' he said, directly to Morna and Nuala. 'I won't have her in the house.'

'Go? Go where? Tormod, you can't—'

'You'll arrange something. But I won't have the results of a fornication in the house.' His eyes were wild and his lips were working as if he might be whispering prayers to himself. 'As for any child – a child of sin and shame, an abomination before the Lord – I can't have it in my house.'

'Tormod, Jessica was attacked – the poor girl was violated—'

'We want to ask the doctor for help—' began Nuala.

'You are not to consult any doctor,' said Tormod, speaking with such cold fury that Nuala flinched. The flesh seemed to have fallen back from his face, throwing into prominence the jutting nose. He was hunched forward, his bony shoulders making him resemble a massive bird of prey as he sat in the wing-chair and glared hatred at them. Almost to himself, he said, 'It's Catriona's evil all over again,' and then he slumped back in his chair.

It was not until later that evening that Morna said, 'We'll ask Donal to help us.'

*   *   *

Nothing Jess could do or say would change their minds. They insisted that Donal must know anyway – dear goodness, did Jessica think a thing like this could be hidden from him? Of course he must be told, and no call for embarrassment or being ashamed, because Donal would have encountered this problem in his parish, and he would tell them what to do. Jess saw that the habit of asking Donal what to do had become so ingrained in them, that even the thought of telling him was making them feel better.

She was helpless. Morna telephoned Donal that night, and he arrived in Kilcarne two days later.

It was the false, deceitful Donal who came, of course, and who sat with Jessica and the aunts, listening as the aunts stumblingly and awkwardly explained what had happened.

He made shocked sounds of sympathy. When Aunt Nuala dissolved into tears, he gave her a clean handkerchief, and when Aunt Morna wanted to string up the man responsible and leave him to die slowly, Donal said this was an understandable reaction, but they must be charitable and try to forgive.

Only once did he look directly at Jessica through all this and, meeting his eyes, Jessica shivered and cowered back in her chair, so that Nuala was instantly concerned, asking did she feel sick, or had she a pain anywhere?

'I'm all right. Don't fuss. I don't want to be here, that's all. I don't want to be anywhere.'

'I wondered about one of those places where unmarried girls are taken in and the babies sent for adoption,' said Morna, tentatively. 'Hostels. The nuns might know of somewhere.'

'But if we talk to the nuns it would get back to Tormod,' said Nuala. 'You know it would.'

'I've heard bad reports of some of those places,' said Donal. 'They can be quite severe.' He made a rueful gesture. 'Even these days, they can be very spartan. We want somewhere nearby, so we can look after Jess ourselves. Keep an eye on her.'

'But without Tormod knowing where she is.'

It seemed to Jess that the aunts exchanged worried looks at this. Then Morna said, 'But we should be putting Jessica first. We should, Jess, it's no use crying all over again. You should be having tests. Scans and things to make sure you're all right. Well, and to make sure the – um – the child's all right. Only at the moment I can't see how we can manage that without it getting out. Getting back to Tormod.'

Again the look passed between them.

Donal said, lightly, 'Oh, I shouldn't worry about scans and tests. Not for the time being. Very overrated, so I'm told in my parish.'

The aunts accepted this at once. Donal would know about these things – his work would have brought him into contact with many young mothers.

'But, Jess, you'll have to be away from school for quite a time,' said Donal. 'Have any of you thought how to cope with that?'

The aunts had. They thought they could tell the nuns that Jessica was visiting relatives for a long stay, and that she would be going to school there for the rest of the current term, and perhaps part of the next.

'We can let it be thought she hasn't really recovered from witnessing the car crash,' explained Nuala, eagerly. 'We think they'll accept that. Oh dear, though, it's a terrible thing that we'll be lying to the sisters and Mother Superior.'

'But we're protecting Jessica,' said Donal. 'And we're avoiding Tormod becoming agitated and risking a second stroke.' He looked at Morna and Nuala very intently for a moment. 'That's right, isn't it?' he said.

'Oh, yes.'

'Then what we need,' said Donal, 'is a safe place for the next four months or so. It is four, isn't it? It was January when it happened?'

He said this as if he had to search his memory for the exact date, but his eyes flickered to Jessica, as if sharing the memory.

'Yes, January.'

'A place of sanctuary,' said Donal, sitting back in his chair and looking at them. 'That's what we want.'

Sanctuary . . .

As soon as he said that word, *sanctuary*, Jessica knew what he was thinking. She saw that the aunts knew it, as well.

Because there was a house, here in Kilcarne, a house set apart
from all the others at the end of a remote lane, but easily
reachable, barely five minutes' drive, no more than ten or
fifteen minutes' walk from their own house. A house that
would be empty for a long, long time, because its owner had
suffered a terrible and double tragedy. Mrs Drury had returned
to England and was not thought likely to come back to Tromloy
– to the house people said she and her husband had spoken
of as serene.

'Tromloy,' said Nuala, in a whisper. 'Oh, but we couldn't
put Jess there.'

'Certainly not.'

'And even if we could get in,' said Nuala, 'supposing we
were seen? Because that poor woman, Mrs Drury, won't have
left the house to itself without having someone to look in from
time to time. It could burn down – gypsies could get in.'

'Or tramps,' said Morna, in an acid tone. 'But I don't know
that it's a question that would arise. Mrs Drury always telephoned Dunleary's shop before coming over – to order in
groceries and milk, and to have the electricity switched on at
the house. And isn't Oona Dunleary the biggest gossip in
Kilcarne, so if Mrs Drury were to be returning, everyone for
miles around would know about it inside five minutes.'

'That's true. And we'd have enough time to get Jess away.'

'And,' said Morna, 'Oona told me she's been asked to keep
an eye on the house – not going inside or even having a key,
but just walking or driving out there on a regular basis, to
make sure the roof hasn't fallen in, or the place burned to a
crisp.'

'For a fee, I daresay,' said Nuala, rather caustically.

'Oh, none of the Dunlearys ever do anything unless they're
paid. But what she's doing, she's driving up to Tromloy every
week, when she visits her sister in Connemara. Wednesday
afternoons, when Dunleary's is closed.'

'So Jessica would need to lie low on Wednesdays,' said
Donal. 'There'd have to be no signs of activity within the
house. But that should be easy enough.'

'It's not the right thing to do,' said Morna. 'It's wrong,
however you look at it.'

'And even if we agreed, how would we get inside Tromloy?' said Nuala.

They looked at Donal with the trustful air of children. He smiled at them, and Jess hated him all over again.

'Getting inside will be easy,' he said. 'Just before he died, Niall Drury gave me a key.'

The aunts looked at one another.

'We'll think about it,' said Morna, firmly. 'We won't make any decision yet, but we'll think about it.'

Jessica hated the possibility of returning to Tromloy and living there on her own for so long. She was frightened Donal would come out there and she was afraid of what he might do to her. Perhaps the aunts would think of another solution, though.

It was difficult to sleep that night, knowing Donal was just a few steps along the landing, and that he could creep into her bedroom without her hearing him. She lay awake for a long time, listening to the small sounds of the house, and the occasional scratching of a bird in the eaves. When she did slide down into an uneasy sleep, she could feel Donal's hands on her body again, pushing beneath her skirt, insistent and hurting. She could hear him gasping and sobbing as he slumped against the sofa afterwards, praying for forgiveness.

Father forgive me for what I cannot help . . . No, that was not right, the words were, 'Father forgive them for they know not what they do.'

I am sorry and beg pardon for all my sins, I detest them above all things . . .

Jessica half woke, gasping and hitting out at the dreadful hands, then came up out of sleep properly, sitting bolt upright in the bed, her heart pounding, clutching the sheets around her. It had been a bad dream, that was all. The sobbing had vanished with the dream, so it was quite all right—

It was not all right, though. There was someone in the bedroom – someone was standing close to her bed, half leaning over her . . . Watching her and reaching out with thin mutton-bone fingers . . . No, of course there was not anyone, it was only a shadow cast by her dressing gown hanging behind the door. She leaned back on the pillows, the sheets still pulled round her. The shadow moved, and Jessica gasped, because he was here, in her bedroom – Donal was here. His eyes were glinting in the darkness, and his hands were gripping the bedrail. His shoulders were hunched over, and just for a moment he resembled a crouching bird of prey. Tormod had looked exactly like that earlier on—

Tormod.

It was not Donal who was in her room. It was Tormod. And he was sobbing and gabbling the Act of Contrition, even as his thin hands were reaching for her. Jess began to scream.

'It's the stroke turned his brain,' said Morna, after Donal had come running in and helped them get Tormod back to bed. 'It made him start sleep-walking,' she said. 'There's no need to be frightened, Jess.'

'It's very common after a stroke, sleep-walking,' said Morna, firmly.

'I never heard that.' Donal had poured himself a glass of brandy, and he was sitting in the kitchen with them. Jess pulled her dressing gown more tightly around her.

'Oh, yes, they told us about it at the time,' said Nuala, quickly. 'Night terrors, they said.'

'It seems to me that it's Jessica who's having those,' said Donal, with unusual sharpness, and Jessica was aware of a faint stir of gratitude to him.

'So there's no need to be frightened, Jess. Not of Tormod.'

But Jessica knew the aunts were just as frightened of Tormod as she was. She finished her milk and said she was all right now, and she would go back to bed. She thought she would drag a chair across her door, so that if Uncle Tormod came back he would fall over it and wake everybody up.

'We'll be nearby if you want us,' said Morna.

'And I'm just at the end of the landing,' said Donal. He put down his brandy. 'I'll go up now. I'll look in on Tormod to make sure he's all right.'

'And you go up as well, Jess, dear. Take the milk with you.'

Jess nodded, and made a slow way out of the room.

*   *   *

'He'll do it again,' said Donal the next morning. 'You do know he'll probably do it again.'

'He doesn't know he's doing it.'

'That's not the point. It makes it even more vital to get Jessica away from him. And,' said Donal, 'to make sure we keep this whole thing very quiet indeed.'

'Do we need to tell anyone about Tormod?' said Nuala, her eyes filling with tears. 'He's a sick man, Donal.'

Donal hesitated, and Jessica saw that he was thinking that to have enquiries made into the family – even medical enquiries – could blow the whole thing about the child wide open. When he spoke, she knew she had been right.

'I think it was a single incident,' he said. 'Finding out what had happened to Jessica disturbed him very deeply, you know. If we can just get Jessica out of his way, he'll settle down. Then, afterwards, we'll think what to do.'

They went out to Tromloy later that same day, choosing the early afternoon when Tormod would be having his nap, and when no one was likely to be around. They took Jessica with them – Jess supposed they were afraid to leave her on her own with Tormod. She was afraid of being on her own with him, anyway.

'We won't take the car,' said Donal, 'because it might be noticed. If anyone sees us it'll just look like an afternoon stroll.'

'If we're ever found out—' began Nuala, then stopped.

'We won't be found out.'

'I'm hating it, though,' said Nuala. 'We're lying and pretending, and it's wrong.'

'Not to mention all the laws we'll be breaking.'

'It's on my conscience, dears,' said Donal, and there, again, was the faint echo of memory.

It'll be my sin, Jessica, my sin not yours, and I'll do penance for it . . . I'll take it on my soul . . .

And last night, in a darkened bedroom, Tormod had whispered the ritual words of penance. *I am sorry and beg pardon for all my sins . . .*

'I'm hating it as well,' said Donal, in answer to Nuala. 'It's only for a short while, though. And I told you that afterwards we'll decide what to do on a long-term basis.'

For Jess, the journey to Tromloy had a dreamlike quality. Here was the chunk of stone with the house's name engraved on it, and here was the sharp curve that brought the house so suddenly into view. As they went towards it, Donal produced the key.

The door swung open easily and smoothly, and although it should have felt wrong to be going into somebody else's house without it being known, it did not. Jess had the curious feeling that the girl she had seen die in the car crash – Abigail, her name had been – did not mind her being here.

She had been afraid she would relive that dreadful day when she had fought against Donal before the deep old fireplace, but she did not. Walking cautiously around the rooms, she thought she would not in the least mind being on her own here for large parts of each day. She could dream and read and draw. She would be away from Tormod. How about Donal? Might he come out here to visit her?

But the aunts were already working out the plan. They would call into Dunleary's at least every other day, because if Mrs Drury was coming to Kilcarne, Oona Dunleary would be telling everyone. They could not have the electricity switched on at Tromloy, of course, but it was the summer, so very little heating would be needed. If it did happen to turn cold they might risk lighting a fire in the hearth. A kettle could be boiled across it, in fact – there was an old trivet in the woodshed at home which could be brought along. They would try to get a battery-operated radio for Jessica as well.

Food and milk could be brought here every day, and they would buy large thermos flasks. Good, nourishing stews could be made and put into a flask. Jessica, listening to them telling each other – telling Donal – how one of them would be coming out here every day, began to feel a bit safer. Donal would not try to do anything to her with Morna or Nuala likely to turn up any minute.

In one of the bedrooms – the girl's bedroom almost certainly – there was a photograph of Abigail Drury. Morna and Nuala examined it with interest and sadness. Such a lovely, unusual-looking girl, with that chestnut hair, and those bright, intelligent eyes, they said. Morna thought they should offer up a special intention for Abigail at Mass on Sunday. And for her father who had died with her, of course.

There was a rocking chair in the room, and a deep padded window-seat with soft cushions. The shelves had books and sketching things. Nuala said it was easy to imagine that poor child curled up here, reading or sketching, listening to her music on the stereo player by the window.

'It's a wide mixture of books,' said Morna, inspecting the shelves. 'Even some poetry. You don't get many girls of that age reading poetry.'

Jessica, installed in Tromloy, sometimes wondered if she had fallen into a dream – not necessarily her own dream. She slept in Abigail Drury's bed and tried not to feel like Goldilocks in the three bears' cottage. The bed was very comfortable, and from the pillow she could look straight at an old photograph of a man standing on a stage. She liked the photo, and she would like to have met that man. Sometimes she thought up little conversations between them – pretending he was her grandfather or her great-grandfather. The books on Abigail's shelves had marvellous stories and poems in them. Several had inscriptions written inside.

In the bedroom was an old fire screen with photographs and old papers and newspaper cuttings pasted on to it. The faces in the photos were interesting – Jess liked looking at them and thinking who the people might have been. On the second night she moved the screen to beneath the theatre photo, so she could look at all the people together.

It was Donal who asked about the birth itself. How would that be dealt with?

'We've thought of that,' said Aunt Nuala, eagerly. 'We'll hope we don't have to call an ambulance, and once it – um – starts to happen, Morna will drive Jess as fast as ever possible to University Hospital in Galway. I'll go with them, of course.'

'I've practised the drive twice,' said Morna. 'So I know about one-way streets and the car park at the Emergency Wing and the like. It won't take us long to get you there, Jess, and it's big and anonymous – far enough away from Kilcarne for no one to find out. You'll be an emergency case, so they won't waste time asking questions. Not at first, anyway.'

'And afterwards we'll ask them to arrange an adoption,' said Nuala, eagerly. 'They'll tell us how we do that, won't they? They'll know about forms and legalities and things. But until then—'

'Certainly, they will. But I might be able to help there,' said Donal, and he sent Jess a look that made her feel as if a shard of ice had been skewered into her spine.

'Jess has a mobile phone, which we'll keep charged,' said Nuala, 'so she can call us in a crisis. But we'll be calling in every day, of course.'

'And phoning every night.'

Donal said, 'Tormod hasn't asked where she is, has he?'

'Not once. He sits mumbling to himself each evening,' said Nuala. 'Sometimes he shivers and shudders.'

'It's my opinion he exaggerates it all to get attention,' said Aunt Morna. 'One day I shall tell him so.'

But Jessica knew Aunt Morna would not do any such thing. She knew both the aunts were too frightened of Tormod.

Crouched in the darkness of the ice pit, Jessica could remember how clearly she had seen the aunts' fear of Tormod.

How much time had passed since Donal had imprisoned her down here? Would it be anywhere near the three hours he had said, yet? Could she even trust him on that?

Once she would have thought that she could trust him. But then once she would not have thought that Donal was capable of committing murder . . .

TWENTY-TWO

It was a dull storm-laden evening when the birth happened. The aunts had said there was plenty of time; they had counted up weeks and days since – well, since the day of the attack, said Aunt Nuala. There would be plenty of warning.

But there was not.

Aunt Morna had just gone home, leaving Jess with some of Nuala's lamb stew – a bit heavy perhaps for an August night, she said, but nourishing and substantial, and Jess must be sure to eat every morsel. There was one of Donal's herb drinks, as well. He had arrived for a short stay that morning. If Jess felt up to seeing him, they might bring him along tomorrow.

Jess had eaten the lamb stew, which was very good, but afterwards had felt it lying like a lump of lead on her stomach. Or was it the baby, indignant at being overwhelmed by all that meat and gravy and vegetables? Lately, she had been thinking of it as a real person, a tiny boy or girl. What would it look like? Would she be allowed to give it a name before the hospital took it away for adoption, which was what the aunts said was going to happen. Best thing for everyone, they said. Don't cry, Jess, dear, you'll get over it in time. You have all your life ahead of you.

But would her life still have Donal in it, and those whispered threats? Would it have Tormod, who had crept into her room while she was asleep, and stood at the foot of her bed, his eyes hooded, his hands curved round the bedrail like claws? When Jess tried to think how many years there might be until she could leave Kilcarne and go to the GMIT, sick despair closed around her. Four years at least. She was not sure she could get through four years. Would she even be able to go to GMIT then?

The feeling in her stomach was starting to be a bit more than discomfort, and Jess got up to walk about, hoping to ease it. She would go up to the bedroom and lie on the bed, where she could see the photograph of the actor and the people in the old fire screen.

She was halfway up the stairs when pain – dreadful, spiking, red-hot agony – sliced through her. She doubled over, gasping, the room spinning around her in a sick blurred whirl as warm fluid, streaked with dark blood, gushed down her thighs.

She did not remember phoning the aunts, but she must have managed to do so, because after what felt like a lifetime of agony, they were there, running anxiously up the stairs, calling that it was all right, Jess, they were here, she would soon be at the hospital.

But downstairs were men's voice as well, and through the pulsating waves of pain, Jessica was aware of a different panic.

'Who's that—?'

'It's your Uncle Tormod and Donal. Donal was coming with us anyway, and we couldn't keep it from Tormod. He insisted on coming. But they'll both stay downstairs.'

The pain swept in again then, and Jessica no longer cared who was in the house.

The aunts wrapped a blanket around her, trying to rework their original plan, because they had not allowed for this kind of emergency, certainly not so soon. Jess swam in and out of consciousness, struggling weakly against the clenching pain. Time blurred and seemed unimportant, but at one point she was aware of the aunts saying they must get her to the infirmary.

'Donal will carry her downstairs and out to the car,' said Morna.

Being in Donal's arms again – smelling his skin – feeling his body . . .

'No,' said Jessica on a gasp of pain. 'Not Donal—'

But they did not seem to hear. Nuala was saying that, once they were on the road, she would phone ahead. 'That way they'll be ready for her.'

As they started to help Jess off the bed, calling to Donal please to come up, heavy, slow footsteps came up the stairs. Jess gasped and shrank back, fighting off the aunts' anxious hands.

'Tormod – he's coming up here . . . I don't want him . . . I don't want either of them—'

But Tormod was already there, standing in the doorway, staring at her. His shoulders were hunched and his mouth worked. Behind him was Donal.

Aunt Morna said, firmly, 'Tormod, would you go back downstairs while Donal carries Jessica to the car.'

'You will not take her to any infirmary,' said Tormod. He did not move from the doorway.

'Perhaps you're right. Perhaps it's already too late for that.' That was Aunt Nuala, trying to make the best of things.

'Emergency ambulance,' said Aunt Morna, reaching for the phone. 'We didn't want to do that, but there's no alternative now. While we're waiting for it to arrive, Nuala, you light that fire, for the child's shivering fit to break apart.'

As Nuala knelt to put a match to the fire, Morna reached for the phone, but Tormod took two paces into the room and knocked it from her hand. 'Will you let the whole of Kilcarne know what's going on?' he said, his voice thick with fury. 'Have Tromloy lit up like a blazing beacon, with sirens and wailing ambulances, bringing everyone up here inside of five minutes wanting to see what's happening. You will not phone anyone.'

'Tormod, please . . .' Aunt Nuala got up from the hearth, still clutching the poker she had been using to stir up the fire. 'You must let us get help.'

'Tormod's right,' said Donal, stepping into the room. 'We've kept the secret all these months – don't let it out now.'

'No! We must call the ambulance,' said Nuala, but as Morna tried to reach the phone lying on the floor, Tormod snatched the poker from Nuala's hands, and held it up. For a moment Jess thought he was going to hit her with it, and Aunt Nuala clearly thought so as well, because she flinched and put up her hands to shield her head.

Aunt Morna said, very briskly, 'We'll manage. The fire's burning up and we can boil water on it. I'll fetch towels from the airing cupboard – they can be burned afterwards. And isn't giving birth the most natural process in the world?'

A quick glance passed between the aunts, and Jessica saw

that Morna was going to try to get help from beyond Tromloy – perhaps to find Jessica's own phone, or even to drive or run to a phone box. But would Tormod let anyone leave the room? He was still there in the doorway, still holding the poker.

Then the pain tore through Jess again, impossibly and viciously strong, and she screamed and writhed, trying to escape it. One of the aunts – she no longer knew which was which – held her ankles, and then, as the pain threatened to rip her into two pieces, it felt as if something burst inside her, then fell out on the bed with a soft squelch. Jess gasped, but the pain was releasing its claws and there was only a cold, wet emptiness.

For a few moments she was aware of nothing except deep gratitude that the pain was rolling away, and she lay back, gasping, the sweat cooling on her face. But there was something wrong somewhere – something in the room that was very wrong indeed. What was it? Was there something that was not here but should be? She fought through the dizziness and weakness.

The child. The child should be crying. Didn't all babies cry when they were born?

She managed to half sit up in the bed – Aunt Nuala put a pillow behind her – and saw that Aunt Morna was holding something wrapped in a blood-smeared towel – something that was still and silent. Tears were streaming down Aunt Morna's face, which was dreadful, because Aunt Morna never cried. But she was sobbing helplessly, and saying, 'Nuala – oh, Jessica – this poor little thing – I can't bear this—'

Nuala was at her side; she gasped. 'Dear God.' Then she said, 'It couldn't possibly have survived – not like that—' She too was crying, but through it, Jessica heard her say a terrible word. 'Incomplete.'

The word spiked into Jessica's mind. Incomplete. The child – the poor, unwanted thing, made from that day of fear and pain – was incomplete.

The aunts looked at one another, and Jessica understood neither of them knew what to do. She started to ask them to let her see the child, but before she could get the words out, Tormod was at their side.

His face was contorted and twitching with rage, and he grabbed the towel-wrapped bundle from Aunt Morna.

'Tormod – no . . . We should—'

'It's as I said it would be,' shouted Tormod. The firelight fell across his face more strongly – or was it just the firelight? Wasn't it blood flooding into his face, turning it red, then crimson? 'Look, both of you. Look at it! The abomination before the Lord. Exactly as I said it would be! A child of sin and shame – unnatural.'

'It's dead,' said Nuala, very quietly. 'It must have been dead for a long time.'

'It can't ever have drawn a single breath, but Donal can baptise it and arrange a discreet funeral in his parish, can't you, Donal?'

'Hardly anyone would need to know,' said Morna, almost pleadingly.

But Donal did not speak.

The crimson in Tormod's face deepened, the thick colour bleeding into his eyes. In a voice that sounded as if he was speaking through flannel, he said, 'Nothing Christian . . . Won't allow any churchyard to be defiled . . .' Half to himself, he said, 'Catriona.'

The name blurred, and broke up like splintering bone, and Tormod frowned. His face was changing – it was as if it were made of wax and the wax was melting, running down, reshaping his face into a dreadful, distorted mask.

He made a clawing motion at the air, as if fighting something off, then his hand flopped down by his side, as if a string inside him had been cut. But he's still holding the baby with his other hand, thought Jessica, horrified.

Before the aunts could stop him, Tormod had stumbled to the hearth, lurching and falling as he went, so that Jessica thought he was going to fall straight on to the fire. There's something dreadfully wrong with him, she thought. But he's still got the child, and I must see it – I *must*— Incomplete . . .

'Donal, stop him,' cried Nuala. 'Donal, please—'

But still Donal did nothing. He stood aside so that Tormod could get to the fireplace. When Morna tried to reach Tormod, Donal grabbed her hand and pulled her back.

In a terrible smeared whisper, Tormod said again, 'Catriona.'
Then, with the hand that still had its use, he threw the dead
child straight on to the fire. As the flames roared upwards, he
fell to the ground.

As the fire burned up, there was a nightmare moment when a
small outline was silhouetted against the flames. Jessica cried
out, and fought her way from the bed, forcing back the weakness
and the sick dizziness. The pain was still dragging at her and
the bed was bloodied and smeared, but the pain was bearable
and she needed to reach the fire, because none of them seemed
to realize that what was burning in there might still be alive—

One of the aunts grabbed her arms to pull her back on to
the bed, and she thought Donal was there as well, but Jess
threw the hands off impatiently.

'Jess – dear child – it's dead – it really is . . . You can't do
anything —'

Then Donal's voice. 'Jessica, do as your aunts say! It's
dead! Leave it be! Let it go!'

Somewhere in the distance she thought someone – Morna?
– was sobbing into a phone, saying something about an ambulance being needed, but none of it mattered – all that mattered
was reaching what was burning in the grate.

The hearth had a row of small black bars jutting up from the
hearth – a miniature fireguard – and Jess reached for them, not
caring if they burned her hands, only wanting to reach the little,
lost thing that Tormod had called an abomination, that Donal
had let him fling into the flames without trying to stop him.

Incomplete, they had said. Dead for a long time. But she
must be sure of that, she *must* . . .

As her hands closed around the black bars, there was a
dreadful sizzling and the stench of burning, and somebody
started to scream. Pain tore through Jessica's hands, and
dizziness began to spin her away from the room.

The last thing she was aware of was Aunt Morna pulling the
fire screen across the hearth to hide what burned there. Then
she tumbled down into a world where there was no longer any
pain.

*   *   *

There was no pain in the dark, enclosed space of the old ice pit, but as the memories swirled around her, Jessica felt as if the pain she had endured two years ago was clawing at her again. With it was the fear and the panic, and that desperate compulsion to get to the child, just in case . . .

The aunts had said it was incomplete. That it was dead – that probably it had never drawn breath. But was that really true? thought Jessica in new agony.

Threaded through it all was the knowledge that Donal had done nothing to save the child. He had stood back as Tormod lunged forward, and he had allowed the child to be flung into the flames. He wanted it to happen, thought Jess. If Tormod had not done it, Donal would have done it, because he wanted there to be no trace, no evidence.

He had not committed a murder that night – nobody had committed a murder, because you could not murder a creature that had never lived, never drawn breath . . .

But he was capable of it. The slow, creeping suspicion that Donal was not going to come back to let her out of this place took a firmer hold of Jessica.

TWENTY-THREE

When Bea heard the sound of a key turning in the lock of Tromloy's door, and then the soft footsteps coming along the hall, panic had sliced through her. She forced herself to think. The only way out of the cottage was by the stairs, and anyone down there would hear and see her. Her phone, which might have summoned the Garda, was marooned in her bag on the kitchen table. The bedroom window was too small to get through, even if there had been a friendly tree she might have scrambled into like a wayward heroine in an old book. And there was a twenty-foot drop straight to the ground below.

All that was left was to hide. She stepped back into the narrow space by the window, into the small alcove created by the wardrobe and the window wall. She waited, listening, trying not to shiver, almost trying not to breathe.

Who had come into the house? Who had a key? Was it the man she had seen with Jessica Cullen? It must be. And there might be a perfectly innocent explanation for him having a key and coming in here, although Bea could not think what it could be, and she could not think why anyone, engaged on a harmless task, would not knock on the door first.

Whoever he was, if he came up here and looked into this room, he would not see her. Not from the door. Or would he? If he did, what would she do? She risked darting out of hiding to snatch up a paperweight lying on the dressing table. It was solid and heavy and, although it was a bit bizarre as a defence weapon, it would deal a hefty blow.

The floorboards below creaked. He was walking along the hall. There was the sound of the sitting-room door opening, and then the kitchen.

The memory of the man she thought of as Maxim Volf came strongly into her mind. But he had not got a key – he had said so. When he came into the house, he had done so through the

window with the faulty catch – the window she had had repaired
a couple of days earlier. And he had said he would not come into
Tromloy again. 'You have my promise,' he had said, before melting
into the darkness, and although it was completely irrational, Bea's
instinct was to trust him on that score.

This was surely the man she had seen with Jessica Cullen.
The man who had had that unmistakably furtive demeanour.
He had seen her take those photographs, and he had not liked
it – that had been clear from the way he turned to look at the
house. Bea took a firmer hold on the paperweight, which she
probably would not be able to bring herself to use, but felt
slightly braver for having it.

He was coming up the stairs. There went the loud creak of
the floorboard that had creaked ever since she and Niall bought
Tromloy. And now he was walking along the landing. Abi's
room was the first one he would come to – would he go in
there? But he did not. He was looking for her, and he knew
where she was, because he had seen her at the window. He
was coming straight to this room. Bea shrank against the wall,
her heart thudding so violently she was afraid it would give
away her hiding place.

Then the old floorboards just outside the bedroom creaked
again, and a soft voice said, 'Beatrice?'

Bea felt a deep shiver go through her entire body, because
this was every horror story, every macabre Gothic fright-tale
ever written. The intruder, entering the locked house, and softly
calling the beleaguered heroine's name. *Knowing* the name.

'Beatrice Drury,' said the voice. 'There's no point in hiding.
But there's no need to be afraid. I'm Jessica Cullen's cousin,
Father Donal.'

Bea did not move, but he came into the room, and a shadow
seemed to fall across the window. And then he was there in
front of her. He was younger than she had thought, and he
was wearing the conventional dark suit and white priest's
collar. It should have been reassuring to see that, but it was
not. It was the eyes. They were wrong – so very wrong, so
very much filled with sly calculation. No priest should look
like that. No human being should look like it.

Bea said, 'How did you get into my house?' and was grateful

to hear that her voice came out with an edge of annoyance. My house. How dare you come in here uninvited?

'I have a key,' he said. 'Your husband gave me a key about an hour before he died.'

'You knew Niall?'

'Slightly. He was returning to England that day, and I was going to look at the faulty window for him, to make sure the house was secure until someone could fix it.'

The faulty window catch Niall had never got round to having fixed. The window catch that Maxim Volf had used to get in. Oh, Niall, thought Bea. You've caused so much trouble.

She stood up a bit straighter, and said, firmly, 'Yes, I see. I'll have the key back, please. And then I'd like you to leave.' When he did not speak or move, she said, 'I met your cousin, Jessica, just briefly.'

'Briefly?' said Donal, softly. 'But wasn't she here with you all of yesterday afternoon? And didn't she talk to you about all kinds of things?'

'Yes, she was here, but—'

'She talked about me while she was here,' said Donal. 'She told me she did. So I was coming to see you. To explain that she's a confused, troubled little soul. To tell you she's given to making up wild stories, and that she'll probably have to be put somewhere safe and quiet and peaceful.' He took a step nearer. 'And that's what I would have told you, Beatrice, if it hadn't been for—'

'What?'

'If it hadn't been for the fact that not fifteen minutes ago you stood at that window and you watched me. You saw where I took Jessica, didn't you? You even took photographs.'

'I didn't see anything. I was photographing the mist over the trees and the mountains,' said Bea, forcing anger into her voice. 'I'm an illustrator – it was for my work. You – you and Jessica just happened to be there. I saw you both, but I thought you were taking a walk.'

'On your land? Didn't you think that a bit strange?'

Bea said, 'Not particularly. And if you want the photos I

took, you can have them. Take the camera and go. I didn't
see anything.'

'I'm very used to knowing when people lie,' he said. 'It's
part of my profession. You know what I did because Jessica
told you. And today you watched where I took her. That's all
too much knowledge, Beatrice, and I'm not risking my career
for you, or for that stupid creature, Jessica.'

'But I didn't see anything!' cried Bea. 'And Jessica didn't
tell me anything! I keep telling you that!'

'You do. It's a pity I don't believe you,' said Donal, and
stepped forward.

Phin parked the car on the track below Tromloy, switched off
the engine, and looked at his companion.

'D'you want to stay in the car while I go up to the house?
It's fine if you do.'

He had expected Maxim would remain in the car, but surprisingly he said, 'I'll come with you.' His voice was expressionless,
and Phin had no idea what he was thinking or feeling.

But he just said, 'Good. We can leave the car here. It doesn't
look as if it's blocking the path.'

'No.'

As they walked up to Tromloy, Maxim indicated a small
hatchback parked outside the house.

'Bea Drury's car,' he said. 'So it looks as if she's at home.'

'And there's a light on in that room,' said Phin.

'Sitting room.'

'Is it?'

'Yes.' As Phin glanced at him, he said, 'I told you I got
into the place. Several times.'

When they knocked on the door there was no response, and
although Phin tried twice more, no one came to open it.

'There's a kitchen door around the back,' said Maxim. 'We
could try that.'

'All right. She might be in the kitchen with the tap running
or something.'

'She might not actually be in at all. She might have walked
somewhere.'

'Let's try the back anyway.'

But the kitchen, when they peered through the window, was deserted.

'There's a jacket thrown over that chair and a handbag on the table,' said Maxim. 'As if she was about to go out.' He stepped back from the door and stared up at the window.

'What's wrong?'

Maxim came back to the door, and lifted a hand indicating a warning. 'She's up there,' he said. 'At the bedroom window. And there's someone with her.'

'Well, if she's in the bedroom with someone, we'd better go at once and hope we haven't interrupted—'

'It's not that,' said Maxim, impatiently. 'The man who's up there is . . . he's dragging her across the room.'

They looked at one another. Phin said, a bit uncertainly, 'People do go in for weird bedroom games—'

'Phin, the man who's dragging her across the room is the man who came out to the Sexton's House and tried to get in! He stared in through the window at me! And whoever he is, he's bloody dangerous – I saw his face just now,' said Maxim, and a different note had come into his voice. 'Whatever's happening up there isn't a game, Phin. I think she's in real danger.'

'All right. Do we call the police? Or try to get in?'

'Both.'

'Are you sure? I mean – we aren't misjudging the situation?'

'I'm very sure, and I'm the one who saw it, and I'm not misjudging anything,' said Maxim, curtly.

'I'll call the police – Garda,' said Phin, accepting this, and thrusting a hand into his pocket. 'Hell, I've left the phone in the car. If I sprint back to get it and call them, can you break a window and get in?'

'I could, but it'd take some time – that's a very small window,' said Maxim. 'He'd certainly hear. And if he panicked, God knows what he might do.'

'All right, you stay here, and I'll get to the car for the phone. I'll be as fast as I can.'

'There's no time. We need to do something now. We need to reach her – Beatrice—'

'If we could get into the house without alerting him,' said Phin, frowning. 'But there's no other way in that I can see—'

Maxim turned abruptly away from Phin, his shoulders bowed as if a massive weight had suddenly been dropped on them. He stood like that for several seconds, then put his hands up to his head, almost as if he was trying to hold it in place. In a soft voice he said, 'Oh, God. Oh dear God. I can't believe—' Then he straightened up and turned to look at Phin. 'There is another way in,' he said, and his whole demeanour had changed so completely that Phin could almost have believed a different person stood there.

But there was no time for questions; he said, 'Another way? Where? How?'

'Come with me.' Maxim was already half running across the uneven ground, and Phin went after him.

'Where are we going?'

'To the old ice pit,' said Maxim.

His voice is different as well, thought Phin. I don't know what's happening, but there'll be time enough later for explanations. 'Ice pit?'

'It was part of the old Kilcarne Manor. Used for storing ice blocks in summer – nineteenth century. Before that, even. It's shown on the old plans. The main entrance – where they used to carry down the ice – is in the grounds, just about here, I think.' He walked around impatiently stamping on the ground. 'But the thing is that the pit itself comes out inside Tromloy.' He looked at Phin, his eyes unreadable. 'Tromloy used to be the housekeeper's wing of the manor house.'

'How on earth—?'

'There should be a trapdoor sunk into the ground,' said Maxim. 'We have to find it fast, Phin. I must reach Beatrice, because . . . Hold on, I think it's here.'

He knelt down, and Phin saw the small square door, like the underside of a loft door. It was set flat into the ground and there was a ring handle.

'It must be it,' said Maxim. 'It's exactly where I—' He broke off, and said, 'Listen.'

'What?'

'*Listen.*'

Then Phin heard it as well. From beneath the ground,

someone was shouting for help. They both reached for the
handle of the trapdoor and began to haul it up.

Jessica heard the footsteps overhead, then the scrabbling
sounds, and at first she shrank back against the hard-packed
earth wall. The prospect of Donal's return was now very
frightening indeed, because now that she remembered everything that had happened, she no longer trusted him to let her
out of this place.

But there were two people up there – she could hear men's
voices, and surely Donal would not have brought someone
with him.

She drew in a deep breath, and shouted, 'Help,' as loudly
as she could, over and over again. 'Help me – get me out—
I'm shut in—'

The voices came again, then the trap's hinges creaked and
a thin thread of light showed around the edges. Jessica saw
for the first time that she had fallen further from the trap than
she had thought, because it was not directly overhead as she
had been visualizing it.

She called out again, and one of the voices said. 'It's all right.
We're getting to you.' It was a nice voice a voice you could trust.

The trap was dragged back, and the light poured in, painful,
almost blinding, after the long darkness. Jess put up a hand
to shield her eyes.

The first voice said, 'God Almighty, you poor child – how
on earth . . . Never mind, just hold on, we're coming down
and we'll get you out. Phin, put that lid all the way back, flat
to the ground.'

There was a dull thud as the trapdoor hit the ground outside,
and Jessica, still trying to adjust her eyes to the light, struggled to her feet.

The man who had called to Phin to fold the trap back,
dropped down next to her, and took her arm. He said, very
gently, 'You're all right. Quite safe with us. Are you hurt?'

'No.'

'Good girl. We haven't time to explain now, because there's
someone in danger up there in the house—'

'At Tromloy? Mrs Drury?' Jessica tried to take in what was happening.

'Yes, Mrs Drury. And there's a way into the house from down here, if only I could bloody find it . . . Phin, will you get down here and help!'

But the other man was already in the ice pit with them. 'Are you all right?' he said to Jess at once.

'I think so. Yes.'

'Good. I'm Phineas Fox, and the person prowling around in the dark corners is Maxim Volf.'

'Um, I'm Jessica Cullen.'

'We'll get you out in a minute, Jessica, but first we need to get through to the house. Maxim, have you found the way? Because this looks to me like a dead end.'

Maxim turned from the far corner. For the first time Jessica saw that his face was badly scarred – burned. But even with the scars, there was something about him that made you want to go on looking at him and listening to what he said.

What he said, in a voice of suppressed fury, was, 'It is a dead end. Oh God, Phin, I've got it wrong! There isn't a way into the house from here – probably there was once, but it's been blocked up! And Beatrice is trapped up there by that bloody man!'

'By my cousin? By Donal?' said Jessica.

'I've no idea who he is, but we need to get to her.'

'If it's Donal, you certainly do,' said Jess. 'It was Donal who put me in this place. If he's got Bea—'

'Phin, you go hell for leather to the car for the phone and call the Garda. I'll break a window and get in. If he goes for me, at least it'll take his attention from Bea.'

Jessica said, 'I could get the phone and call the Garda. That'd leave both of you to deal with Donal.'

'Could you? Are you sure you're all right?'

'Yes, of course,' she said impatiently. 'Give me the car keys. I'll be more help doing that, and I know the people so I can explain what's going on.'

Phin exchanged a quick glance with Maxim, and Jess saw that they were thinking she would be safer out of the action anyway. Phin said, 'Good girl. Here's the car key. Button press there to unlock it. The car's near the foot of the track – a red hatchback. All right?'

'Yes.'

'The phone's in the glove compartment. Can you get out of here on your own, or shall I go up and help you? Oh, wait, there's a couple of ledges just there – footholds, almost. If you use those you should be able to reach up and get out. I'll give you a hand.'

Jessica, grasping Phin's hand and climbing on to the footholds that somebody must have hewn out years ago, was able to reach up and grasp the edges of the open trapdoor very easily. Phin waited while she clambered through and on to the grassy land beyond.

'I'll run all the way to the car,' she said, kneeling down for a moment to look back at them.

'Make sure you keep out of sight of the windows. And when you've made the call don't come back up to the house,' said Phin. 'Keep running down to the road and meet the Garda there.'

'I will.'

It felt incredibly good to be out in the fresh air again, and to see the sky and the trees. Jess felt a bit peculiar and slightly light-headed, but there was no time to give in to this. Bea Drury was being threatened by Donal. It's because he thinks I told Bea what he did to me, thought Jessica, running towards the track, careful to keep out of sight of Tromloy. I'll feel dreadfully guilty about that later, but for the moment I'll concentrate on reaching the car and calling the Garda.

She ran a bit, slithering down the track, and saw with relief the small scarlet car, parked just off the track as Phineas Fox had said. The door locks blinked as she depressed the key, and Jess tumbled thankfully inside and reached for the phone. Not long, Beatrice, she thought. But Phin and Maxim will get to you in a very few minutes, anyway.

In the ice pit, Maxim had pulled himself out on to the ground above, and Phin was about to follow, when he stopped.

'Maxim – look back down here.'

'What? Where?'

'It's a door,' said Phin. 'It's half covered with earth and roots, but I'm sure—'

Maxim leapt back down. 'It is a door,' he said, as Phin pointed. 'It's got to lead up to Tromloy.'

'Can we get it open?'

Phin was feeling all round the door's edges for a handle or a lock, but Maxim said, 'Sod that. Stand clear.' He stepped back and aimed a fierce kick at the door's side. It protested, and clouds of earth billowed up.

'Maxim no – you'll never do it. It might be locked.'

'I don't care if it's guarded by the three-headed hound of Hades,' said Maxim, and he kicked the door a second time. There was a splintering of old wood, and a harsh grating sound of hinges snapping. The door swung slowly inwards, and stale, bad-smelling air gusted into their faces.

'All in the best Gothic tradition,' said Maxim. 'And now we go as softly and as stealthily as we can up into the house, and we grab that evil bastard before he knows what's happening.'

It was dark beyond the old door, but it was not as dark as the ice pit had been. Faint chinks of light came in from overhead, and after a cautious walk of perhaps fifty yards, they came to a flight of stone steps.

'They've got to come out somewhere in the house,' said Maxim, starting up them. 'But I don't know exactly where.'

'If they used ice for cooking,' said Phin, following him, 'then surely the tunnel – those steps – would come out in the kitchen?'

'There's a big larder in the kitchen,' said Maxim. 'And it's got one of those old-fashioned marble slabs for cold stuff. Oh, God, I wonder if it's a lid in itself, that slab.'

'Maxim,' said Phin, 'exactly how much do you know about Tromloy?'

'A very great deal,' said Maxim. 'Keep quiet now, will you, because we're at the top of the stairs.'

'Pray God we get up there before Donal Cullen tips over the edge.'

'I am praying,' said Maxim.

The minute Donal Cullen reached for her, Beatrice raised the paperweight above her head. Then she froze, because it was suddenly sickeningly easy to imagine how it would feel to bring the heavy marble crunching down on bones and nerves and flesh.

In that second of hesitation, Donal knocked the paperweight from her grasp, and snatched her wrists, holding them together tightly.

Beatrice fought and kicked out at him. 'Let me go! Get out before I call the Garda. I don't give a stuff what you've done. For all I care you can have broken all the commandments and committed every sin in the calendar!'

'I probably have,' he said. 'But we're beyond the point where I can trust you. So since you got on so well with my weird little cousin, I think it'd be a fine idea if I took you to spend some time with her now.' His grip on her hands tightened and he began to pull her out of the cramped alcove.

Bea fought him with every ounce of strength, but he had her hands in an iron grip, and he was starting to pull her across the room. It was useless to scream because there was no one to hear her, but she did scream.

At once Donal Cullen brought up one hand and hit her very hard across the face. The blow missed her eyes, but Bea felt the hard bruising pain across one cheekbone.

'There'll be more of that if you scream again,' he said.

'Let me go!' shouted Bea again, and with the words there was a sudden massive crash from somewhere downstairs, followed by the sound of footsteps – two pairs of footsteps – running hard up the stairs. From outside the house was the sound of wailing police sirens. It was all right. She was going to be safe. The knowledge gave her a sudden burst of extra strength, and she twisted out of Donal's hands, and pushed him back against the wall.

The bedroom door was flung open, banging against the wall, and two men were in the room. One was a complete stranger, but the other— Bea gave a gasp, partly of shock, partly of relief, and half fell against the wall, dizzy and trembling as Donal bounded towards the door. He was down the stairs before either of the two men could stop him, then the younger one – Bea had no idea who he was – went after him.

The other man looked at her. 'Are you all right?'

'Yes.'

'Good. Stay there. I'll be back.'

Then he was gone, running down the stairs after Donal Cullen.

TWENTY-FOUR

A t first Phin thought they had lost Cullen – he thought the man had melted into the trees and the mist-shrouded gardens behind Tromloy.

Then Maxim shouted, 'He's over there – can you see? Running along that sloping bit of ground.'

'Shouldn't we leave it to the Garda?' The police cars had drawn up at the front of the house, and the men were getting out, talking on crackly radios, and issuing directions.

'He'll be gone before they can reach him,' said Maxim. 'And I'm not letting that bastard escape. Stay with me, Phin.'

He went towards the trees, and Phin followed.

Donal Cullen was running like a fleeing hare, and Phin thought they could never catch him. But he had reckoned without Maxim. Maxim went after Donal like a man possessed – he covered the uneven ground as if he were flying across it, and Phin struggled to keep him in sight. Once Cullen stumbled on a jutting root or a rabbit hole, but he regained his balance and went on again.

Phin gasped out, 'He's mad – he must know he'll be caught.'

But Donal did not seem to know it. He ran across the ground, and Phin had just realized he must be almost at the ice pit, and he was remembering they had left the trapdoor open, when Donal gave a sudden shout, and plunged below the ground.

Maxim checked his stride, then went on again. In a dozen strides they had reached the old pit, the outline black and stark against the thrusting grass.

'He's down there,' said Maxim, kneeling on the edge of the pit. 'And what wouldn't I give to slam that door down on him, and tell the Garda we've lost him.'

'You won't do it, though.'

Maxim looked up at Phin. 'I won't do it,' he said. 'But—' He broke off, and leaned down further, peering into the darkness.

'He is there, isn't he?' Phin knelt down to look as well. He would not have been surprised if Donal had suddenly reared up and grabbed them, pulling them down with him, but he did not.

He did not, because he was lying on the ground, full length, with his head at an ugly, impossible angle to his body. When Phin moved slightly, to allow a vagrant shard of light to lie across him, his eyes were wide open and staring.

Beatrice had stayed where she was in the bedroom. She had managed to get up off the floor, although her legs felt as if all the bones had been pulled out of them, and she was sitting in the button-back chair by the window. She had assured the Garda she was perfectly all right and she had politely declined offers of paramedics.

'I'd like to just stay here quietly, if you don't mind.'

Stay there . . . That was what he had said, flinging the words over his shoulder before he went hell-for-leather down the stairs after Donal Cullen. *Stay there . . . I'll be back.*

Maxim Volf. The man who had been in this house that first night – the man she had thought of as belonging to the shadows, and the man who had failed to save Abigail.

Bea leaned her head back against the chair. Time slid along – it might have been minutes or hours or even longer before she heard his step on the stair.

Maxim Volf.

He came in quietly, and stood for a moment looking across at her. There was such humility and such hope in his eyes that Bea felt as if something had seized her by the throat and was wringing every drop of breath from her. But as he came towards her, she stood up, and waited. He reached for her hand, and the instant his fingers closed around hers, Bea knew unquestionably, with an instinct that overrode everything else, who he really was. She forgot the bitterness she had harboured for the last two years; she forgot the anger and the aching loneliness and the pain of loss. She forgot the infidelities and the deceptions that had gone before, as well, and she only remembered that this was the man who could weave dreams and spin enchantments and who could quote lyrical poetry that caressed your mind even while his hands were caressing your body . . .

Abigail's father. Beatrice's lost, dead love.

In a voice that seemed to come from outside her, and that was barely more than a whisper, she said, 'Niall.'

And fell forward into his arms.

The fire in the deep old hearth had burned low, and the Garda had finally gone, taking reams of statements with them. Phin Fox had taken Jessica home to the gloomy house with the faded ladies.

And Bea and Niall were alone.

'I don't know where to begin,' he said. 'But I'll begin with Abigail. I didn't save her. You know that, of course. But, oh, Bea, I really did try.'

'I know that now.' Bea touched the scars on his face very lightly. 'It's a curious thing,' she said, 'but there've been times when I pretended it wasn't Abi who died. That there had been someone else in the car, and that the wrong person had been buried. That Abi had wandered off with no memory, and I'd still find her one day. And I got it nearly right, didn't I? Except it wasn't Abi who got mistaken for an unknown person, it was you. Who's in your grave? Don't shiver like that, it's only a form of speech.'

'I only know fragments,' he said. 'I truly didn't remember until – well, until Phin and I came up to the house today. But I know there was a tramp who used to wander around Kilcarne in those weeks. A bit of a local character, I think.' He frowned. 'That girl – Jessica – ran into the road – she was running away from someone.'

'Donal,' said Beatrice, very positively.

'It's the likeliest answer. The tramp was running away from him – I swerved to avoid them both – it was the hire-car, and I wasn't familiar with it, and—' A violent shudder shook him, and Bea said, quickly, 'Don't go on if you'd rather not.'

'It's all right. I remember I flung my left arm across Abi to keep her in her seat.' He shivered again, and Bea reached out to him. His head came down on her shoulder, and as she put her arms round him, she felt his tears soaking into her sweater, and his hands clinging to her. There was nothing to be done but to hold him, and after a short while, he raised his head, and said, 'Sorry to be so emotional.'

Bea reached for the whiskey standing on the low table, and refilled their glasses. 'Don't be sorry,' she said. 'I'd hate you if you didn't have that grief.'

'I know it happened two years ago, but for me I've only just heard about it. Bea, will I ever come to terms with losing Abi?'

'No. I shan't either. I don't want to come to terms with it,' said Bea. 'I don't want to stop missing her and being bitterly regretful and resentful that she didn't have more of life.'

He turned to look at her more intently. 'It must have been unbearable.'

'Yes it was. But it'll be better now.'

'Now that I'm back?' His voice was bitter. 'Fine prospect I am. No money, no real job . . . Looking like something from a bad horror film—'

'I don't care about the money or the job. And you don't look anywhere near as bad as you think. Even if you did, I wouldn't care.'

He smiled at that. '"Love is not love/Which alters when it alteration finds".'

'I might have known you'd hide behind a quotation. As for a job – could you write, do you think?'

'God, no!'

But something had sparked in his eyes, and Bea said, 'Not fiction, necessarily. But something about legends and myths. Remember all those tales you used to spin for Abi?'

'Tracing the origins? Linking the sources between countries? Comparing them? Abi once said we'd do that. She said she and I would write it, and you'd illustrate it.' His tone was offhand, but a light was back in his eyes.

Bea said, 'It's still a good idea.'

'You and me working together?'

'There have been unlikelier collaborations.'

'True. I'll think about it.'

But as he reached for the whiskey glass, Bea could see he was already starting to think, and that he would go on thinking.

Abigail's Stories, she thought. That's what we'd call it. But she only said, 'Go on about the crash. You swerved to avoid the tramp. You thought he was running away from Donal?'

'Yes, but I can't think why he would be doing that.' Again there was the frown of concentration. 'A lot of it's still confused,' he said. 'But I remember a terrific screeching of metal, and the feeling of being somersaulted across the road.'

'You were thrown out of the car?'

'I must have been. The next thing I knew I was lying in the road – I wasn't sure where I was or what had happened. But I remember seeing the tramp running towards the car – I remember he had a bright red scarf on. Did he get to the car—? Yes, yes, he did! I saw him half climb in through the driver's side to get to Abi – that door had been torn off in the crash, and the car was lying on the passenger side. But that was when the petrol tank went up.' Again the shudder shook him. 'I think I had got up from the road by then, and I started to run to the car, but it was blazing like an inferno. I couldn't get near. They both burned. Abigail and the tramp.'

Bea said, carefully, 'The body next to Abi was too badly burned for definite identification – but since it was in the car with her there was no reason to think it was anyone other than you. The police told me about you – about how you tried to get them out—'

'I've known for the last two years that I tried to get to Abi, but that I couldn't. But that's all I've known. Everything was wiped from my mind.'

'The shock of the crash and the fire?'

'The doctors thought so. And I had no papers on me, nothing at all. No name. So I stole an identity I found here in this house.'

'Maxim Volf,' said Bea, softly.

'Yes. I suppose at some level I remembered Tromloy and that's why I came here.' He set down his glass and took her hands. 'About Abigail,' he said. 'It was over so quickly. It's probably the one bit of . . . of solace I can give you, but it really was only moments.'

'Yes.' Bea stared into the embers of the dying fire, then she said, 'There's a great deal we still don't know, isn't there?

Such as why Donal Cullen attacked me – or why he imprisoned Jessica in the old ice pit.'

'Phin's talking to the police and Jessica. He's coming out to Tromloy tomorrow, so we might find out more then. I'm not sorry that bastard, Cullen, is dead, Bea. God knows what he was going to do to you this afternoon.'

'If you hadn't got in through the old ice pit – if you hadn't suddenly remembered the old plans of the house—'

'Let's not do the "ifs".' His arm came round her, and Bea leaned against him. The room was warm and quiet, and the firelight glinted on the glasses. 'We used to do this in that other life, didn't we? Drink whiskey by this fire.'

'Yes.'

'And then I'd carry you upstairs to our bed. But now—' He broke off and drew back, putting a hand across his face in a partial gesture of concealment.

Bea reached for his hand. 'I don't care about the scars,' she said. 'I wish I could take them away for you, but I don't care about them. You're still—'

'Still Niall?'

'Not quite. Not any longer. I think you're Maxim now,' she said. 'And I think I might find it very easy to get used to that name. Would he – the real Maxim – mind that, do you think?'

'I don't know. I've found out a bit about him through Phin, but not very much.'

He was staring into the fire, and after a moment, Bea said, 'Can you still negotiate the stairs to the bedroom, do you suppose?'

In the light from the fire, the smile she remembered – the smile she had never forgotten – touched his eyes. Bea felt as if something had punched into the pit of her stomach, and delight and longing sliced through her.

'Oh, yes,' said Maxim, softly. 'Oh yes, my darling girl, I do suppose I can still do that.'

Nuala had not stopped crying since Jessica had been brought home, and the Garda had told them that Donal was dead.

As for the circumstances surrounding his death . . .

'It will be a mistake,' said Nuala, sobbingly, when the

sergeant had finished the account. 'Donal couldn't possibly commit any kind of crime.'

'He's a priest – good and devout and hardworking.' Morna had listened to everything that was said, not crying, but plaiting her hands together over and over again. 'It must be a dreadful misunderstanding.'

'Mistaken identity, even,' said Nuala, daring to hope for a moment.

But there was no mistake. And after the sergeant had left, listening to Jessica, it seemed they could not have known Donal at all.

'We thought it was that tramp who attacked you that day,' said Nuala, in a faltering voice. 'Donal even suggested that.'

'I know. But it wasn't the tramp. And,' said Jessica, leaning forward, gripping her hands tightly together, 'you do believe me, don't you?'

'I'm shocked to hear myself say this, but I find I do believe you,' said Morna, and Nuala nodded. 'But I shall never find it in my heart to forgive Donal Cullen. Or to forgive myself for not knowing what was going on.'

'Jess, why didn't you tell us?'

'Donal said if I told anyone he'd say I was mad,' said Jessica.

'For goodness' sake, no one would have believed that!'

'He said my mother was mad,' whispered Jess, and she looked at Morna and Nuala with such trust and such fear that Nuala cried all over again, and they both flew at Jess and hugged her.

'A black, wicked lie,' said Morna. 'Catriona was never mad, not in a million years. She was lively and imaginative – exactly as you are – but she was as sane as anyone I ever knew.'

'If only we'd known the truth.' Nuala could hardly bear to think of Jess going through all this by herself, frightened and confused. 'We could have helped. We'd have done anything.'

'And then the birth itself—'

Memory flared between the three of them, then Morna said, 'Donal stood back and let Tormod do what he did. He could easily have stopped him, you know. Arranged a proper funeral.'

'He was afraid to let the child's existence get out,' said Nuala. 'He simply wanted it destroyed. Out of the way and forgotten.

He didn't even give Extreme Unction – pronounce the words of the Last Rites. That should have been almost a reflex action for him.'

Morna said, 'I've tried to forget what Tormod did that day. I really have.'

'So have I. But—'

'We won't say it,' said Morna, quickly. 'He's our brother.'

'And he was starting to be ill – the stroke he had straight afterwards,' said Nuala, eagerly. 'Let's remember that.'

Jessica said in a thread of a voice, 'The child . . . It really was dead, wasn't it?'

'Yes.' Morna's assurance came instantly and definitely. 'There's no question about it. I promise you that, Jess.'

Jess nodded gratefully, and Morna said, 'But we were cowards afterwards, Jess. We were grateful when you – well, I don't know the right word, but when you blanked it all out.'

'We thought it was the best thing for you. We thought we were doing the right thing – protecting you – encouraging you not to remember—'

'Letting the nuns – everyone – believe you were being given home lessons.'

'Donal dealt with that,' said Nuala. 'He told us not to worry – that he'd talk to the education people. The lies he must have told!' She looked at her sister, and in a whisper, said, 'But now – how are we going to tell Tormod what's happened?'

They told him that night after supper. It took a great deal of courage, but they told him everything – how Donal had taken Jessica up to that house – Tromloy – two years earlier. How he had forced himself on to her. And then threatened her that if she told, he would cause her to be shut away.

And how he had died today because he had been trying to silence both Jessica and Beatrice Drury, so the truth would not get out.

At first Morna and Nuala did not think Tormod had understood. He did not speak, but his hands gripped the handle of his walking stick tightly, turning the knuckles white.

Then he whispered the name he had whispered in the firelit bedroom at Tromloy. 'Catriona.'

The sisters glanced uneasily at one another, then Morna said, 'No, Tormod, it's Jessica we're talking about.'

'Catriona's daughter,' said Nuala. 'Jessica.'

Tormod shook his head, but whether to disagree with them, or to shake off something he could not understand or could not bear to remember, they had no idea.

'Catriona,' he said, again, and the dreadful crimson colour flooded his face. Before either of the sisters could do anything he fell sideways in the chair, his face distorting, froth appearing on his lips.

When the paramedics, summoned by Morna's frantic phone call, arrived ten minutes later, Tormod was still murmuring Catriona's name.

Phin went back to O'Brien's, his mind whirling with everything that had happened – with the knowledge that Maxim Volf was the believed-dead Niall Drury; with Donal Cullen's vicious behaviour and Beatrice Drury's narrow escape. And with the discovery that Roman Volf and Feofil Markov had been one and the same person, and that Roman had been alive in 1921 and at The Genesius Theatre. And that his last performance might be captured on cine film.

What about Antoinette? Who had she been, and how did she fit into all this? There's something that's still there to be uncovered, he thought, but I don't know if I'm going to uncover it. He frowned, then put Antoinette to one side and checked his phone for messages. There was a voicemail from the rugby-playing neighbour who was, it appeared, still enthusiastically planning the promised party. As for holding it without Phin, they would not think of any such thing.

'We'll wait until you're back in London, and as a matter of fact, my cousin Arabella is coming to stay, and I know she wants to meet you. She saw you moving in last month, and she went into transports – and trust me, old boy, when Arabella goes into transports . . . She said – let me get this right, because she's apt to be a bit butterfly-minded, my cousin Arabella – she said you looked as if you might occupy a scholar's ivory tower for most of the time, but she suspected that on occasions you were exquisitely wild and sinned with the angels.'

Phin flipped on the laptop and spent ten minutes trying to trace the source of this line, eventually concluding it was a skewed blend of Longfellow and Shakespeare.

It might not be so bad, after all, to go to the neighbour's party. Just for an hour or two. Purely to be polite, and nothing to do with meeting a butterfly-minded female who wove a patchwork of poetry. (How did you sin with angels, for pity's sake?) Before he could change his mind, he left a message on the neighbour's phone, saying he would be back in his flat in about a week.

While he was making the call, an email came in from the red-haired Canadian editor who had told his agent he had silver eyes. She would be in London in two weeks' time, she said – she was staying at her favourite Bloomsbury hotel, so perhaps Phin would like to take her to dinner one night? Any night would do. Here was the hotel's number. Phin smiled, and tried to think what restaurants he knew in Bloomsbury.

The curious thing, to Jessica, was the calm way in which the aunts accepted Tormod's illness. The doctors had been sad and sympathetic and had said the outlook this time was a poor one. A massive stroke, they said, and Mr Cullen's sisters, no matter how devoted, could not possibly look after him. He required specialist nursing – there would be tubes, assistance with breathing, various nursing tasks. Better by far, kinder by far, to hand him over to the people who knew what to do. The infirmary in Galway had splendid facilities, and the family could visit as often as they wanted.

Jessica steeled herself, but it was as if, having dreaded it for so long, now that the worst had happened the aunts were almost relieved. They did not say they had been afraid of him for years, and they did not say they had never been able to forget or forgive what he had done to the poor dead baby at Tromloy that day.

Instead, they reminded one another that poor Tormod was not actually dead, and that they would be able to visit him regularly. Perhaps they would not do so every day, they thought. Twice a week would be enough – even once a week. Not in the depths of winter, of course, when the roads were icy. But they would go regularly, and they would talk to Tormod, they would tell him all the local news. The doctors had said he would not be able to hear them, but you never knew.

Nuala said they might even make a day of it each week. They might have their lunch out, and even go to a cinema or a theatre.

'I think that's a very good idea,' said Jessica, encouragingly. She looked at them both, and said, 'Specially if I'm studying at GMIT next year.'

There was a pause.

'It really could happen, could it?' said Morna, hesitantly. 'GMIT?'

'Bea Drury thinks it could. She knows one of the lecturers or heads of department there. She's going to have a word.'

Nuala said, 'It will be a very good thing for you, Jess. We'll be very proud of you.'

Jessica smiled. 'You can ask Bea Drury about it tomorrow,' she said. 'You are still coming with me to Tromloy, aren't you? Bea's really keen to meet you.'

'I thought I'd wear my coffee lace blouse,' said Nuala.

'And the cameo brooch.'

Bea thought it was almost like old times to be preparing for guests – to be setting out cups and saucers, and to see Maxim uncorking a bottle of wine. Bea knew he would deliberately sit in the least-lit corner of the room, but at least he had not refused to meet Jessica's aunts and to see Phin Fox again.

Phin arrived a bit early. 'I'll go out again and drive round the block if it isn't all right,' he said. 'But I wanted to ask one or two questions, and I didn't want to do it in front of Jess and the Cullen ladies. I don't want to risk upsetting them.'

Maxim waved him to a chair. 'Ask away.'

Phin said, 'It's about Donal,' he said. 'I think I understand why he attacked Bea – it was because Jessica told him that Bea knew about the rape, wasn't it?'

'Yes. And Jess is still apologizing for that,' said Bea, handing Phin a cup of tea. 'I think she'll feel guilty for the next five years. I've been trying to tell her there's no need – that bastard Donal Cullen was about to push her into the ice pit, and the poor child thought if he believed someone knew the truth, it might stop him.'

'Yes. But,' said Phin, drinking his tea, 'what I don't understand is why Donal went out to the Sexton's House that day. Have we got any clue as to his motives?'

'We think so,' said Maxim. 'Bea's more or less pieced it together.'

Bea said, 'Donal attacked Jessica in this house. She's talked to me about that. I'm not pushing her to talk, but I'm listening when she does, and I think she's finding it easier to talk to me than to her aunts. It appears that the tramp – the man who died in the car crash – saw the rape. Jess doesn't know how much he actually saw, but he was at the window – she thinks he wanted to help but wasn't sure what to do. But it's clear he saw enough to be a threat to Donal. Donal certainly thought so. He went for him – the tramp ran away, and Jess ran after them both.'

Bea glanced at Maxim, as if handing the next part over to him. He said, 'But then came the crash. Afterwards, the tramp was never mentioned – probably no one even knew he was around that day. All that people knew was that there had been a crash, and a passing stranger tried to help with the rescue. Nobody made any connection between that stranger and the tramp. There was no reason why anyone would.'

'But Donal made the connection,' said Phin. 'He knew the tramp had been there. Yes, I see.'

'When I went to live in the Sexton's House, people started to talk. They thought I was the tramp come back.' Maxim smiled. 'I probably looked like a tramp most of the time, anyway.'

'You probably did,' said Bea. 'But according to Jess, Donal heard the speculation – there was something about a supper party and gossip—'

'Grania O'Brien,' said Phin, grinning.

'I think after that Donal decided he might need to silence Maxim to stop him talking,' said Bea.

'So he came out to the Sexton's House to see if I was the same man.'

'Yes. And he saw it wasn't the same man at all, so he went away. I'm very glad indeed about that,' said Bea. She glanced towards the window. 'That looks like Jessica and the aunts now. Maxim, will you put the kettle on again while I let them in.'

Morna and Nuala had brought a huge bunch of mop-headed chrysanthemums for Mrs Drury, and they were very pleased indeed to be meeting her, and to be able to thank her for all her kindness to Jessica.

They accepted cups of tea, and sat together on the sofa, both thinking how lovely it was to be seeing Tromloy properly, without the need to creep around with candles and torches. They had discussed anxiously whether they should tell Mrs Drury the truth about how Jess had lived here for those months, but Jess had said not. It was too sad a memory to print on to Tromloy, she said, especially now, when Bea's husband had so remarkably come back into her life. Morna and Nuala thought she was right, although they would feel dreadfully guilty.

Mrs Drury – she had said to call her Bea – made them very welcome indeed, and it was nice to see how relaxed and friendly Jessica was with everyone. They had both been a bit nervous about meeting Mrs Drury's husband, and Nuala particularly noticed that he took a seat with his back to the light, but in fact he was very charming, and neither of them could imagine how anyone had ever taken him for a vagrant. The burns were distressing, of course, but the odd thing was that once you started talking to him, you forgot them, almost to the extent of hardly noticing them.

Nuala asked a bit hesitantly, about the old fire screen propped against the wall.

'It's very unusual, isn't it?'

'It was here when we bought the house,' said Bea, and it seemed to the sisters that Jessica leaned forward to listen very intently, as if the screen might mean something to her. 'But I've no idea how old it is.'

'I always wanted to throw it out,' said Maxim. 'But it's got a quaint charm of its own. And Bea likes it.'

'Yes, but I damaged it a bit the other night,' said Bea. 'I wanted to examine one of the glued-on pieces more closely – I was as careful as I could be about taking it off, but it still tore part of the base.'

'Oh, but that could easily be repaired,' said Nuala, eagerly, pleased to be able to offer a suggestion. 'You could cover those small tears – use a good glue, and then a new coat of varnish . . . Could I look more closely, Mrs Drury? I'll be very careful.'

'Yes, of course.'

Phin said, 'Do you recognize any of the photos or newspaper cuttings?'

'Well, they're a bit before my time, Mr Fox,' said Nuala, slightly apologetically.

'A lot before it, I should think,' said Phin, smiling at her, and Nuala blushed, and thought how much nicer and friendlier he was than the image she and Morna had had of an aloof British academic.

'That looks like something from one of the old wartime concerts.' Morna was examining the screen and pointing out a small playbill.

'Quality Quince again,' said Maxim, glancing at Phin and grinning.

'The man was everywhere.'

'See, if you just slide this old programme out where you've chipped away that section,' said Nuala, 'it can be trimmed back. It won't damage anything, because it looks as if it's the entire programme, not just the cover. Or is it padded underneath by some sheets of paper?'

'Do be careful,' said Morna. 'There's writing on those sheets – they might be valuable.'

Maxim said, 'It's probably somebody's old shopping list,' but both he and Phin were leaning forward.

'It looks like part of a letter,' said Nuala, and with one voice, Phin and Maxim said, 'A letter?'

'Yes, rather graceful writing. It's folded – there are several pages—'

Phin and Maxim were both kneeling next to her by now.

'Can we get at them?' said Phin. 'Without damaging them?'

'I'm not sure, but if I'm extremely careful . . .' There was a brief pause, then the dry rustle of old paper. Nuala sat back, beaming with triumph. 'There you are.'

'Miss Cullen, you're brilliant,' said Phin. He glanced at the others, then looked straight at Maxim.

Maxim said, 'It's the same handwriting as my two letters, isn't it?'

'Yes.' Phin touched the paper with a fingertip.

'Can you see the signature? But,' said Maxim, 'you don't need to see it, do you?'

'No.' But using extreme care, Phin unfolded the sheets of paper until he came to the last one and the signature.

And there it was. Antoinette.

TWENTY-FIVE

The room had fallen into a deep, waiting silence, and as Phin flattened out the sheets of Antoinette's letter, he realized his hands were shaking. Antoinette, he thought, don't let me down. Please have put all the answers in this letter. And Roman – Feofil – don't have put your own slant on this. You must have translated it, but please don't have edited out what you thought shouldn't be known.

As if from a long way away, he was aware of the two Cullen ladies murmuring something apologetic about leaving – this would perhaps be a family document – and of Bea reassuring them, and asking them to stay.

Then Maxim's voice reached him. 'Read it, Phin.'

'It's your house. Your letter,' began Phin.

'But it's your work, Phin,' said Bea. 'Please read it.'

Phin took a deep breath and, as he began to read Antoinette's words, the past poured into the room, exactly as it had done before.

My dearest Roman

Again, I send this to your apartment house, and again I have the assurance it will reach you.

I have hesitated about setting these details down, but I cannot see any other way of telling you what is about to happen.

It's said that the most successful plans have, at their heart, simplicity, and I think there is great simplicity about this plan. But there are two weak links in the chain I have forged.

Two of the guards at the fortress have been bribed – this is the first weak link, for one or both of them may have questionable allegiances, be playing a double game, or be offered higher bribes. But I hope the money given them – with the promise of a further payment afterwards – will be sufficient.

You are held in Cell No. 9. In Cell No. 6, close by, is a man convicted of murder and rape – a crime that happened just before the tsar's assassination, and that received scant notice

as a result. Still, he was sentenced to death – rightly so, I am
assured – and he is to hang, in a week's time. He will hang
in your place. When the executioner comes for you, the numbers
on the doors will have been turned upside-down, so that No. 6
will appear to be No. 9, and the man inside will be assumed
to be you. Like you, he has become unshaven and unkempt,
and he is of the same colouring and similar build. But the risk
of it being realized he is not you is the second weak link.

The man knows he is to die, and his silence and compliance
has been bought by the promise that his sister – the only
person for whom he has ever shown any real care or affection
– will be provided for. I have already done that. My father
had many faults, but he was always generous, and there are
sufficient funds.

There will have to be a very macabre addition to the execu-
tion. It is to be partly public – people are to be allowed into
the courtyard to witness it. That, of course, is one of the Family's
ploys to demonstrate how they deal with the people who killed
the tsar. They have stirred up a great deal of hatred and bitter-
ness against you – they knew how loved and revered you were,
and they will not risk any kind of protest. So the execution is
to be watched by several hundred people. There is still the old
mechanism for public execution in that fortress, and it will be
made use of. The guards will let it down from the window of
what is called the hanging room, which overlooks the courtyard.
It will remain like that for the execution, jutting at right angles
to the wall, suspended some thirty feet above the crowd.

While the death procession walks to the hanging room, you
will be taken from the real Cell 9 and through the prison until
you are outside. More bribes have been paid to ensure that
all doors will be unlocked.

I dare not be there to take you away. Once you are outside
the fortress, it must be your ingenuity and courage that gets
you away. But you have my word that I will take Maxim to
safety. Already I have arranged a new identity for him, and
I will impress on him the absolute need to forget that 'Maxim
Volf' ever existed. He is an intelligent boy and I will make
him understand. I will not risk you being caught, and I will
not let your son's identity be known. My family are hunting

down the assassins – they have sworn to find and execute every last one. If they come to hear of Maxim's existence they might try to find him. It could create a trail that would lead them to realize you did not die on the gallows. They might even mete out punishment to Maxim himself, purely for who he is. I will not risk any of that.

The execution will be on the day after tomorrow at nine o'clock in the morning. I think the plan will succeed. You will smile now and say I am being fey, but – but, Roman, in my mind I can see you, far in the future, on a stage somewhere, pouring your marvellous music into an auditorium. Sprinkling its brilliance on to dark water. Do you remember once saying that to me?

I don't know how or where or when it will happen, that far distant stage and that unknown theatre, but I believe it will be so. I hope I can be there to see it. But I do not think it will ever be possible.

I do not forget my image of that theatre of the future, though, with you on its stage. Sprinkling the brilliance.

Do you remember how, in Odessa, looking at the ruined Skomorokh Theatre, you were so passionate about saving it from its dereliction – about saving all theatres from dereliction? That money I placed in a trust account is still there, Roman – if not for the Skomorokh, perhaps for some other theatre.

My family believe I am travelling to England to escape the unhappy and unwise marriage I made. There is a man in England I have met, who talks of marriage. He is one of the St Leger family, and he is wealthy and influential. If I marry him, I would have the title baroness.

If things had been different, Roman, you and I . . . But I know it cannot be, not now. Perhaps it never could.

But the reality is that I am forever yours, as I always was, and always will be.

Antoinette.

When Phin laid down the letter, there was a long silence.

Then, finally, Maxim said, very softly, 'The plan worked, didn't it? She got him out.'

'Yes.'

'Who was she, Phin? Because there's another name now – St Leger. Can we look her up? Bea, is the laptop on—?'

But Bea was already at the dining table, and the laptop's screen was already lit. It seemed to Phin that as Bea typed in a search request for Antoinette St Leger, the ghosts crept nearer, leaning forward to hear and watch – not because they wanted to know; they already did know. But because they wanted the people in the room to know.

Then Bea said, 'I think this is it,' and Phin sat in the dining chair next to her.

'Read it,' said Maxim, and Jessica and the aunts leaned forward eagerly.

Bea began to read.

'"Antoinette St Leger, born Antoinette Bayer on 20 June 1856, at St Petersburg, Russia. She was—"' She stopped, then went on. '"She was the illegitimate daughter of Alexander Nikolaevich Romanov – Alexander II, Tsar of Russia – by his mistress, Wilhelmine Bayer. Antoinette married Federico Stolte in 1873, but they were divorced before 1881. In October 1881 in London, she married Richard Flemyng St Leger, after which she was known as Baroness Antoinette St Leger. She died in January 1948, aged 91".' Bea scrolled the web page down slightly. 'There's another paragraph about how she and St Leger created a kind of centre for poets and musicians and writers in the Swiss part of Lake Maggiore, but that's all.'

Maxim said, softly, 'So that's who she was.'

'An illegitimate Romanov,' said Phin. 'Of course she was. And the family – in that letter she gives it the upper case F, by the way – the family wanted to demonstrate how they dealt with anyone who attacked one of their number. I'd guess they found out about Antoinette's affair with Roman—'

'And disapproved?' said Bea. 'That's a bit steep considering old Alexander had – wait a bit, it's here somewhere . . . Yes, here it is. Wilhelmine Bayer was one of seven known mistresses of Alexander II.'

'Other times, other manners,' said Maxim.

'We'll probably never know the exact truth,' said Phin, 'but it's a reasonable supposition that even though Antoinette was a bastard sprig of the imperial tree, the Romanovs didn't much like her association with such a flamboyant and public figure as Roman Volf.'

'It wouldn't be the first time a murder charge was faked,' said Maxim, dryly.

'No. I shouldn't think Roman did play any part in the assassination, but the theatre world's a curious mix of people and Russian Society in that era . . . Roman could have been in the company of one or two of the plotters a few times,' said Phin. 'If so, the Romanovs might have seen that as their chance to entangle him in the list of the real killers, and get him away from Antoinette that way.'

'In those other two letters,' said Maxim, 'Antoinette says something about wanting to force her way into the courtroom to give Roman an alibi. You remember that, Phin?'

'I do.'

'She said they would believe her "because—". She broke off the sentence there, though. She must have meant the court would have believed her because of who she was.'

'The tsar's own daughter,' said Phin.

'Why didn't she do that?' said Bea. 'Because she didn't dare? Because the other Romanovs prevented her?'

'Either or both,' said Phin. 'But what she did do was make sure Roman wasn't hanged. And that his son – that real Maxim Volf – was taken to safety. She even changed his name so that he couldn't be traced.'

'He became Mortimer Quince,' said Maxim. 'And he lived in this house.'

'I think he must have done.'

'I've looked on the Title Deeds,' said Bea, eagerly. 'The name doesn't appear. There is a Russian name, though – someone who owned Tromloy for several years in the early part of the twentieth century.'

She looked at Phin, and he said, 'Feofil Markov?'

'Yes.'

Phin said, very softly, 'Which means that Roman Volf once owned and lived in this house.' He sat back and looked round the room.

Jessica said, very hesitantly, 'Might there be anything else in the fire screen?'

'It's got so many old photographs and newspaper cuttings,' said Nuala, almost apologetically.

'You're right.' Phin sprang up from the chair. 'Always return to your original source,' he said. 'Let's see what there is. Bea, if we do any irreparable damage, I promise it'll be made good a hundredfold.'

'I'll hold you to that,' said Bea, getting up to help them.

The Cullen sisters were careful and neat. Slowly and painstakingly, they chipped at the old varnish, and even more slowly and painstakingly, they removed the cobwebby fragments and handed each one to Jessica.

'A shame to litter up your lovely room,' said Nuala to Bea, as Jess laid each piece on the floor.

'I don't care if you turn the whole house upside-down,' said Bea.

It was an hour before the contents of the screen had been removed, but, finally and at last, there they were. The chronicles of the rich, romantic, bawdy, vagabond life that had been Mortimer Quince's. It was all spread out like the shards of a Persian prince's carpet, or jigsaw pieces snipped from a lost century. The memories of the music halls, and the taverns, the cider cellars and the pub rooms, the press cuttings and the photographs and the song sheets.

'Marvellous,' said Phin, cautiously picking up programme covers from theatres whose names had vanished, and brittle old newspaper cuttings of concerts long forgotten. 'And also priceless.' He looked at them, his eyes shining. 'Quince once wrote that one day he hoped to create his autobiography,' he said. 'I tried – unsuccessfully – to find it. I didn't know then – probably he didn't, either – that the operative word was "create".'

'He didn't write it,' said Bea. 'But he did create it. This is his autobiography. Can you – I don't know – but can you assemble it into something for people to see, Phin? A book or a programme or something?'

'If I can't,' said Phin, 'my agent will make sure somebody else does. In fact he'll fall on all this with such . . . You'll all be credited in whatever comes of it, of course,' he said, looking up, and Morna and Nuala turned pink with delight.

'And so,' said Maxim, sitting back, 'the revels ended here in Kilcarne. The insubstantial pageant faded.'

*   *   *

It was not until the following night that the last shred of Roman Volf's life reached out to Phin. It was the smallest of shreds, and news of its existence came through modern technology in the form of an email.

The sender of the email was the secretary of the Irish Film Society, and the subject heading was, 'Old cine footage.'

Don't expect anything, thought Phin, almost afraid to read it. It'll be too far back – they won't have kept film footage from that time.

> Dear Phin Fox,
>
> I'm delighted to tell you we have found the old footage you emailed us about yesterday – the clip of The Genesius Theatre, in Galway, from 1921. The quality has deteriorated with time, of course, but the images are still surprisingly good.
>
> Could you contact us as soon as you can, because we would be more than happy to arrange a viewing for you.
>
> It was, as you thought, recorded on The Genesius' opening night – it was very helpful to our search that you gave us an exact date! – and it features an unknown violinist called Feohl Markov. We understand that sadly Mr Markov died later that night, so whoever he was, that evening saw his final performance.

The final performance. So that had been the night when Roman stepped off a concert platform for the last time. The revels had ended there, in The Genesius, but the insubstantial pageant of Roman Volf's life had not faded. That final scrap of his brilliance had been trapped on a sliver of cine film. Phin would be able to see it for himself. Other people would see it.

And, thought Phin, reaching for his notes for the TV programme, in the weeks ahead, Roman Volf's name would be cleared of murder.